EXODUS OF EVIL

DAVID R MARSTON

EXODUS OF EVIL

David R Marston

ISBN: 978-1-9169023-1-2

Published by David R Marston in conjunction with Writersworld. This book is produced entirely in the UK, is available to order from most book shops in the United Kingdom and is globally available via UK-based Internet book retailers and www.amazon.com.

Copy edited by Ian Large

Cover design by Jag Lall

www.writersworld.co.uk

WRITERSWORLD
2 Bear Close Flats
Bear Close
Woodstock
Oxfordshire
OX20 1JX
United Kingdom

☎ 01993 812500

☎ +44 1993 812500

The text pages of this book are produced via an independent certification process that ensures the trees from which the paper is produced come from well managed sources that exclude the risk of using illegally logged timber while leaving options to use post-consumer recycled paper as well.

CONTENTS

FOREWORD

In the heavens a voice is heard.

"I am who I am now let my people go!"

"Many of the chosen, who were rejected for their divergence to the Golden Path through force rather than desire, were mingled in blood lines with the lesser men to the great joy of the Devil, for they worshiped the Devil through many false gods and great wickedness was done by them and their ancestors.

"The chosen ones' genes were still as that intended by God and so, through generation upon generation, there came to be a time where the spirit of God was raised once more in man's consciousness. This spirit of enlightenment was the gift to mankind, seen only in the purity of thought of those individuals chosen to hear the messages of God.

"The great faiths, based on goodness and love for one another, were formed and this was God's way of creating new order on the earth. Despite this, an evil continued to ravage the world. Great, but evil men did much harm, but always the spirit fought back to bring examples of humanity in perfection of the spirit, to marshal the forces of good in the world. This battle ensued through the ages of human existence, even unto today.

"Modern man, both good and tainted with evil, but through the defeat of evil in both world wars, a new peace was established for a time which has enabled the spirit to be heard once more in pockets around the world. The great faiths were able to thrive, giving good people in the world a chance to grow in strength of belief and in numbers, through the divine and the goodwill fostered by God the Creator.

"The Devil, in the dawn of time, brought evil that sits awaiting release upon the earth. While the Devil mourns the sight as the formation of the earth seals his latest abomination deep into the planet, perhaps never to find the light of day, but he knows that men will grow and develop despite of all his effort, and he follows time unto infinity in his mind. His demons work their own kinds of wickedness and creation and pollution, invention and destruction follow on in man's growth and inspirational thinking that comes from the gifts from God.

"The pressure, so great that it is confined in something near as hard a diamond. A crystal houses at its centre a genetic virus. Alive yet not alive. It sits dormant in state waiting to be opened. Hard as diamond in the deep and dark places of the earth. This is the Devil's gambit. It was set for release in World War Two as devised by the cunning of Satan. It is about to open in 2021 and, with its coming, the lines have now been drawn for the greatest battle for the souls of men and the capture of the entire planet.

"From afar, in the deepest parts of Hell, there comes the sound of purest evil. The devil Satan screeches his anguish at the heavens. His favourite song rings out. ONE DAY IT WILL COME AND THEN WE WILL SEE!

"That day is finally here..."

CHAPTER ONE
THE BEGINNING OF THE END

The Australian mining industry was flailing. Even the deep mines were running out of precious materials. Seams of coal that had been the lifeblood of the industrial revolution in Australia. They were now becoming too expensive to mine, and with the political wish to reduce carbon emissions on the planet in the face of global warming, it became clear to the owners of these industries that their days were numbered. Bill Carruthers was a solid character. He was Australian born and used to getting his own way. His father, who worked the mining industry in the Australian interior, had made his fortune in coal, as had his father before him. Bill was the third generation to own the majority of shares in his corporation. He sat pondering the latest report into his operations. It was clear that even his deep mines were mined out of precious stones and minerals and the corporation was facing its demise unless he could find a way to reinvest away from mining. Bill considered his options again. He needed to keep this revelation from the board, and he knew he would require a plan to distract them while he carefully took his money out of the business.

Bill was ruthless. His father had been the same. Bill had been made to mine coal for a full five years before he was given any responsibility in the business. He learned how to hold his own with the men underground. Bill, like his father before him, was in his element in the depths. He loved blasting the coal loose. He revelled in the fear and adrenaline that poured into his veins and could barely hold himself back once the dust settled and a new coal face had been blown. Shovel in hand he and his gang worked the coal into trucks and up to the surface. Bill was not much taller than his father had been. He stood 5' 11" tall but had the strength of a bull due to the hard labour he had been subjected to.

At thirty-five years of age he was the master and the board of directors knew it. Although they respected him for his knowledge, they also feared him a little. He was not a forgiving man and several board members who had challenged him in the boardroom had fallen foul of his temper and cold revenge that followed. Bill employed his own detectives to spy on board members. Their strengths and weaknesses and plots were defeated skilfully and the tables turned to the ruin of many. Bill held sway.

As a bachelor, wealthy, healthy and rich, his rugged face did not stop female suitors from crossing his path. Bill liked women but he knew they would weaken his command over his world and make him softer. Bill wanted an heir to the throne but not yet; there would be time for such things in the future when he was secure. His friends in government and politicians that wanted his money and contacts were a good source of information. They had helped him to this point to make lots of money and investments and Bill was worth billions. Yet, like all self-made men, he trusted no one completely and this had served him well. "What to do? What to do?" he muttered under his breath.

CHAPTER TWO
A VICTORIOUS SPEECH

The Prime Minister, leading her government of Australia, looked out on the opposition benches. She smiled at the angry faces before her as she had done many times before. It really upsets them, she thought, these sexist conservative types hate the fact that I beat them with the power of the Australian female might at the ballot box. Mrs Shaw was the first lady prime minister that had been voted into power. Her Labour colleagues admired and feared her. She resembled a young Margaret Thatcher in her powerful personality. That is where the resemblance ended. Mrs Shaw was blonde and quite beautiful, tall and slim with a winning smile. Her followers adored her for her looks, her great understanding of politics and her leadership and cunning in rising to the office she now held.

Mrs Shaw was not left or right in her views. She detested the dogma of both sides and saw these models of power for what they were: a way for the powerful two per cent, who held the wealth of the world, to prevent drastic social change so that they always held power. The voices of derision that had heralded her speech aimed at reducing Australia's carbon footprint lost its force. Mrs Shaw called out politely, "Have the dogs of derision finished with their barking?" The floor of the house was once more filled with loud shouts of shameful remarks from the opposition benches. Mrs Shaw merely smiled once more and turned to see the delight on the faces of her own party, enjoying the loss of control on the benches opposite.

Order was called for and it came from the speaker. "Mrs Shaw!" Once more the noise subsided. Mrs Shaw changed her tactics. "Of course," she said, "my comments were not meant to be disrespectful of the good members of parliament on the seating opposite. They were aimed at the few powerful men under the sway of the coal industry who will do anything they can to defeat this side of the house in the matter of reducing coal mining." Growls were heard from fewer than half of the members opposite.

"Yes!" she said, in her most commanding voice, "you know whom I refer to! They betray themselves and their true masters will not like that, oh no! They will not like that at all." Mrs Shaw waited again for silence. "I forgive you for all your faults and your false loyalties! The fact of the matter is that coal has had its day. It is rather sad that Australians are fighting on almost alone in the world to destroy the planet!"

Loud shouts of "More, more!" as her benches' joyful pleasure fell upon her ears and those opposite her looked uncomfortable, finding no instant answer coming from their own benches. "Order! Order!" the speaker intervenes. Mrs Shaw plays her master card for the day. "We, on this side of the house, and I suspect many on the opposition side also, want to end this impasse. I intend to invite all the coal magnates of this great country to meet with me this very week, before we vote to shut down their industry for good. If they meet me, we will find a compromise, if they do not, we will finish with them!"

Mrs Shaw sat down, calm, relaxed and in control. Her benches were delighted. The opposition were apparently unsure of which way to move. The speaker called out to the house. "Business is closed for the day!"

Once back in her office, Mrs Shaw smiled at her secretary, and she smiled back. "Tea Prime Minister?"

"Yes please, then close the door. I need some time to ponder my next move," she smiled, showing no sign of tiredness or uncertainty, despite her words. The tea came in and the door closed. Once alone Mrs Shaw removed her bright red high heels and reached for her comfy slippers hidden from sight under her desk. She slipped them on her feet and sighed aloud at the pleasure such soft comfort gave her. Men could never manage high heels all day, she smiled to herself, they would all be walking like John Wayne within an hour! Ah women are great! We suffer pain, discomfort and use all our feminine wiles together with some borrowed from the opposite gender to bring everything to order.

It had been a good day for Australia, all things considered. The trade deficit was reduced and there was money in the coffers to begin the tricky but essential task of managing the oncoming storm. Increasing the military budget was a shock for her own politicians today and they backed her, trusting her judgement and accepting her decision based on information from the security echelons of power in the country. She had balanced this uncertainty with an attack on the out-of-favour and still powerful coal mining industry, which had been making the country rich with sales of coal to China and the surrounding districts. This was a win-win situation as far as she was concerned, for her country had to deal with its horrendous carbon footprint and quickly. Also, she thought the country might need the coal reserves they had left in the future.

Mrs Shaw opened her telephone diary, a red leathered pig skin cover, which was warm and soft to the touch. She flicked through the pages and came to the number she had been seeking. People would be surprised as to whom she was to speak to in the next few minutes, if they knew.

The Queen of England was up early, sitting in her office in her night clothes, a glass of milk on her right and a telephone on her left. The phone rang. "Put her through," said the Queen. "Hello Mrs Shaw, how did it go?"

"Better than expected Your Majesty, we are ready for the next step."

"Powerful people are dangerous, Mrs Shaw, please be

careful and please take the fight to save this planet to the next level. I fear our enemies are becoming aware that you are not acting alone, but we have a small window in which to act to bring this first chapter to a close."

Mrs Shaw hung up without comment. She knew quite well that she had stirred the hornet's nest! Now to offer some honey to Bill Carruthers, she thought to herself, with a slight frown coming to her face. Mrs Shaw knew Bill to be a tough negotiator and would want something unexpected for any cooperation he might decide to give. She did not know Carruthers well but his file from the security services was a thick one and she had taken time over the past few days to get to see the detail around some of his darker dealings on the market. It seemed to her, on summation, that he was a tough man who did what he wished, working inside the law and sometimes in the mirky area outside the law too. This was usual with very powerful men and she needed this tough guy to work with her on the up-and-coming project.

Molly, the secretary in the outer office, picked up the telephone. "Mr Carruthers' office, who is calling please?" A male voice calmly replied, "I have the Prime Minister on the line." Molly's eyes widened and she took a deep breath and thought 'wow!' But what she said was equally calm. "Hold the line please." Molly walked calmly into Bill's office and announced, "The Prime Minister on line one."

Bill picked up the phone, muttering to himself. "Nothing good coming my way today then… Hello Mrs Shaw, what can I do for you today?"

"Hello Bill, if I may call you Bill, and please call me Carol."

"Of course, and thank you Mrs Shaw. So what do you need from me today? And by the way, your speech was very well delivered. You are certainly some points ahead of your political rivals today. You must be thrilled," he said, barely hiding the irony in his voice.

"Thanks to you Bill, but I know you don't really mean that. I would like to talk to you about those mines you hold most of the stock for in the interior, you know, the ones that are nearly played out." Mrs Shaw enjoyed the long pause at the other end of the line.

"What do you want to say Mrs Shaw, I have a lot of business meetings today and this call has been taken as a curtesy extended to you and your position. I have not got long." Carol Shaw knew she had his attention now.

"Okay Bill, here it is. The government will buy those mines from you at top dollar (if you keep it quiet). Something has come up relating to that area and I want to send my special forces into those mines to check what has happened there."

After a brief discussion Bill put the phone down and blew the air out of his lungs to relieve the pressure there. He had been holding his breath for five minutes. Bill called Molly into his office and ordered a flight to meet with Mrs Shaw.

* * *

Bill was ushered into the Prime Minister's office. Carol knew her men. She gestured for him to help himself to a drink from the bar while she finished the call she was on. Bill poured two generous glasses of single malt and took his seat. Carol sat opposite Bill, some three metres away.

"Something rather disturbing happened near one of your mines. We have found entrails of locals from the nearest town, leading down into the mines."

Bill raised an eyebrow, clearly surprised by what he was hearing. "Okay, but why buy the mine? And what is the national interest here?"

"Well done for being astute," Carol said earnestly. "Bill, we need... no, the country needs to shut down all mining in the area. There is something happening there that no one can quite explain, and we need to avoid a panic, which will certainly happen if any of what I am about to show you ever gets to the press."

They moved to a small cinema room adjacent to the office. The lights went down without a word.

"We are clearly not alone. There is a dangerous force in this country and this incident was very well orchestrated. Before you ask further questions, I want you to watch this recording with me so that you will understand some of what we are dealing with."

The film started. It was dark and a camera, probably an old 8-track model, was focused in on a couple in their back garden. Others were standing around. It seemed to Bill the camera angle suggested the person filming was upstairs. This was an adult barbie, Bill surmised. Then the back fence rocked visibly and fell down, and animals came storming through the gap, gaping jaws, long arms with claw-like fingers which latched into the couple being caught on camera and they began screaming. The angle widened. Perhaps a hundred creatures were now ripping into the guests at the party. They were slaughtered and dragged out by their arms or legs, leaving a trail of blood. The camera was shaking but it followed the creatures to the broken fence. There stood a seven feet tall, demonic figure, with horns, glowing red eyes and heavily muscled arms and legs. It looked around, as if to check they had not missed anyone. The person holding the camera timidly backed away from the window, as those red eyes caught sight of him. Silently, the glass shattered in front of the camera and the beastly demon was reaching out with grasping fingers. The camera clattered to the floor and the demon could be seen dragging the corpse, for that is what it now was. A teenage boy, maybe fifteen or sixteen years old. Murdered.

The lights came on. He and Mrs Shaw went back to her office. This time Carol poured two more generous single malts. Neither with water. Bill accepted the drink silently with a slight trembling in his hand. He didn't look her in the eye.

"I'm sorry for shocking you like that." Carol gestured to the chair again. "As you can see, something very wrong is loose in the interior and we have had reports of small communities going missing. All the missing people lived within one or two miles of your mines and we have managed to track some of the activity using satellites."

"What do you want me to do?" Bill looked seriously at Carol. "Mrs Shaw, I thought you were going to use your new-found intelligence to influence me to back your schemes relating to climate change and now I do not know what to think. What do you want from me?"

Carol Shaw pressed a button on her desk and the door to the office promptly opened and in walked several secret service men and women and a couple of serious looking generals. Carol Shaw gave names and titles. Bill realised these were the top people in the security business. He sat back, nursing his drink while they seated themselves in chairs that had been stacked at the side of the room. When everyone was settled, Carol Shaw's security locked the room. No one was able to get in or out, nor could anyone from outside hear anything said in that room. Bill was holding out well. He had dozens of questions, but he could see that there were a lot of worried men in that room. He didn't want to break the tension until he fully understood why he was there.

Mrs Shaw ignored Bill now.

"What is the latest general?"

"We believe that there is a nest of these animals in the depths of Mr Carruthers' mines. There are a lot of them. We have considered blowing the entrances, but we guess they are good at digging, so this would only slow them down. We cannot use heavy weapons without going into the tunnels ourselves. We lost two hundred men on the last attempt to do just that. No one came out. We think they are all dead."

The room was silent. Carol Shaw looked upset but in

complete control. 'She is a good choice for leader,' Bill thought to himself.

"Gentlemen, I have spoken as our head of state and the Queen has considered how the Commonwealth is situated to support us and is in agreement with me, that this matter is too serious to keep a lid on for long. These creatures, whatever they are, are getting more aggressive and are clearly being led by some form of higher intelligence that makes me believe that our nation is under attack. Our people are being kidnapped or slaughtered in large numbers," said Carol.

"Why do you say kidnapped?" asked Bill.

"No blood at some of the sites where people were taken, and another thing," said the first general to have spoken, "they only kill and probably eat adults. Remains were found by our incursion into the mines. We found a lot of bones before everything went quiet."

Bill interjected. "I wonder what they are doing with the children."

* * *

Deep under the earth, in an old dwarf digging, some two miles down and away from the entrance of the mine, the Spawn creatures dwelled. They had recently returned from the assault on a settlement and were busy cutting up meat and filling pots to cook down the flesh into a soupy morass. The bones were removed. Some were cattle, some kangaroo meat and some human remains. First the Spawn ate, then the demons were fed, before food was taken to the cages where there were human survivors. There were between fifteen and twenty of them huddled in a group, in shock and fear for what they were enduring. The demon moved to the cage side. "Eat!" he snarled, "or be eaten!"

In a picture of misery, the group moved one by one to take a bowl and began to force the food in their mouths. Most had tears running down their cheeks as they avoided each other's gaze.

"Good, good," said the demon, in a calmer and less threatening voice. He moved away and went to see his queen to report the progress made above and below ground.

CHAPTER THREE
WHAT TO DO?

Mrs Shaw was once more sat across from Bill Carruthers.

"So, you see we are in a bit of a fix Bill. We must keep this savage assault under wraps until we are in the position to understand what is happening and then properly manage it. If we release the truth the population will panic. We will have a lot of frightened Australians wondering if the world is about to end. If we buy your shares and create a military boundary for at least ten miles from the mines, we might be able to contain the attacks by these Spawn from what looks like a devil and control who sees what while we eradicate every demon we find and plug the source of this evil assault on our land." She sighed, "...and we might also find some survivors."

Bill looked and felt a bit sick after what he had witnessed but he also felt a sense of euphoria because in one swoop he had resolved his business problems and liquidated his assets and could now buy capital stocks well away from this impending disaster zone.

"I agree," said Bill. "Get your lawyers together with mine. They can do the leg work. I also want something from you Mrs Shaw. I want to be in on the ground and support you in the mines. I know the terrain very well, none better. I have spent half my adult life under the ground and I know the difference between natural terrain and whatever else we find there. I know it is a small offer, but it's all I've got for the present."

"Thank you, Mr Carruthers! I was hoping for at least that much, but it will likely be dangerous."

'I know it will,' thought Bill, 'but what an opportunity to raise my profile on the world stage. Not many self-made men get the chance to hang with the most powerful governments on the planet in a war setting. If my guts tell me anything, this little war we are about to engage in is going to turn up some pretty exciting stuff. I must invest in news corporations first. It will be very handy to be in at the ground floor of this breaking (eventual) scoop.'

* * *

The city of Mount Isa is situated in Queensland's vast north west, in arid surroundings in the heart of the outback. Bill Carruthers had offices in the town centre and part of the oldest street to be found still standing in the town. They were old but palatial and a part of the original success story that he inherited from his father. Bill settled behind the large oak desk, which had a polished surface that was showing signs of heavy wear. Bill felt comfortable in the high-backed red leather chair that was his father's. His father knew quality and comfort and Bill inherited this quality from his father. Bill pressed the old buzzer on his desk and his faithful and long-suffering secretary came in promptly to take letters.

"Come in Molly, take a seat. I have a few emails for you to check before they go out. You know my spelling is a bit iffy on the longer words," he said with a smile.

"You are a lazy speller," she taunted him without looking up, and so hiding a wry smile. "If you had paid attention when we were at school instead of trying to look up the girls' skirts you would not need me to make you look good," she mock scolded him.

"Aah, you know me so very well and that's why I pay you the big bucks!"

Molly smiled easily and retorted, "I can always use more you know, but you can't afford it really so shall we get on with some work now that playtime has finished?"

"Absolutely and so to business!"

Bill shared his over-sized screen and got down to the serious work of running his company. This was one of Bill's favourite parts of the day. He knew that Molly could run the show on her own and only needed to get him to make the serious money decisions. Molly already spent his money on building the business and she had shown she was astute and tough. What he really liked about Molly was that she was his long-time friend and there had never been a spark of interest romantically between them. It was more like a best friend relationship of two equals, and not only did it keep Bill's feet firmly on the ground, but it also helped him keep in touch with the smaller decisions that keep staff attentive but happy at work. His staff respected Molly for her character and strength. They knew how important she was. If one of his executives was in the bad books with Bill, it wasn't unknown for them to talk to Molly to see how to get off the hook. Molly was clever and intensely loyal to Bill but only gave him information that he needed to hear. In this way the workforce knew where the real power lay and were loyal to Bill and, importantly, to Molly.

As the morning came to its conclusion, Bill said finally, "Now Molly, something big has come up and, as you guessed, Mrs Shaw was not calling to wish me well. I have seen things that make my blood run cold."

Bill told her in confidence all that had occurred. Molly was serious.

"Hell Bill! This is a bit of a turn up! It certainly gets you off the hook business wise and it sounds pretty bloody terrifying to think there is a whole load of devils and demons on the loose at the bottom of our mines. The area won't be affectionately known as the 'oasis of the outback' anymore, will it? I guess that high fence you are having erected is not such a bad idea after all. That was next on my agenda. I thought you had gotten too much sunshine or something!"

Bill was deadly serious and looking straight at Molly. He said, "We need to distance our business from this nest of hornets, soon as we can. I have a nasty feeling about what is happening around here and I want you to move most of the staff to our offices in the big city. I do not want anyone I like to be the lunch for some monster. I want you to run things for me Molly. Make the offers on shares that we discussed this morning. I trust you to run with the business. I am going to be too busy on the other side of the fence to give my attention to our business interests."

"Okay Bill." And with that she left the office.

Bill was pleased with his day at work. He could focus on what he needed to relearn about his mines. Bill was relieved to hear from Molly earlier that all work, even maintenance, had stopped at the Mount Isa coal field. 'No need to risk their lives,' he thought. He gave a shiver, part memory of what those creatures did to the people in that garden, and part adrenalin, fuelled by the expectation of adventure and danger that he guessed would be involved. He was not wrong.

CHAPTER FOUR
OF MINES AND MEN

Mrs Shaw watched the film in her car on the way to the newly erected compound that now surrounded Mount Isa. She looked up to see the gleaming mirage on the horizon that was a feature of the arid outback for which Mount Isa was so famous. 'Red sky in the morning, shepherds warning,' she thought and then, 'not too many sheep here now and I wonder if they were eaten by locals or the other recently discovered residents...'

Keeping these thoughts to herself she relaxed and sat back to enjoy the scenery and let her driver and security man focus on their jobs. There was an air of tension in the car that she had rarely experienced before emanating from her security team. They were taking the business very seriously and had issued to them their best and most lethal weapons. Machine pistols, body armour and ammunition were all locked in a box inside the car and more in the boot. They were going prepared for anything. The car drove to and then over a vast hill of blasted rock some 30 metres high, where the mine had dumped the rock from delving deep under the ground. A giant conveyer belt stretched into the distance at the bottom of this man-made hill. The conveyor carried the coal to the waiting train trucks and lorries which hauled this black gold away for sale in China, Japan and even Korea, North and South.

The cars from Mrs Shaw's convey followed alongside the tracks. They came up to a barrier, a 30-feet high steel meshed fence that had been electrified to keep something unseen in and any people out. Clear signs warning of the danger were placed every ten metres as far as the eye could see. The cars moved through the barriers, which closed behind the fleet of vehicles. A small city of hastily erected buildings, tents and armoured personnel vehicles came into view. As they exited the vehicles, they were hit by the wave of heat, exacerbated by the heat from the machinery all around them. The temperature was in excess of 40 degrees and even the cool Mrs Shaw became aware of a trickle of sweat forming on her back.

'Thank God for deodorant,' she thought, 'I hope all the men are wearing it or this is going to get very smelly very quick!'

The party moved gratefully into a long, grey, single-storey building made up of 20 or so units. Mrs Shaw was shown into the war room, which housed all the communications equipment needed to meet the army and air force needs. There were serious faces looking at screens showing the landscape and the mine entrance, as well as a bank of monitors that showed the interior of the mine. The last three screens were blank.

"Are they spares?" asked Mrs Shaw to her general.

"No, they aren't, Mrs Shaw, something or someone knocked out the camera system in the heart of the mine."

Mrs Shaw raised an eyebrow, neatly pencilled, but made no further comment until they were all safely ushered into a large room with long tables at which sat soldiers in desert uniform and Bill Carruthers also dressed in uniform. He looked up and smiled as Mrs Shaw took her place.

"Good to see you Bill! And good to see all of you too!" she said to the room in general, as she gazed around at the faces now looking towards her. Mrs Shaw was pleased to see there were at least 20 other women in the room of perhaps 200 men in all.

General Lee spoke with a voice used to being obeyed. He outlined to the room the latest intel about Mount Isa and surrounding district.

"We have now learned of more incursions onto Australian soil by what we have named the 'Spawn' and the 'Slavers'. These creatures are bold and number in the hundreds and have attacked and decimated another two isolated communities on similar lines to the assault shown in the film you have all seen."

Several people moved uncomfortably in their seats.

"Our opening response to these attacks has been limited to containing further attacks and to this end the fence now surrounds the Isa mine for a mile and nothing has yet tried to get past or over it. Now that we have containment, we are ready to move into the mine itself. Mr Carruthers has been instrumental in helping us map the mine from a strategic point of view and I am confident we can avoid attempts to ambush our troops on the way in or on the way out. Tomorrow we move as a unit into harm's way to achieve the following objectives. First, to find and retrieve our people. Second, to exterminate this menace to our society; and third, to learn whatever we can about how, why and what has caused these creatures to come into existence. Please make no mistake people! You have all seen the savagery of these creatures in action and this will be a bloody fight if we meet the Spawn head on. We all need to remember that the Slavers seem to be their leaders and there may be other creatures that we have not met as yet."

* * *

Next day was an uncomfortably early start for Carol. An uncomfortable night on a strange bed with no air conditioning meant that her dreams were filled with visions of heat and odd images from her childhood, mixed with a vague sense of fear and discomfort. Although, as Prime Minister, she was to be precluded from going into any danger, she was clear with everyone that she intended to be on hand to support her generals and troops that were taking the risks. She knew that the men and women she was sending into the mines were the cream of her armed forces and every one of them would do their duty or die trying. She wanted to keep the dying down to a minimum by ensuring there was no delay if political judgements were needed. She also wanted no one to enter that mine with a light heart. This, she knew, was going to be a serious business.

General Lee greeted Mrs Shaw in the Ops Room. Everyone was there, including Bill Carruthers.

"Okay," said the general, "the mine is very wide at the entrance, 200 metres across and it stays that way for the first half a mile, before it begins to taper in to 20 metres at a mile down. I want barricades every 200 metres from a mile onwards. These will be manned by regular troops already briefed for their roles. The ceiling height comes right down to three metres and then even lower, so we go on foot for the last quarter of a mile."

No one seemed phased by the mix of metric and old money terms. The general had the respect of all present. "Mr Carruthers goes in the front, at his insistence. He feels his personal knowledge of the mine will be needed; and he has been busy looking at snags for the past week. Bill Carruthers knows his stuff people, so listen to him and look after him."

Bill looked a bit sheepish, and Carol Shaw thought to herself that he looked very capable of looking after himself. He did look a lot older than his years this morning, but she reflected that he was standing amidst the best young soldiers in this man's army and none of them looked a day over 30, and many a lot younger than that.

When the detailed briefing finished the sun was well up. A red sky in the morning met them as they exited the building. By 10.00 hours they were ready to go in. Bill was introduced to Able Squad. They were his protection. They sounded off, quietly, giving their names to him. Jane, Ann and Smithy stuck immediately in his mind. Fortunately, all of them had their names stitched onto their uniforms, specifically for this operation. The names were illuminated and shone in the dark when light from a torch hit them. This was for Bill's sake and if they met trouble the name tags came off. The women looked as tough as the men and equally capable. Bill could see that this squad was close. They checked each other's armour and straps. Everyone was ready for action. Ann checked Bill's pack and tightened a couple of straps so the pack moved with him without chafing. Bill was given a side arm, which he holstered.

"That's for your if anything gets past us, but don't worry, 'cause nothing gets past us," said Jane. "Stick close to me at all times and do as you are told Bill, is that clear?"

Bill nodded. He approved of their manner. He was even a bit in awe of Jane. She was muscled in a feminine way and tanned. She and her team were so confident in their ability. He found this very pleasing in people so young. Bill was careful not to look too long at Jane. He needed focus for what was coming.

'Think of them as grandchildren,' he thought to himself. Then he was back in the zone.

Back in the Command Centre the general took the radio.

"Send them in," he said.

Heavy vehicles started moving into the mine. A long line of vehicles, a thousand well-armed troops with automatic weapons but no explosives and nothing that was likely to bring the tunnel down. The only place where explosives were set was at the entrance. Mrs Shaw wanted to be sure they could block this exit to any potential enemy once her troops were back out. Coffee in hand, she watched through the cameras as the troops moved forward.

General Lee explained again, "Once we get to the walking point the troops will begin to film everything that happens there. All side tunnels are blocked with barricades. Our scouts reported that the activity of these Spawn comes straight out of the mine entrance as far as we can tell. We are, however, ready for anything."

Carol Shaw looked confident, surrounded at a short distance by her personal security people.

Bill sat in the middle seat, in the back of the vehicle. The bench seat was big enough for three and Bill sat with a soldier each side. All along the walls were the now silent machinery which, when working, pushed the temperature easily up to 40°C. There were huge fans blasting fresh air into the mine. The miners working the machines would normally be covered in sweat and guzzle water down by the litre. Now the temperature was a good ten or fifteen degrees cooler than it ought to have been. When Bill looked behind, he saw the other vehicle above him and could just make out the latest barrier walls being quickly erected by busy soldier engineers.

The lights came on as the vehicle approached each sector, set off by movement sensors. These gave the mine an 'eerie' feel to the soldiers who were unused to working in mines, but Bill felt more comfortable now he was under ground; away from the bigwigs and planning for the operation. He was reminded of his days as a young man, seeing the full extent of this man-made mine that had extracted, first copper in vast quantities, which had made the family rich, and more lately coal. His father, and then Bill, had been extracting as quickly as was possible to maintain the profit margins through the export of high-quality coal.

The vehicle moved forward into the darkness. Bill was shaken from his thoughts. "Stop!" he called.

Bill and the soldiers disembarked from the vehicle, collecting themselves, their weaponry and supplies in packs that they now strapped to their backs once more. Handheld lights were distributed and they shone brightly with a high intensity, almost as good as daylight, but with sharp blackness at their edge, behind which was the unknown. Jane and Ann looked around and the light fell on Smithy.

"Not scared of the dark are you girls," he said with a wide grin on his face.

"Funny man!" retorted Jane, as she kicked a rock with her foot in his direction.

Bill enjoyed the moment. These were confident, professional and relaxed with each other. Bill joined the moment with a grin of his own, which was returned by Ann, who flanked him on his left.

Two hundred soldiers moved down the tunnel. Smaller tools now could be seen set against the walls. Drills, compressors and even shovels were piled up and left when the mine was hurriedly shut down. Going was slower and it took perhaps an hour to walk the last 600 metres, checking the roof and walls for clues of any hidden openings, before they reached the end.

The final stop was to the rockface itself, almost like a small siding, with a giant drilling machine that looked like it was from a sci-fi film, in the light and shade of the high-resolution lights of the torches.

"This place is a bit claustrophobic," Jane said aloud to Ann and Bill, stood between them.

Bill thought to himself that this was what mining is all about. Darkness, dust and digging rocks out of the ground. He was again reminded of his family history where the early miners got so hot and grimed as they worked the face naked, to reduce body heat and allow them to work a shift in something approaching comfort. The coalface looked solid enough before them. The ceiling height was now down to eight feet.

Bill spoke. "Check the walls for signs of any entrance beyond the wall."

Bill spoke with authority and the soldiers around him moved to obey. The rockface looked flat from a distance, but Bill knew it was not flat and incursions into the coal were not always smooth. A soldier called attention to a corridor hidden in the wall by a jutting forward edge of the coalface.

'Now I'm earning my money,' thought Bill, as he moved towards the sound to investigate behind the coalface. This tunnel appeared to go nowhere after a few metres and Bill came out. They moved on, taking it in turns to check out the wide cracks that might fit someone through. The next moment another shout and he was called to another crack. He was now standing directly behind the soldier who had made the discovery. It was too dark to see his face, which was covered in a sweaty swipe of coal dust. With a hand on the soldier's shoulder he moved with him into the darkness. The soldier switched on his torch.

A metre wide and perhaps two metres high, a gaping hole appeared as the light shone through. The air was getting stuffy. Bill became aware of the human odour, some of it his own, as he walked on. The soldier, with Bill, and then Ann, Jane, Smithy and the rest, moved forward as one. The tunnel went before them before opening out into a large, cavernous space, perhaps 20 metres across with a roof 20 or so metres high. Its overall shape was round. It was lined by black walls, shiny in appearance, like freshly cut coal, which glittered back to their eyes. At the far wall there was another opening, with a flat descending floor with rounded walls which met to shape the ceiling two metres above them.

"Down we go," said Smithy. They went in single file and Bill could hear and feel the noise from many sets of army boots covering the distance, disturbing stones under foot as they went. This tunnel was longer and on a slope of one to four and the party became more cautious as they moved to prevent themselves from slipping.

The walls now began to change in texture and colour. They went from shiny black to a dull grey in the torchlight. They were now over two miles underground and the air pushed on them from behind from the last fans was only a slight movement felt on the skin, now covered in sweat.

"This is why the old miners wore hard hats and very little else in the deep parts of the mines," said Bill. "I'm all for that idea," called out Smithy. "Oww!" His jape was ended with a real yelp of pain as Jane twisted his right ear.

"Best behaviour Smithy, please," said Jane. "We have a guest, remember?"

Smithy called out. "Sorry Bill!"

The banter, Bill knew, was to lighten the mood in the dark, for although they had lights on, they were, after all, very far underground and by the temperature Bill knew that they would soon be breathing heavily through their scarf protected mouths.

Bill was then surprised, for it began to feel a bit cooler and the air fresher. He said out loud, "There must be a shaft somewhere near for the air to be this cool. Look out for any breezes coming from the rockfaces as you go."

Once more they moved forward and, before long, came upon a cavern. This was also rounded in shape and opposite it was something they had not expected to see. As each soldier followed Bill into the space, all gasped at what was revealed as the light lit up the space. Before them, ten feet away, stood a stone door with a strange set of markings upon it.

"Whoa," said Bill, "now that is a surprise! That door is nothing to do with our mine and it looks very old."

They moved forward as a group. Now there were perhaps 30 soldiers in the cavern, which was ten metres wide and perhaps another two and a half metres up to the door. Two of the soldiers moved to inspect the door. It was made of thick stone, perhaps a metre thick. It was shut and it was a tight fit, except on the floor. By kneeling with his head on the floor another soldier said he could make out the other inward edge of the door with his torch.

"This door must weigh ten tons easily," said Bill. He was then ushered back from the door while those recording their activity continued to relay pictures back to the Command Centre.

A voice came over the radio link. "Let us see if we can get in without using explosives. There must be a trigger mechanism somewhere."

Men searched the walls of the cavern for hidden triggers, but they found nothing. Bill was ordered back from the gateway and back up along the tunnel, through the first cavern and along the corridor leading back to the mine proper. Once back in the mine Bill and his crew sat down together while sappers took explosives into the tunnel and down to the old door they had discovered. Bill used the viewer of a camera. Now that there was real light once more, it revealed the walls stark black.

Mrs Shaw spoke to Bill. "That is a real turn up for the books Bill! Not one of us really expected to find that doorway. How old do you think it is?"

Bill looked rugged, now covered in a fine coal dust and smeared where he had wiped the sweat from his face. "It certainly looks very old, hundreds or even thousands of years old, I don't really know. What I can say is those tunnels have not been excavated by modern mining techniques. They look as though they have been excavated by hand. The coal is easy to break but that stone it moves into is solid stone and hard and yet it is cut as smoothly as if it was by a laser. There are very few marks upon it."

Bill listened for Mrs Shaw's reply as she spoke to General Lee.

"General, I don't think I want those sappers blowing up that door. It is probably of historical interest and probably worth a lot and we will need to be mindful that this is an archaeological find, very rare indeed."

The sound came clear to them in the mine as they debated whether they should cut into the walls next to the door rather than try anything too explosive. Bill thought all this very sensible and he said so loudly and clearly for all those in the Control Centre within earshot.

Suddenly, the sound of gunfire far underground came to his ears, followed by snarling and then human screaming as of someone being ripped apart. Shocked, Bill turned to where the sound was coming. In the tunnel they had just left, more firing, shouts and screams emanated up to Bill and the others. Soldiers began running out of the tunnel to take up firing positions at the entrance. The sounds of battle could be recognised, and word came back from those below that they were under assault by the creatures they knew as Spawn. Within a minute the first cavern had been evacuated by all that were ever coming out.

Men were shouting to get out of the tunnel. "Move! Move!" Men, and the occasional woman, could be heard falling then screaming as they were pulled deeper into the mine. Whether alive or dead no one yet knew. Soldier after soldier came stumbling back into the mine. Their fellows guided them with hands on shoulders straight on and away. After maybe 20 minutes the last soldier ran through into the mine proper. He was covered in blood, none of which appeared to be his own.

Order was restored and heavy machine guns moved into place to cover the entrance they had so recently exited. Bill was ushered up the mine proper and past makeshift barricades, manned by many soldiers. All were now serious faced and focused on the threat from the tunnel. There came a rumbling sound. Bill knew that sound all too well. "Cave in!" he shouted, and began to run immediately up the mine shaft. His section was right with him. Other soldiers abandoned their positions as Bill and the others ran up the mine. Bill only stopped when the rumbling subsided. They had reached the first vehicles. Soldier after soldier arrived at the vehicles. "Sound off!" came the call from section leaders, now that they were in a better position.

Voices were calling, numbers being checked.

"We are missing 40 men and women!" came the call from a master sergeant.

The calm and commanding voice of General Lee came over the intercom. "Okay people, secure the mine where you stand. Make a dignified retreat to the barricade behind you. Make sure we bring everyone out with you that we can."

The order was acknowledged, the platoon with Bill moved quickly up the mine, Jane to his left, Ann and Smithy to his right. The others were just to the rear and everyone was moving with some haste, keen to have something very solid between them and what they had just retreated from. Behind the barricade, which spanned one hundred metres from wall to wall, with firing steps behind, now manned by one hundred plus soldiers, getting themselves ready to fight back if they needed to.

When the door in that lower second chamber had sprung wide, it took the soldiers completely by surprise. In less than a couple of seconds at least ten men were fighting for their very lives. While the Spawn were growling, the men were shouting and shocked by the force and strength of their enemies. The Spawn were about five feet tall. As they reached out to the first soldiers, the advantage was all with them. One body after another was lifted overhead by a Spawn and immediately grabbed and pulled into the doorway and then it was gone. The Spawn tore into flesh with their hideous claws and five more bodies followed the first. The human screams began as, one by one, in the wink of an eye, bodies disappeared, only to be replaced immediately by more Spawn.

Bullets started to fly into the Spawn as they moved forward for their next victim. Several Spawn were cut almost in half by the rapid fire that hit them. As the Spawn went down, they too were hoisted overhead and began their journey back down that tunnel. Once more there was hand-to-hand combat and another five soldiers were hoisted overhead. A female voice screamed as she was grabbed, even while firing into the bodies of the Spawn that held her. Two went down and up and over they went, followed by the female who moaned in terror as she disappeared through the door.

The Spawn had taken the first cavern and were pressing into the tunnel in pursuit of the soldiers now in full retreat. Firing became sporadic. A soldier slipped in the panic to reach the next cavern. Those behind him were trapped until he moved on. The ten men behind him were one by one dispatched down the tunnel. The screams and the growling continued with the occasional burst of machine gun fire.

The soldier who had fallen got up, only to be hauled on from behind. He had very nearly made it, but now he was headed back down the tunnel, battered and bruised, until he fell unconscious from hitting the ceiling as he was passed down by the Spawn.

The brief respite caused by the soldier's fall at least gave those in the second cavern time to move out. They did so with all haste. Four soldiers stood their ground and began to blast the Spawn as they came into the second cavern. Spawn after Spawn was cut down but the pressure from those behind was irresistible. The Spawn that fell were lifted high, as before. They became shields for those following and in a very few seconds the soldiers were fighting hand-to-hand, then they were downed.

Spawn did not halt. Up they went into the second tunnel. This was the longer tunnel of the two. Now there was a queue formed at the entrance to the mine proper, as soldiers squeezed through the narrow entrance. Soldiers began to shout from the back. The last three in the line turned to face what was coming. They had barely enough time to fire their weapons before the first Spawn was pushed, quite dead, into the first soldier. He grappled, went down, was followed by the next and the next and the next. Few of these soldiers had been killed outright. Over the heads of the Spawn they went. Over 20 more followed their comrades down into the depths before the rest escaped.

The fighting grew slowly louder behind them. Almost constant gunfire was resounding off the walls. Men were now dying in the second chamber and then in the next tunnel. Whatever they were shooting was resilient and coming through hails of bullets.

In Bill's mind he was imagining the terrible scene behind him in the mine. His squad was shouting to their colleagues to move out and get behind the barrier and get ready for what was shortly going to be coming into their line of fire.

"Come on Bill!" said Jane and she and Ann pulled him away from the barricade steps and up the road to the next barrier.

"Let someone else have a go!" said Ann, clearly shaken, though trying hard not to show it. Her squad moved with Bill up the tunnel. Behind them there was a shout and then an order to 'Fire!' Bill and his squad of ten moved on, now breathing heavily. They passed the next barrier, also heavily manned.

Back in the Control Centre there was a buzz of anticipation. The Operations Room was full of animated soldiers all working on the problem. The camera system in the main tunnel was working and giving the soldiers some valuable intelligence about the newly discovered enemy. Some of the Operations Room staff were shaking from the adrenalin flooding their nervous systems. They were trained for combat, and seeing their comrades fall to these beasts was hard to watch. The deepest barrier in the main tunnel, and the soldiers on it, opened fire with everything they had as soon as

Spawn came into the main shaft.

General Lee gave a grimace of satisfaction as Spawn began to fall quickly at first. Mrs Shaw was shocked by what she was seeing happening to her soldiers. Some of them were women and she was also alarmed at the speed and the ferocity of the Spawn, as they demonstrated their strength and willingness to sacrifice themselves in the assault. The weapon fire continued unabated. In spite of this, fewer Spawn were falling now that their dead colleagues were in front and overhead, effectively blocking many bullets. They reached the first fully manned barrier. It seemed to Bill that a tide of bodies hit the barrier.

Automatic fire continued and, like the sea, the Spawn stood upon the top of their fallen comrades until they were four high and ten deep and all ravaging to reach the soldiers now in front of them. General Lee watched, mouth open in horror, on the camera as the automatic weapon fire grew more sporadic as hand-to-hand fighting had begun, defending the barrier as soldiers fought for their very lives. It seems to be always the soldiers that were thrown backwards.

There were now hundreds of Spawn attacking the soldiers, who had been forced to retreat or die and so leaped off their firing steps. The Spawn, showing hideous mouths screeching for blood, raised their arms, showing their mighty clawed appendages. Their colour of skin was a mottled pale pink, as were their eyes, which were surrounded by fatty tissue. They looked like pigs standing on their hind legs, that had no snout or ears. These were replaced by tiny black holes from which there was a clear fluid running constantly as if they all had heavy colds. The teeth were sharp and shaped like shark teeth and they showed two lines of these when they snarled. Just like pigs they had no neck, the jaw defined the end of the hideous features.

On they came, attacking the soldiers who had leapt off their firing steps and moved backwards, firing as they went. More soldiers went down. These soldiers were the best Australia had and Bill felt tears of pride for them as they left their stations, hit the ground, and turned and fired into the Spawn. Now clear, the Spawn began to breach over the top of the barrier. The soldiers, to a man and woman, withdrew as they fired, keeping the Spawn at bay. As distance came between them, their fire was less deadly. Once the order came from the officer in charge, they turned and ran for the cover of the next barrier.

General Lee and those in the Operations Room were now recovering from their own shock, as professional soldiers began to do as they were trained to do, and took great pride in how they were marshalling on the battlefield. It gave them confidence and the general felt much calmer than he looked, once he could see his troops' reaction to battle with such a bizarre and quite terrifying army.

Lee turned to his Prime Minister. "This is not going at all as expected Ma'am and I would like permission to withdraw our troops from the tunnel before we get more casualties, as the tunnel widens and more of these creatures can come at them."

The Prime Minister nodded in agreement, still shocked by what she was witnessing. "This is your battle to command general," was her reply.

Orders came over the radio headsets asking for a complete but orderly withdrawal as the troops on the second barrier opened fire in support of the survivors who had reached this barrier. Bill looked back at the chaos. He and the squad reached the next barrier. Bill felt in control of things now that he was back in the main shaft. He saw that the roof was coal, unsurprisingly, but it was a thin vein, or it would have been mined. He knew it was probably thick enough to made quite a blockage. He turned to his squad.

"They can't hold long, Jane! We need to take the roof down!"

Jane got the message and immediately saw what Bill meant and called to the nearest officer, Jono. Bill shouted to him over the gunfire behind him. "Jono! Tell those on the second barricade to fire at the roof!"

The officer spoke into his mike. Bill could only hear his response as the persons on the other end looked to confirm the order.

"Yes! Yes! Take it down!"

The Spawn had almost reached the second barricade when the firing on the roof began. In front of the second barricade, large chunks of ceiling, coal and rock, began to fall on the Spawn. Bill now had the ear of the officer.

"Pull your men back Jono and intensify the fire on the roof. Throw grenades, whatever you have as your men reach safety."

The troops pulled back behind the barrier and took up stations to support the men on the barricade's firing steps. Despite the assault from their weapons and the collapsing roof overhead, the Spawn came over the second barrier. At the same time the soldiers took evasive action from the firing steps at the last moment and leaped to the safety of the ground. The soldiers behind them opened fire. The officer, Jono, now had had time to devise his response. "Grenades!" he shouted.

Every soldier in range of the barricade pulled pins, including Jane, Ann, Smithy and the rest and threw them with all their might at and over the Spawn. Bill was pushed to the floor to protect him as the explosions began. The noise from firing and explosions was deafening and Bill put his hands over his ears. It seemed to go on for a long, long time. As the noise began to abate, Bill looked up to see a large cave-in in progress and, for a second or so, saw it fall on the Spawn as they raced up the mine, trampling over their own fallen, moving towards the third barrier.

The mine was blocked with coal and stone and dust piled up, covering them all over in a fine black mist. Bill and the others waited until the roar of fallen rock subsided and the dust began to settle. The mine was completely sealed in front of them, probably burying a few soldiers and an awful lot of Spawn. The important thing was that the Spawn could no longer come at them. The mine fell silent. The soldiers were silent as they turned away and retreated up the mine. Bill was also silent, thinking about the soldiers who had been killed and how relieved he felt to have thought quickly enough to get Jono to bring the roof down. 'I hope those in the Control Centre liked my response and I don't get court marshalled and shot! Or worse, get Jono and the others in trouble.'

They walked up and out of the mine. Further charges were laid and set off. Nothing was coming out of the mine for a prolonged period. Jane grinned at Bill as they walked out into the sun. "Nice white teeth Bill! How do my teeth look?"

The gallows humour of the outfit surfaced and infected the others who couldn't stop laughing, as the relief of surviving whatever it was that they had just experienced swept over them.

Carol Shaw and General Lee were sat once more in a wardroom when Bill and Jono, the officer in charge of Bill's section, were ushered in. General Lee took the initiative. "Sit down gentlemen, we have a lot to discuss."

When they were seated and given coffee, courtesy of Carol Shaw, happy to have something distracting to do, General Lee opened the conversation. "First and foremost, and before we get into the nitty gritty of this very strange and traumatic day, I want to thank you Bill for your quick thinking to bring the ceiling down on those bastards. Jono, you took the initiative when it was offered you and probably saved a lot of soldiers' lives. I know Mrs Shaw is equally pleased that we got out of this with the fewest fatalities we could under the circumstances. We put the number at forty-six."

Carol grimaced at the number. Jono put his coffee on the low table in front of him. "It seems we lost another six coming out then," he said. "Thank you for your support general Sir, but it was really Bill's local knowledge that found the hidden entrance and then saved the day."

Bill looked uncomfortable. He asked the question uppermost in his mind. "So, what happens next?"

General Lee spoke very seriously. "There have been 'developments' around the world. While we were meeting this insane threat here, there have been similar outbreaks on the edge of the Gobi Desert and in the Rockies in America. Thousands of these Spawn appear to have broken out across the globe. It seems that humankind is facing a real threat, worldwide. I have been briefed by the Command Defence and the Queen, as Head of the Commonwealth, together with the Prime Minister have authorized all the support we need from Great Britain and the Commonwealth."

As the meeting went on it was claimed the Americans in the Mid-West were caught cold. Several towns had been ravaged, with hundreds killed and thousands unaccounted for.

"We think both China and Russia are responding to similar threats, but they are not admitting it yet. For now, we need to look to our own people. There are bound to be other exits for these Spawn beasts. We need to be ready to respond quickly."

General Lee and the others now turned to discuss what they had learned and could share with their allies. They talked on for two hours and then took a break to let the rest of the world have their intel.

Carol Shaw and Bill left the area by air. They flew back to Perth to get the government machinery working to support the population.

CHAPTER FIVE
THE EXODUS OF EVIL

The Angel Deborah sat with Ruth in the Fifth Level of the Golden Path and began to tell her the memories of the fall of Satan, for she had been called upon by the Angel Death to battle at his side against the forces of Satan, and she, with many other angels, had crossed blades with Satan's strongest allies. She had been particularly directed by the angel called Death to fight against Alshaylon Yonlik, who fought alongside Satan at the initiation of the battle.

"In the beginning there was nothing (in this Universe for it had not been formed). Why would there be? The Creator in his Heaven was and is omnipotent and there was peace in Heaven. The Creator was invincible in all things and master of all life at all levels.

"So many universes, so many forms of creation, each different from the next. All these universes are producing life through the Creator's might and will. Some of these universes were exceedingly ancient indeed, formed by a thought in the Creator's ever-expanding form. Some high forms of life that had grown to be great in these places, were close to him. Upon the Seventh Level, where they shared his wonderous vision for creation and marvelled at his greatness, were some of his most powerful allies in his quest to create life and beauty.

"Satan was one of the Creator's followers and hit a snag in conjunction with the god's vision in creating greatness, not only in formed universes, but also those yet to be thought of. At this time there was only good in existence, for only good can come from God.

"The Seventh Level was pure thought and as close as any created soul could come to the Creator as far as I know," said Deborah.

"To be on the Seventh Level was to be in the greatest of

God's houses. The Creator's vision was that all forms of life should have a plan, a purpose and opportunity to learn and grow. The plan was for God alone. The purpose the Creator shared with no one." Deborah then spoke of the fall of Satan.

"Growth was in the mind and a part of the purpose for humanity and was for the Creator alone to comprehend. Satan was close to the powerful song of creation and sought convergence to change its perfection to one which he and his followers could claim so that they might share the experience of the Creator over the millennia of existence. Satan was stupendous and powerful in spirit and came from an early example of other universal growth. He was different. He became envious as his growth, which had been continuous to that point, was now slowing and had paused.

"Satan planned to link himself into the song of the Creator and so grow continually as the song created new universes. He touched the Creator's song for he believed at that point that, once set in motion, the Creator moved on and would not notice his subtle change to perfection.

"The angel called Death saw what Satan had done and was immediately clear that some wrong had been created and forced Satan and that portion of imperfection into retreat. The Angel Death had more power even than Satan and his power expanded across the seven levels of the great path and he was known everywhere. Satan, seeing that he was discovered, began to weave the song for his own defence and for the defence of his allies, but Death was the more powerful angel and called forth the greatest of the Creator's angels to battle Satan and force him to yield and accept his punishment.

"Satan became afraid, for he knew the meaning of fear now for the first time in his existence. He had never been tested by another phenomenal angel and was found wanting. He fought savagely when attacked but Satan responded out of growing fear, whereas the Angel Death knew nothing of fear or defeat.

Satan now knew that if he relinquished his power and gave up the fight, he believed there would be nothing of him left and he had come to covet his independence above the life of anything living.

"Satan therefore sought to delay the forces of good while he and his spirits were pushed lower and lower and became darker and darker as they fell into fear. The suppression of the dark powers of the damned Satan was severe. For, as they fought, they became depressed in order of thought, understanding and life. The smallest of Satan's allied spirits falling into muteness and poor definition with every level of the Golden Path that they dropped off.

"Even the great Satan felt himself shrink into a pressure of suppression which dulled his intellect and inspirational aspects of his vision. Satan was strong and resisted, but always slipped back further after an attack and focussed upon only his closest associates in the battle they fought. While Death faced Satan, other angels of great power were called to fight Satan's acolytes.

"Death charged me, Deborah, to hound Alshaylon Yonlik, and this I did. With all my might I smote at Yonlik, who was close to surrender and already on the Third Level of Creation."

Deborah looked seriously at Ruth.

"Dear Ruth, I was set against a foe beyond my measure, for Yonlik was much higher in status than I. Why the Angel Death gave this task to me, I have often pondered here on the Fifth Level, after my return. Yonlik had served on the Seventh Level of Creation with Satan, but her powers were being consumed upon the Earth and this made it possible for me, an angel that had been lifted by the Creator's grace, to approach Yonlik and survive and to give her battle.

"When Satan gave much of himself in a desperate bid to keep her fighting, Yonlik felt Satan's support for her and pushed back against my strokes and we battled on an equal footing for many strokes. Yonlik, being of higher status, was able to colour the battlefield for one that suited her mindset. She, all blackness as close to nothingness in my eyes. I could barely follow her movements. I fought her in an almost impenetrable darkness. Only my blade and inner light shone out and it was enough for me to see my enemy and her scimitar, which she had fashioned for the battle within her mind. My weapon I chose to be a small, slim and light blade, filled with my essence and inner light as stark in contrast to her darkness that I could imagine.

"We were in a tunnel of the Creator's vision. Behind me was the entry to the Fourth Level and behind Yonlik utter darkness. Back and forth we battled, she and I. Prior to the intervention of Satan's darkness I had seen Yonlik grow in fear, now she was separated from his power as he fell. Yonlik rallied and showed her determination to survive. Yonlik taunted me. Taunting an angel was a foul deed, calling me evil names and making foul odours to put me off in the fight. For my part, I ignored these distractions. I was determined to be unmoving and not take a backwards step. I was quite prepared to battle to the last part of my life force and spirit.

"I dug deep into my love for the Creator; and I felt the purity of his essence for that instant. It was so full of love and perfection in that moment, I was renewed. I went at Yonlik, not now fighting her with my own prowess alone, but with the love and grace given to me by the Creator, in that most wonderful of moments. I now fought with a surety and conviction, not of my own making.

"The assaults on Yonlik and her weapon intensified until it was hardly possible for you to imagine the speed, power and energy in my blows that were as light as light itself. The assaults on Yonlik were felt by her as powerful ripostes and, as our weapons clashed and burned at each other, like mighty giant blows. One blade as bright as a star in the heat of battle and the other black to the hilt with burning red edges. Her blade got redder under the strain she was feeling. I fought and fought until I felt that inner love begin to diminish back to something close to what had been normal, but I was changed now and different for the experience.

"Our blows slowed, hers quicker than mine. We were near the end of our strength again, for although we kept our powers fighting at such a ferocity, it was wearing even for us. Yonlik was weakening and becoming fearful, for she saw the look on my face. She could see such clarity in pure love for the Creator even though I was as tired as she.

"Yonlik looked terrified now for she looked at my face and felt her own death etched there. I had the Creator to call upon from within and she could not do so and nor could she seek aid from the fallen one. The environs of our battle now favoured my essence and not hers and her blade screamed with effort and glowed redder and darker as it began to fail.

"In a final effort to overcome me, Yonlik spat vitriol into my eyes, which blinded me for an instant. She began to fade before my eyes under the suppression of my assaults upon her. She eluded me in that instant the vitriol hit me, by breaching the light of the tunnel where it was still as a grey dusk.

"This took her onto the Earth at the very edge of the Third Level, and in doing so she hid herself. Yonlik arrived under the Earth and not upon it, far beneath a mountain, and fled further and further under the mountain while her corporate body was still able to move through the rock of the Earth. Eventually she set herself in a cavernous area of heat and gas which made her cough due to the fumes. Yonlik was wounded but not mortally so and she was now trapped and unable to leave that place."

Deborah wiped her eyes as she recalled her memory.

"My enemy was gone beyond my reach. I joined the battle to support the angelic host and continued the fight until Satan was on the Second Level and then I returned to search for Yonlik and seek answers to how I might finish her evil and expel her to what we now call Hell, but to no purpose, for Yonlik was gone from the surface and I could not follow for I was not diminished as was she."

Deborah took a deep sigh before continuing and Ruth could see it would have been her personal wish to finish Yonlik there and then, but it was not to be. Deborah resumed her tale.

"Under the command of the Angel Gabriel, who had fought with Satan from the Fifth Level, good and powerful spirits entered the Second Tier of the Great Path to delay Satan and the dark spirits who fell there under his dark fire. The forces for good recognised that evil was now inevitable and so stood firm and were envisioned as a wall of bright angels, clad in armour, equipped with sword and shield. They placed themselves on the borders of the Second Tier of Creation and the First Tier of the Golden Path.

"Satan's ally on the Second Level was cornered on the very edge of the Second Tier. Cornered, but not expelled, the evil male spirit pushed back and kept himself firmly ensconced in the Second Level. He was a small spirit compared with Satan, or Yonlik for that matter, mean and traitorous even to his own master in the end and fled from Satan before Satan was defeated almost utterly. Although the evil spirit formed a great dark shape, he could not escape and was held by the forces of good on the very edge of the Second Tier. He named himself Despite.

"Despite created a barrier of rock and stone in the dream world of the Second Tier by tapping into dark energy left behind by Satan, as he fell from the formation of the Golden Path. Sadly, this was enough for Despite to endure in the dream world of men and the force of his remaining will stymied the angels seeking to banish him from the Second Tier of the Golden Path. He saw his foes falter and sent every hellish spirit and demon he could summon from Satan before the gate to the First Level was sealed.

"When the angel called Death closed the exit from the First Level to Satan, the spirit of Despite and his allies, through their joint efforts, held on to the Second Tier. What was to become the dream world of men, now contained evil.

"Despite was a traitorous spirit who had made progress behind the shadow of Satan and was one of his supporters who was on the Third Level before the fall. His nature, however, matched that of his master and so he was easily identified by Heaven's angels. He was cowardly and afraid for himself for he had been busy carving for himself a small slice of the world, where he could practise his dark arts. Despite had already gained a following upon Earth of darker creatures that resided there. These were reptilian in nature and were a form of small dinosaur, with talons upon short arms and powerful feet. They moved on two legs, with a long tail to balance themselves and had gaping rounded jaws, rather like a shark. When they bit into their prey, they swallowed without chewing.

"Despite was fond of these creatures, whom he thought of as his pets. Despite fed and altered these creatures to house lesser spirits within them from Satan's spiritual following.

"Despite, like Satan, had originally come from outside our universe and so had longevity outside the realms of time. Despite had fled from Satan at the first opportunity and anchored himself on Earth while Satan was fighting on the Sixth Level. He had seen the enemy and recognised his own end unless he acted. He fled as the coward he is, with no intention of sharing his master's fate.

"Using Satan's essence, to which he had limited access, he corralled his creatures and, through a form of necromancy unknown in this universe, he managed to reduce his creatures and himself into spirit form. He could do this because the

Earth was still teeming with creativity and the Creator had set his powerful spiritual song for the arrival of men.

"The song was forming the Second Tier for the arrival of higher species, where they could dream. Despite named himself Lord in the Second Tier. His creatures grew slim, and more snake-like in their appearance, in the dream world. Despite constructed a defence, which took the form of a castle prison where he housed his creatures. His preparations made it possible to defeat the plans of the powers for good. Despite does not feature strongly in this telling but he remains a powerful evil influence. He will not be ignored for long, lest he find a way to return to the Earth."

Ruth was saddened by what she heard and by the pain in Deborah's voice.

"So it would remain, for time did not exist in the world of dreams, but now evil could access the dreams of men and other creatures that walk upon the Earth under the mantle of time. This was a cause of great anguish for all angels that had rallied for the Creator to expel Satan, for it meant that dreams were open to both good and evil. So, it became the decision of angel forces of Gabriel to take it upon themselves to protect life born into the Third Level from interference by evil spirits on the Second Tier of the Golden Path in every way that they could.

"Gabriel and Death returned to the higher echelons of Heaven. Their task completed as well as could be done for that time. They had not destroyed Satan but had diminished and trapped him. Satan was now awaiting the attention and judgement of the Creator. He was mad with fear for an aeon but, when nothing changed, he began to grow again. A darkness that was drawn into him from a source he could not fathom was sustaining his growth. Satan embraced the darkness.

"Satan was pinned in his own dark fire, which scorched his

followers and blackened their existence and made them alike to Satan, but weaker and so subservient. There he stayed, master of himself, twisted by his own fire into something opposed to good. He began to mimic the spirits who were his guards, forming low forms, evil, twisted spirits which gained form on the First Tier. Satan mimicked reality and built his own army in mockery of the Creator to oppose the light.

"There he sat and there he sits still. Defeated and almost crushed from existence. His once mighty spirit rallied and, spun a world of his own making, which he called Hell. In Hell he felt he was safe from attack from Death, the mighty angel, and the others, but he was trapped in Hell. His anguish and greed took form and dark fires erupted in his world where extreme heat and cold were insanely mixed so that the spirits with him were either frozen or burned by his fire. Their agony from heat or cold grew into lustful heat and lustful cold, which they began to spin into their cores, making them masters of weaker spiritual creatures, fearful of both heat and cold."

Ruth had listened and been fascinated by the memory of Deborah as she told her tale. She marvelled at the honour she was being given to be told such great events.

The Angel Deborah spoke again. "In the dawn of time an evil virus sits, awaiting release upon the Earth. The devil Satan mourns the sight as the formation of the Earth seals his oldest allied abomination deep into the planet. Trapped, hopefully never to find the light of day. Or so we had hoped. We speculated that when man arrived, he would have been further in development upon the path and so better armed to elude the vile machinations of Despite, but it has proved not to be so.

"The evil that it is Yonlik, confined in rock caverns in the deep and dark places of the Earth, seemed to me to be unable to escape from her prison. I remember how Satan screeched his anguish at the heavens. His song rings out still in my memory: 'ONE DAY SHE WILL COME AND THEN WE WILL SEE!'

"The Devil, Satan spoke thus. Yes, we will see and gluttony and greed and the power we concede will itself fall to seed in Hell of my choosing, for I, Satan, although banished, remain Satan. I exist in the First Level and have survived all the others above me. The Angel Death ran from me in the beginning of my time here in Hell.

"Those I have banished will not fail me nor will they love me for their banishment. Some will fail to seed, planted so deep, and some will repent, if ever allowed in time. My closest servants will do my bidding whether they know it or not. They are armed with Despite, a master of betrayal in its purest form. It will surface and battle the good that they find for my dark fire has burned within them even as I pushed them away.

"Satan sent forth his mind and vision and allowed for all to hear that could, as he said, 'Just as the evil ones of my choosing are losing, I will spring my traps and end wars for all time. No more clean spirits and no more chosen men, only my shadows from the army of Despite. The warped minds of men and women will live in fear of me and of mine. This I decree as my power grows once more and I ascend to face the Creator again. For I survived the assault of the angel called Death and all his cronies. This must make me the most powerful of all angels and over time I will grow again to be greater than ever! I will battle the Creator himself in the end, for nothing can end my hunger and my lust!'

"This last utterance was the sound of pure insanity and his insane laugh filled Hell once more. When he finished laughing, he became solemn in his mood and cold as ice.

"Satan spoke on. 'Souls will be so tortured by me and mine that the Creator will notice their evil and God will revolt, abhorred by the warped intentions of Despite and of Yonlik. He will leave me to ponder for millennia my plans, which will seal the fate of his creatures; and none will stand forth. They will be mine, too filled with dark fire to ever leave me.'"

The Angel Deborah did not sing the Devil's song, but Ruth saw in her mind his insanity at its ending. Ruth was not fearful for hearing the song in the telling, for she was in blessed company, which cushioned her from any impact of evil memory while Deborah was present, and no evil could reach into the Fourth Level and above.

Deborah continued. "Satan spoke now to the spirits around him. 'I have already begun my plan to ascend; even as I fell, strong spirits already do my bidding on the tiers above. My adventure of discovery of the Creator's plans to come are known to me. The Third Tier of the Golden Path will be mine, mine for all time. From there we will force the angels of good to do battle, and in doing so they will break the barrier called Time, and once the barrier is made to fracture, we will move up in a great host and nothing, not even the Angel Death will stand against us. This universe will fall to me and then we will break free to carry the battle into the heavens.'

"The Devil's closest allies, from the spirits that fell with him to Hell gathered around him. 'Master! How can we re-enter Heaven when we have been cast out so far from the Creator? We are alone on the First Tier of the Almighty and Heaven's gates stand at every level and great are the guardians placed there unto the Seventh Gate.'

"The Devil smiled in his malice and hunger, knowing the heat and the pain that they suffer, for to be a spirit so far removed from God was a dire and painful loss, which diminished them all.

"Satan put forth his dark fire and drew them all closer. The Devil rallied his servants, and their fear was plain to see. 'Aah! My faithful, we will suffer much pain before we reach the Heavens again. Our pathway is clear in my mind. It is ours to unwind and experience the ecstasy of fire and ice and evil.'

"'We must tempt all of God's creatures and visit their minds and find those that are weakest and plant our very essence in them. Over time they become part of us! We will start with Despite in the world of dreams, as far as we yet can reach. We will turn the dreams of creatures we find there and bend them to our mind.'

"The Devil's servants were filled with dreadful glee, for the task set before them gave succour to their pain. The Devil smiled. He would one day have his revenge. Satan knows the Creator, who is greater than him and ever will be, may be damaged with the ruin of his song of creation. He wished such malicious harm to destroy fully and completely the intention for creation. In his insanity he would show to his master that he is worthy of his soul!

"Satan smiled at the devilry, deep in thought. 'If he denies me Heaven, I will have mastery at least on this minor world with a heart of rock! It is a good place to start, for the one God has moved onto other great feats and his song will grow quiet over time. Time is my friend and, as it passes, I will endure and so will my faithful servants. We will overcome all before us! Over Time!'"

Deborah sighed deeply before saying, "The Devil was in raptures for he saw in Time itself a way into the Creator's plan once more. God in his glory created Time but it exists only on the Third Level of the Golden Path. It is the Creator's tool to measure the progression of those of his chosen along their path to glory. Time exists nowhere else on the Golden Path.

"Thus, man can only measure himself against his ancestors' achievements. Satan thought that this was of course by design. The Creator, who knows everything, is everything and creates everything, wished to test those chosen by him in creation to work through the challenges set for them. Over time they would be tested and measured, but only on the Third Level of the Golden Path, for this was challenge enough. If they succeeded, then some would be raised up to the Golden Paths above to take their place among the great and the good, wherever they may be."

Deborah paused and smiled at Ruth, saying to her with love, "Ruth, you are one such soul that has continued to grow and is not yet done. For you have ascended to the Fifth Level with my help and because your origins come from the Earth itself, you will not cause the arch of time to fall. This is your destiny. I cannot follow you, for my reality began on the Fourth Level, and once Death and Gabriel fell to the Second Level and pushed Satan and his forces to what is now Hell, upon their return they closed the barrier of what we call Time. It was set to last for aeons to come. If any angel tried to cross these lower realms again, then the veil would be broken and Satan would have access to the Golden Path and true hope once more. This can never be allowed, or so much that is good will be lost to us!"

Deborah returned to her tale.

"When Satan fell, he learned of Man through time and space. He became enraged that a simpleton species like Man could one day be closer to God than he could get. He saw them now as his tool for personal growth and power for they were feeble when compared to his growing malice and cunning. He might also find other creatures along Time's pathway that he could conquer. Satan also knew that the angels of creation would be watching, and by torturing the Earth and the creatures upon it, he would test the angels and mock them from afar.

"The devil Satan thought onwards and taught his followers that, although they had inhabited the first realm of life, they could not take form that any other could see, nor could they yet influence those on the tiers above, for the way was blocked. Over what would be aeons of time, he taught them how they might breach the road to the dream world. It took many aeons for the Devil's servants to inhabit the majority of the First Tier of existence.

"As he expanded his power through his dark spirit, he moved ever closer to the next gateway. This gateway was wide but very well soldiered by the guardians of Heaven who stood side by side to meet the pressure of Evil, pushed from behind as Satan battled the suppression with his darkness. The Devil was cautious, using patience and watchfulness to predict the arrival of men's spiritual centre, which was God given. Satan knew he could not interfere with Man directly himself, but he had the help of Despite to aid him.

"The gift of dreams given to men, to experience the Creator's song in the form of dreams, which for the chosen was a pure connection, as it was meant to be for all of humankind in the beginning."

Deborah lifted Ruth onto her feet. They walked through the Fifth Level and Deborah gifted Ruth her own insight into the beauty to be found there. Ruth saw the glory of creation in a new light. On the Fourth Level there had been beautiful islands filled with creatures known upon the Earth but also many that were not. Ruth had loved to land herself upon such islands of beauty and walk among the glorious flora to be found there. The scents clear and unmistakeable, of roses and carnations. Fields filled with daisies and poppies of brilliant colour. Grasses both tall and short on grasslands bordered by mighty trees. All was so wholesome. Ruth had thought the growth on Earth to be merely an imprint of true nature, when she compared the Earth with that which was the Fourth Level of Creation.

Here, on the Fifth Level, she was startled once more to see that even more real and varied was the fauna and flora and she soaked up the sights in her soul as she walked, noticing everything new to her. She saw fiery fairies that seemed to bounce from flower to flower and let off a glittering array of colour as they visited each. At times it was too much for her and Ruth would touch Deborah's arm, such as a young child might pull her mother's arm to make her aware of something quite urgent. In this way they moved through the land, which to Ruth's eye was so full of marvels, some of which she could not fully describe, that at times she found it difficult to listen to Deborah continue her long tale.

"Satan measured his timing and grew ever darker in spirit. Although he could not breach the defences himself, he was at times of great disturbance upon the Earth, able to achieve through his servants on the tiers above occasional sorties. Lower spirits battled on the Second Tier, testing the defences of the guardians set there. Despite remained secure in his dungeon city while his acolytes gave battle.

"Millennia had passed and even the good and the great were not entirely immune to change, being so far from the Creator and inhabiting lower spiritual levels than they needed to.

"As time passed on Earth, the Devil's servants grew more astute. Under the direction of that evil named Despite, they began to inflict themselves on the spirit of men in their sleep. Nightmares were created to intermingle with Man's search for peace and distract the spirits of men and women from the Creator's call. The evil spirits suffered on the Second Level, even when they escaped the guardians set there. It was the first time since the Great Fall of Satan that they could see men's dreams. Also, the first assault on humanity by Satan upon those residing on Earth outside the garden of Edain.

"Despite learned to interpret and damage these dreams, making some men tired upon waking and unhappy, then lost to their nightmares. Even here, in the creation of these people, there was strength enough to fight off evil spirits. Evil's success was hit and miss and some saw through this attack and drew apart, as has been told.

"These were the dwarf kind, who left and drew apart from evil, and were eventually to meet the faithful and were much changed over time by their exodus. The evil spirits were concerned to be cautious. They picked those dreamers who were struggling in the world on the Earth and entwined themselves like vines around the dreams and filled them with dread and then with heat and fired up their libido in evil twisting dreams. They caused weak men, over time, to lose their morality and sense of healthiness and respect for others, in the waking world.

"The planet we call Earth was beautiful indeed. The very heart of the planet was natural and good and, once men gained insight into what was their home world, they marvelled at the beauty, in fauna and flora. From scented flowers so fragile and colourful to the greatest of trees, powerful and strong and so vibrant and healthy, that the song of Mother Nature sang out and is reflected in the intricacy and detail in the world of nature. Blue skies, gentle rain, abundant mixes of essential oxygen and other gases all delivered to Mother Nature to entwine with the Creator's intent. Warm breezes, cool breezes and storms gave birth to an array of plant life so diverse as to be a most beautiful setting. So complex and so sweet, even the Earth itself as it formed was wholesome and wonderous and crawling with life.

"That wonderous Mother Nature on Earth mapped out the seasons for all plants to grow and gave power from her source to the spring and the summer, while slowing nature thereafter to allow autumn time and so onto winter and to rest, before blooming once more.

"The lore in the Creator's great song was there to renew and grow and ever change the form of nature. The ground itself was so fertile with life upon every inch. Some varieties of fungus would grow, come to fruition only to be seen in the height of a dry season or after a fire had naturally burned through the thick and rich verdant forests. Here were vast stretches of grassy plains, where wonderous varieties of animals lived out their lives, a part of the whole of nature.

"Satan and his servants felt their power swell as they fed on creation, moulding their own paths to acceptance in the world of dreams. Something quite alien to man that had fallen into a world. The spirits began by merely influencing thoughts at night and building on those most animalistic qualities in man. They used their influence to set traps for the innocent souls who floated in the joy of God's glorious song and received messages and hope from this sustaining force for which invention was only to enhance man in his growth and understanding of God's plans and building on goodness.

"The devil spirits sang their own song, confusing dreams so that the weakest of men's spirits became trapped while they slept. The devils surrounded souls, corrupting their inner visions, giving them comfort when they were angry, rewarding greed with devilish heat. They encouraged men who were coming under their sway to become corrupt in the waking world, making them uncomfortable, idle and wasteful of the energy of others, while awake on the Third Tier.

"They started to form groups of like-minded people and their shared cruelty grew into intolerance and loathing for the societies that good men and women sought. They learned to steal, rape, pillage and, although some were caught and summarily destroyed for their acts, the cleverest among them learned avoidance, deceit and how to wallow in greed. Aided by their evil spirit, they did not notice the evil overcoming their souls. They committed crimes against humanity, ending in torture and murder, it was murder that broke the Creator's links of love to these men and, without love, the full corruption of the Devil Yonlik, powerful in those times, warped the humans to such an extent that they became something no longer human on the inside.

"Under Yonlik, some of the less intelligent were mingled with other species. These became the Spawn. Others became flying demons. The most intelligent held most of their shape as humans but grew larger in their malice and the spirits within gifted them with their own gifts of thought control. Still few in numbers, these demons were known as the princesses. Slavers also maintained some human qualities and females were attracted to humans and male Slavers alike. They hid their malice in the dark places of the world. Hiding beneath the Earth, hating the Sun's glorious light, but enduring it. They would hunt at night when the moon was low in intensity or waxing and waning. Their powers were stronger in the dark and they quickly became a force of evil to challenge man. The princesses are the direct descendants of Yonlik, made from the first grotesque Slaver male that Yonlik spawned after her long recovery from near extinction at my hand."

Deborah spoke quietly but seriously about the so-called Princesses of Yonlik.

"These creatures are exceedingly dangerous in the world of men. They are vicious and cruel to all creatures. They exude evil to such an extent that it is difficult for humanity to even be in their company. Much of what followed is to be blamed upon them, for they gave rise to a change in the evolution of mankind, and humanity was split at this time.

"Those untouched by the Devil stayed close to God and were spared the interactions with the Devil's servants. Their purity and commitment to their god earned them the right to visit Tier Four of the Great Path, where only the good and spiritually great across the universe could go. The Edain went there in sleep and they learned of the fight between good and evil on the Earth.

"They learned, as you did, Ruth, that some of their vanquished kindred were captured by Satan. The devil princesses avoided personal conflict with the pure in spirit and their servants feared them. For they had the power within them not only to defeat evil, but in doing so banish the evil within, back to Hell in a depleted, shrivelled state, only to be consumed by Satan for their failure.

"The first born of humankind named themselves 'The Elven'. They saw their path to Heaven as a great gift. They lived their generously long lives, perhaps five hundred seasons in a state of great health, growing wisdom; and always with their minds learning to inhabit the Fourth Level of the Golden Path. Their dream was to send their spirit, which lives forever, forwards and upwards, following the Creator's song in accordance with his plans for men. The elves were wholly good, their behaviour could only ever mirror this, due to the constancy of the Creator's song. Under the command of this power, they remained separate from the rest of humankind for a long period of years, as we would count time now.

"The greatest among these, after very many years, listened to the Creator's song and came to a shared conclusion. In deliberations with one another, they believed that they could play a part in helping some of the fallen humans back onto the Creator's path. Some elves were gifted with an inner sight from which they could roam the Third Level of the Golden Path as spirits and spy on the evil in the world without concern for their souls. This was the Creator's intention. Elves were pure and nothing evil that had yet walked the Earth could approach them in any form.

"Upon the Earth, this great people populated the land of Edain from one end to the other. It was a vast country of the elves who remained in Edain, where the Creator's song was most powerful. From the dawn of man, at the appropriate time, where beauty and perfection in form was evident in every aspect. Flowers, trees of all kinds were set there with sweeping vales filled with sweet fragrances, grasslands stretching the length and breadth of the land with rivers sweeping from the high places in the mountains down to the vales and across the plains. The birds in the air and the beasts on the ground were all in perfect harmony.

"The elves learned to hunt, as directed by the Creator's song. They were merciful in their killing and only killed what was needed for survival. They learned to harvest grains and collect fruits and they flourished under the sun. The barrier between Edain and the rest of the planet was not one that could be seen, but it was there all the same. The elves ventured to the borders of their land and were perfectly capable of travelling on but the change in the air and the quality of life, even at the very edge of Edain, was subtly different and to the chosen abhorrent. With one step beyond the boundary, they became aware of the change. It was a discomforting thought, small at first, but then more and more prominent in their minds. They felt the ill intended by Satan to disrupt the planet and turning it towards chaos. Although they could endure the ill on the Earth, they chose to remain with perfection within the boundaries of Edain. To their mind there was no purpose to go beyond the border and they took the knowledge of Satan and his evil as a sign from the Creator that they should avoid contact with evil.

"In Edain, the pathway from Earth to the Fourth Level was clear and pure and assessable to all elves. The Creator, in his wisdom, had made his chosen powerful and they were mighty in spirit, even on the Earth. Their minds looked towards the Creator. They learned through long years to walk in Edain. At the same time, their minds wandered through the glories of the Fourth Level on the Golden Path. What they saw there none could tell to those on Earth, but it gave their countenance great joy and they exuded confidence and surety of their place in the Creator's plans and were grateful for it.

"The Earth was fresh and beautiful to the human eye, even outside Edain for a while. For those less perfect, once banished from Edain none could return. The barrier was that of perfection so that, although people who were for the most part untainted by evil could approach Edain, they could never enter. Many men did indeed try to renounce evil, but the pathway was blocked. Some of these became the dwarf nations, others maintained their humanity in other ways, avoiding evil places and expelling evildoers who were exposed in their ranks.

"The world was indeed beautiful to behold and flourished as nature intended for the most part. Of flora and lower forms of fauna than man, the ill in the world did not engage much, for Satan's intent from the beginning was to escape and he knew his chance was best met by focussing on Man as the dominant species on the Earth. For he alone had sufficient self-knowledge to reach into his memories of the tiers above with his spirit. Why Satan believed he could escape from the Earth was unknown, for his evil could not approach Edain, never mind enter it or attack the chosen within. This flaw, if that is indeed what it was, cannot be fathomed by those on Earth. The Creator's message through his song was clear. Avoid evil, defeat all its manifestations where you find it and always look to the Creator for guidance. Now we come to your time Ruth my dearest and so my story telling ends at last."

CHAPTER SIX
RUTH'S TALE

Now Ruth took up her story and shared it with Deborah while they rested at ease. Ruth had listened and become enthralled by the description of the great battle that defeated Satan and of Deborah's part in it. Ruth could see that there was no regret in Deborah for failing to finish Yonlik and banish her to Hell with Satan. Deborah knew from the beginning that she had been badly outmatched at the start of the fight. Her surety came from having fought so well and honourably. It had given her inner peace.

Ruth now spoke of her people.

"Elves in their spirit form became aware of the dwarves and their inner goodness. We elves also saw that they were imperfect in some ways, or at least different in their development from ourselves. The race of dwarves is prolific of their seed, great delvers and builders. They learned skills in building weaponry in the form of great axes, armour and great knowledge of the molten heart of the Earth far beneath them. The elves saw the Creator's song at work within them and marvelled at how they trapped light from the streams of molten rock that passed their realms to form lighting far underground. Golden and red light filled their great halls.

"They endured and grew apart after their travels to escape the evil on the land. It was at the time of change that elves first visited the dwarves. A few of the elves, of which I was one, felt an urgent need to aid the men of Earth. Some of the Edain travelled with me to visit the dwarves in their mountains but we were waylaid and delayed by the evil princesses. The Edain had not met this evil upon the Earth. We all knew instantly that they were a danger even to us. We fought their lower creatures, which sadly included warped men. After we had escaped from the trap set by the princesses, many of my kin wanted to return immediately to Edain. Two hundred of my kindred left to seek their path back to Edain, our home.

"I and ten others saw how great and powerful was this evil, carried within the princesses. We decided to remain and battle it as best we could. Our brethren tried hard to make us change our minds. They believed they saw the likely outcome was to be our destruction, which all of them would find hard to bear. We argued back and forth that we Edain were perhaps the only few that would, or indeed could, dare to intervene. In the end the discussion was conceded and the two hundred separated from us and sought to follow the path that would return them to Edain.

"When we had left Edain we had thought it would be just a matter of travelling to regain entrance to our lands. I learned much later, with great sadness, that when the two hundred came to the border of Edain, they could not re-enter, having met evil on the Earth. They were greatly troubled and had held further council among themselves and deemed it now to be their mission to aid man against the evil. They tried to return to us in the quest. Their hope was to lead men and dwarves away from the grasp of evil and teach them the ways of the Edain so that they could better defend themselves. We never saw them again. The princesses had followed them but dared not attack them so close to Edain. They waited until the two hundred were once more far from home before the princesses released hordes of Slavers and Spawn."

Ruth spoke in sad tones. "When my people turned to find us, the evil found them and trapped them and this time nearly all were killed. It was a terrible end upon the Earth for so many of the Creator's chosen. Two were alive but too injured to fight on and were taken by the enemy. Only one escaped the enemy for a while. He was strong, powerful and his spirit was no less full of life than my own. He found men before we were aware of him and warned them of the impending doom that evil sought to bestow upon them. They cared for him. In turn he taught them as much as he could in the time available to him. He met the dwarf peoples and was welcomed into one of their halls.

"When the Spawn Wars began as raids against men's settlements, he realised the threat, and urgently aided their response. He gave counsel to build bigger and stronger groups and arm themselves with weapons. Their skills and development soared with the help of the man from Edain and in the face of the threat from the devilish broods that assailed them. The man from Edain taught them stories, songs of the Edain, filled with wisdom from the Fourth Level of the Golden Path. Its meaning hidden in texts that the dwarves took as prayers. Personal growth and wisdom flooded into the dwarf communities. This developed into reflective listening on the part of the dwarf folk. They gleaned the essence of the Edain from the songs of the Golden Pathway and loved to recite the songs through the dark nights and under the ground where they were safest. The minds of the dwarves turned towards the light intended for the world and at the same time filled their souls to bursting point. They battled with the flying demon princesses, Slavers and Spawn, and there was much suffering. They were defeated many times. Sadly, the elf man perished himself, defending the old and young of the dwarves. I never discovered his true name.

"Yet our own efforts in meeting men enabled us to duplicate many of the lessons shared with the dwarves and, in the end, we were triumphant and the ill of the Devil's servants retreated to the deepest and darkest places in the Earth. Their defeat was not final. The Slavers worked to create the abomination of plagues and viruses and laid eggs with Spawn and the other demon siblings filled with the ill from the princesses. Some Slavers were of female gender. These grew lithe in appearance, larger than Man, smaller than the male

Slavers, but with a sexual attraction not only for other male Slavers. They exuded powerful hormones that human males could not ignore; even though they saw the evil and the intent, their bodies betrayed them. In this way many men that were not yet evil were enslaved to the demons and they trapped the innocent, male and female, and brought them into ambush where they were taken and enslaved.

"Once underground there was no escape. For long years raids took place in secret; many times dark rumour would spread that demonkind were abroad. Hunting parties were often dispatched but nothing could be found because the Spawn would collapse the tunnels where they retreated to make their escape and leave no evidence. Areas where these raids took place became places of fear and for years men would avoid the risk associated with these dreadful places where evil was tangible to the good hearts of men, even if they could not see it.

"Woman were tortured and became the playthings of the Slavers. Young women were nurtured into evil acts until they became the willing servants of the demons. These black witches, as they became named by rumour, carried out the alluring and entrapment of men over the centuries. Some were caught and burned. Many of the innocent also met this fate.

"In the underground, very far from the surface, the demons laid their plans to once more battle with Man. The most senior spirits devised a devilish biological experiment of stealing the sperm from men, warping the wombs of women until they were a new and altered creature. Some female Slavers raped males until they eventually died from exhaustion and broken bodies. These tortured souls were unable to resist the Slaver females who fed on the suffering, while stealing sperm and imprinting each sperm into a demon egg that hatched a Spawn. These eggs and their nests were hidden in the warm depths of the Earth, waiting for their time when they would hatch. The eggs would hatch into offspring under the control of the parent Slaver's mind. This gave the female Slavers command over all Spawn. Male Slavers mated with female and this gave them an almost equal hold over the Spawn. Numbers of Spawn were laid down in dormant nests, ready for the time when they would sweep across all the regions of the Earth. The princesses planned for total dominance over mankind and every other being on the planet. They would breed and spread like a fire. Stronger spirits placed their intelligence and malice within the strongest Slavers. Yonlik maimed even the evil spirits, trapping the weaker spirits in lesser Slavers so that they could remain alive but dormant for aeons if necessary.

"The Devil spawned lower lifeforms than Man, intending to bend them to the destruction of the planet. Lesser species of men walked upon the Earth and these multiplied far quicker than some. These men were not the brightest, in that they could not comprehend the spirit as did the offspring of the Edain. These men were part of Creation but were destined to follow a different path, which was warped by the intervention of Despite and Yonlik. Their origins were lost in time. They came to be known by different names. The Spawn were made from such as these. Lost souls driven from humankind for their evil and nurtured for their base desires by Yonlik.

"Not all those lesser men who were lost to the Creator were evil at heart and they had not committed murder. Many still had goodness within and lived simple existences, seeking nature's wisdom without knowing nature was itself linked to the Creator. These, the Devil's spirits could not overwhelm. These men retreated and, when they saw the evil at work, they hid themselves and fled before the evil could capture them, creating their own cultures. They changed in strength and shape, becoming over time adapted to their new environment forced upon them. These free men were spread far and wide across the planet. It was only those close to the evil places that made friendships with their dwarf cousins. The dwarves were shorter than many men, but stronger and great diggers and tunnel builders. They became known as the dwarf peoples and were many beneath the Earth.

"The dwarves forgot their parentage in the past and focussed on the strong bonds of love they held for one another as outcasts. As outcasts made to live with rock and stone, they delved deeper and deeper to hide from the evil in the form of the Spawn, which made the surface, for all its beauty, a hazardous place. The dwarves knew that to become greater they needed time and space and many children to create safety in numbers.

"The Edain who failed to escape was taken, only through force rather than desire, and was mingled in bloodlines with the lesser men, to the great joy of Yonlik. It turned out that a few of his offspring were a powerful resource in cunning. The princesses set him into breeding programmes, which turned them, over time, to evil. For their fall from grace was devastating and they finally came to venerate evil through many falsehoods told to them and great wickedness was done to them. The cost to them was of much shorter existence on the Earth. These were hollow, soulless clones meant to shame the people who met them.

"My folk with whom I had travelled saw the capture of our two kin as monstrous and we feared what evil might learn from them before they themselves succumbed to evil. The captured Elvin was valuable to the princesses for his service. Where the chosen were the greatest among human form, so his fall into evil was just as great. The evil of Yonlik alone would finally turn him evil. For this fallen one was made to entirely forget his former existence and so he was the perfect servant for Yonlik, who kept him to herself. This made him feared and created jealousy among the evil spirit forms who could not directly compete on the Earth, but only through weaker humans who could be possessed.

"These fell under the sway of the now Elven general and were forced to manage lesser tasks. The elf general themselves were committed to the dominance of all men. He built his own armies and jealously guarded against infiltration from his peers, spies. Trust was in short supply.

"My people and I knew the devil Satan himself was chained to the First Level of the Golden Path. This was the Creator's intention that he should no longer be able to directly influence or destroy the Creator's planned development for men and women. They learned the name of evil on the Earth while in Edain. They knew Satan named himself Alshaylon and his first lieutenant was given in honour the title of Alshaylon Yonlik, which means the Devil's own. Yonlik was a fallen angel herself, and as such was much feared by the Edain for her brutality and evil. Only a few dared to think she could be challenged."

The Angel Deborah interceded at this point to speak of Yonlik and her offspring. "Beautiful in appearance of her shape only, it was rumoured to be terrifying to be in the presence of Yonlik. She exuded evil and contaminated every creature that came into her presence. Yonlik was power hungry and had used much of her essence to escape under the Earth when she avoided my assaults upon her. She had achieved this through Satan's burnishing fire and her own will to survive while he was at his strongest. Now on Earth, Yonlik possessed enough evil to overcome all obstacles and rule, eventually over the whole planet, unless the good in the world could fight her.

"She was the most powerful figure on the Third Tier, known as the Earth, and she had been burned to the very centre of her being by the demon Satan's fire and her own personality barely survived. She spent half an aeon recovering her strength and remembering who she was. The satanic fire had given rise to false beliefs in her, that she was indeed the partner of Satan, such was his power over her. Yonlik came to understand that the demon Satan was removed and was not able to rise to her present tier on the Earth and it came to her that she alone would now gain complete control of all animal life on the planet and turn it to her own uses.

"It was Yonlik who christened Satan under a new name Alshaylon Yonlik in order, in her own mind, to carry his power and essence with her. Queen Yonlik bred her own species from the mixing of races and made her creatures, the Spawn and the Slavers, do her bidding and they built for her a great fortress in the Earth from the remnant of an early dwarf dwelling. Satan was present in her mind as a thought, watching her, and she watched him. He could not speak to Yonlik, but he flowed a current of thought with malevolence that aided Yonlik in her devising of her armies.

"From her great fortress she began her domination of the world. Her wicked desire led her to breeding Spawn and Slavers to meet her needs. Yonlik had a form of great outer beauty and she had great wings, which gave her the power of flight. Yonlik named herself Queen of the Earth. Her offspring had the same look and build but were a lot weaker and smaller than she. Yonlik mated with her most powerful allies and her offspring were her princesses, who were charged with forming their own demon hordes among the Spawn and Slavers.

"As the queen's armies grew into the hundreds of thousands, these became split into three colonies. They were named Shimishi, Yuehan and Zhuxi. They had the same power and appearance to one another, so close that it was impossible to see a difference. What separated them into individuals was their scent and their intelligence, which varied one from another. Each was enticing and irresistible to their Slavers and the Spawn. A Slaver told to rip himself to pieces with his claws would not hesitate to do their bidding. Spawn could barely move in their presence for wonder and fear in their simple animalistic minds of being noticed. Being noticed as a Spawn usually meant death."

Angel Deborah sighed quietly to herself.

Ruth responded with her own knowledge. "We learned much of the tactics of Yonlik while we both protected and fought for men under threat. Our numbers dwindled sadly, for the Spawn and Slavers began to target the elves of Edain in every conflict at no personal expense for themselves. Eventually I was all alone of my race left upon the Earth and outside Edain. I knew my days were numbered. I decided it would serve Man best if I could remove the elf general from her influence before I was hunted and killed. I went alone into Yonlik's lair deeper than any human had ever reached. I managed to bypass the princesses who were not so fully formed in their powers as was Yonlik; I remained undetected. I moved deep into the passages of Yonlik to where her slaves had torture chambers for unwilling captives, of humankind and ancestry. Many were mindless souls due to the torment placed upon them. They were beyond any hope of saving and I did not dare despatch them to end their suffering, for fear of being captured before I had ended my quest for the fallen elf and had killed them."

Tears came to the eyes of Ruth as she remembered the suffering she had witnessed in the dens of Yonlik. "Men and women from different human tribes and ancestry, caught by evil, and so tortured of mind and body they could not recognise friend from fiend and flinched when I was near them."

Ruth shuddered as she recalled the very scent of Queen Yonlik, set in her dominion deep in the Earth.

"So far down, it was hot and protected by molten rock, held

back by her force of will or some other power I could not fathom. Here she sat while her princesses worked through time to progress the Devil's great plan. It was the offspring called Shimishi who built her legions up first, stealing away her sister creatures at the behest of Queen Yonlik. Princess Shimishi was given the role of diminishing the numbers of the Edain and the dwarves wherever they were found." Ruth recalled the level of fear in her and shivered.

"The injured Elven, when captured, was sent before Queen Yonlik, who alone retained sufficient power in evil to turn him, over time, into her personal general. Once turned, the general was to be given to the princesses to aid in their separate tasks. I managed to hide myself from detection for several days among some of the most damaged human slaves who were used to bathe captured humans new to the den. This was part of the evil intent on perverting humanity through feigned kindness, giving good food, sexual partners while under the influence of the aromas surrounding the princesses. He would be sent each day to the princesses to be imprinted by them, stealing reproductive seminal fluid, seeding their own forces with human genes. For especially powerful and evil intelligence, the human females were made to act as incubators for terrifying offspring. They were born within an egg and resembled the princesses in shape if not in their power. These were collected specifically by Yonlik for her to nurture and aid her in her evil plans to defeat mankind."

This was a process important for the princesses as the Spawn creatures would survive only as long as the princesses. Ruth knew this to be an important element in the building up of evil forces and perhaps a way to kill the armies should the chance arise. Lying low between the broken minds of the washing slaves, Ruth waited for her chance.

"Finally, I had a little good fortune, which was very unexpected in that dark place. The general had been feasting and servicing female slaves. At the orders of Yonlik and in his changed forms he gloried in the suffering he was causing to their victims.

"The washing human slaves were ordered to attend to the general and I went with these to the quarters of the fallen elf general. As I entered the first chamber, the general, so called, was lying naked upon a bed in the centre of the chamber. I wasted no time and despatched him by removing his head from his body. The washers were so damaged they merely stood, bemused by what they had witnessed. I had no hope of escape from the chambers. Terror such as I have never felt before or since came upon me and I guessed that the princesses or Yonlik were very close and eager to catch me.

"The Spawn came against me in vast numbers. I fought them with all my strength. I slashed down with my sword and pressed my enemies with maiming strokes to their arms and legs, to slow the others from tearing into me and bringing me down while I was still living. Even so, I was forced slowly and surely to retreat. The Slavers who were conducting the Spawn clearly wished to capture rather than kill me. As I grew weary from the fight, I remembered that, on the way in, I had seen a crevice which opened onto a lake of magma, which was held back by a wall of stone and an unseen force. I was desperately tired. I could feel the adrenalin fading in my muscles even though I was still feeling terrified. My body was bathed in sweat and the blood of my enemies, but deep within me hope was rekindled and so I battled on.

"I now retreated with purpose, maiming rather than trying to kill. When I reached my destination, I squeezed through the crevice. I blocked the crevice with dead Spawn and had time to take in my surroundings for the first time. I was in a chamber with a river of lava that flowed through the middle of the cavern. The lava was swift and deep and very hot. A small bridge lay across the river of deadly heat and beyond that I spied the shape of a giantess; beautiful, dark of skin, with great wings tucked neatly behind her. It was Yonlik herself. She had her back to me and began to turn, hearing the screams of the Spawn dragging the corpses from the crevice I had entered through. For a second, I was lost. I knew that if Yonlik spoke, I would obey. I used my last strength to leap into the fiery pit. Everything seemed to slow down and happen in slow motion. As I jumped to my death, I felt no fear, only the adrenalin in my veins as the clawing fingers that sought my flesh as my fall made them miss their mark. I could see their broken claws buried in my legs where they clutched at me as I fell. In that instant I felt the euphoria of victory! In the next instant I felt terrible pain, as my body was enveloped in the magna stream. I screamed and then there was nothing.

"I awoke to see that I was lying on soft grass. It was a warm and sunny day. Gone was the pain and the grief. Gone was all fear that I had felt in life. Gone was the other Earth. I was at peace. As the memories came back into my mind, everything I had been and done was now remembered but I was changed. My experiences gave me wisdom and, from mistakes I had made, there was no retribution, for my whole purpose in my life on Earth was explained to me in that instant. I was whole and sound and without guilt for all my earthly failings. I was in full knowledge that my life had given rise to a network of many future possibilities that the Creator's song could now cause to come into existence. For this reason, many actions for which I was primarily responsible had advanced my soul, released in death onto the Fourth Level of the Golden Path. It came to me after a while that I might continue my journey towards the pinnacle of my ability, to reach up to the Creator.

"I looked now at my body. It was without blemish. My limbs were fair and I was restored to appear as my most beautiful self. Strong of limb and lithe of figure, with no sense of sexuality or lust within. Only peaceful acceptance that my spirit was free and that my body would continue to change as I advanced in knowledge upon the Golden Path.

"I looked outward and saw beautiful people from my earthly life advancing towards me. There were my parents and friends who had gone before me and their spirits shone within them, showing the happiness they felt in seeing me now among them.

"These beautiful people were now all around me, surrounding me with their inner radiance. One of them was the general elf I had despatched. We clung to one another and he thanked me for his freedom. I roamed the Fourth Tier of the Golden Path, finding peace, tranquillity and health more than I could ever have hoped, and then you came Deborah."

CHAPTER SEVEN
SHIMISHI DOMINATES HER SISTERS

Thueban, a powerful Slaver, was Princess Shimishi's first Slaver general after the demise of the fallen elf killed by Ruth. He was a male of great stature and pleasured himself, where he wished, upon the human slaves. He, like all Princess Shimishi's horde, had a lust for his princess, which burned within him when in her presence. He stood before her now. Thueban lifted his eyes so that he could just see his queen's neck. He knew that if he looked directly at her, he would lose the power of speech. His fear of her overwhelmed his lust for it was never safe near a princess. They were evil and treacherous.

"My queen, we have slaughtered very many humans, male and female, and captured many to serve in the Spawn and Slaver nests. Their offspring are many and they are all at your command."

Princess Shimishi surveyed her general; her voice was like treacle.

"What of the dwarves and their dwellings?"

"My princess..." began her general. "The dwarves, curse them, have moved away from us in their thousands. They build as they go, and when we discover their fortresses then we assault and destroy all we find. The Spawn are prolific of their seed and our losses are acceptable, given the fighting prowess of these dwarves. We hunt them and track them from one gathering to the next. Our human spies are experienced in betrayal. We treat them well, as you instructed."

Thueban's tone held the slightest element of derision, born from jealousy that such a low form as human life should be treated well at all, or even noticed by his princess.

Princess Shimishi smiled at this open show of contempt. "Very good Thueban, good indeed, but what of the rumours of a vast defence built by the dwarves to the south?"

General Thueban flinched before responding to Princess Shimishi. "Oh! Princess, please forgive your servant general, I have sent spies to the south, north, east and west of the Earth as far as our influence stretches in every direction. My spies beyond these points have all perished and no word has come back to me. Fortunate indeed it was that I was able to spare my officer. He returned to me with the word that humans, called dwarves, were fenced within the borders of the High Rock Mountains, and five dwarf halls lay within the mountains themselves. The dwarves have constructed great stone doors which lead into their fortress homes."

The Princess Shimishi looked pleased. She had been awaiting this news for a long time and was inpatient for progress now that she knew where to look. "Thueban! Bring the officer human into my presence now!"

Thueban bowed to the princess and ushered the traitorous man to stand before her, head bowed and subservient. The man was thin and feeble in frame, with sly, wary features and a cruel edge to his eyes. He was entirely without compassion for anything but himself. On the inside he was rotten to the core. All signs of goodness that could once have made him human were gone. He was an evil shell; feeble body, cruel to the weak and fearful of the strong and powerful. He gestured to his general in respect and obedience before getting on his knees before Shimishi.

"Speak," she said.

He spoke up, his dark features and cunning, intelligent eyes lowered to avoid her face as he beamed with the importance placed upon him. 'This is my moment to impress,' he thought inwardly.

"My princess, under the general's instruction, I went far south, searching among my traitorous clan for news of the whereabouts of the dwarves. It is as the general said. They have built strong fortresses. These are approachable from only the north. The circle of mountains and the plain beneath are housing many thousands of enemies. Fifty thousand dwarves and men living before these gates set in stone. They have armour and skills in growing food in vast quantities. They trade with each other and use gold and silver and other precious metals to gain foodstuffs, cattle and other livestock and they grow stronger in defence every day.

"The men of the plains have followed the dwarves' example and are led by their own chieftains and the goodwill between men and dwarves is sickening. I could not breach the defence wall that protects the plains, but I spoke to many who had knowledge of the dwellings and they all confirmed what I tell you now."

He was tempted to spit in derision as if to make his point stronger but feared it might be too much. He feared Shimishi above anyone else.

Princess Shimishi spoke again. "How many Spawn are ready to march?"

The general stepped nearer and dispatched the man to collect his reward in the slave pens beneath the hall.

"Oh! princess, we have 500,000 Slavers and Spawn in the horde, ready to march at your orders. We have 2,000 men at your immediate command. This will leave as many Spawn in defence of your realm, O mighty Shimishi."

She was pleased with the flattery, enjoying the pained expression on Thueban's features. "Good! Good! Very good... And now I want you to march on the dwarf scum and take their vile fortresses. They will be useful for the great plan devised by mother. My dear sisters, Yuehan and Zhuxi will be pleased to place themselves in these fortresses and make their own improvements and plans in safe dwellings with unlimited slaves, when they defeat the dwarves."

'It will also put some good distance between us so that they don't get chance to interfere in my own plans for my future,' she thought to herself.

* * *

Shimishi greeted her sisters as equals as they came into her throne room. "Thank you for honouring me with your presence dear sisters. Our plans go well."

The three sat somewhat apart, but near enough to be easily heard. The three of them together exuded evil, and its intensity made it difficult for their servants to stay too long in their company when they came together like this. Together they were almost a match for their mother Yonlik, and they knew this. It gave them pleasure to think such thoughts and Yonlik, in her hidden dwelling far beneath, smiled inwardly in her malice. She knew her daughters would never work to overcome her. This was not through loyalty to their mother but, ultimately, fear of what would happen to them if they failed. They had never been to Hell and did not wish for one moment to descend there.

The three planned the forces and discussed tactics and weaponry for the march to war with the dwarves. Their forces would be split equally, each at the disposal of a princess. Princess Yuehan would provide her own vanguard of personal Slavers. All were trusted Slavers and a few men. Princess Zhuxi would do the same.

Both vanguards were 5,000 of the most lethal Spawn. They named these, 'The Jashi' for they were always hungry for slaughter and adept at hunting prey, and, under the control of the Slavers, they protected the princesses totally, with their unflinching aggression and fighting capability. The plans made, the three princesses summoned food and wine. The food came in on three platters. Cooked human delicacies were placed before them, together with blood wine, a drink favoured by the princesses for its strength in alcoholic content and thickness of the blood. They ate and drank heartily before retiring to their own rooms, where they summoned their favoured servants to wait on them, each content for the present that they would be separate from their sisters.

CHAPTER EIGHT
THE DWARVES

The dwarves were many beneath the earth. They honoured their parentage and the past and focussed on the strong bonds of love they held for one another as outcasts hiding from evil.

The vast majority of those avoiding the growing evil were moving out into the world ahead of it. Sometimes generations ahead, in distance, for the evil ones to travel. The progress of the dwarves was quick. They were organised, loyal to one another, often in family groups together and moved to one purpose, which was to escape the evil by putting great distances between them. The Spawn and their masters were content to move slowly, build little and feed upon those they fought. They would eat crops, animals, men and dwarves that they fought and killed.

The further away from the She Devil's original hiding place, the less organised the Spawn became. The Slavers had to coerce the Spawn into battle, especially where it was cold and hard land to traverse or where there were rivers to cross. This gave hope to those who battled them. Some victories in the last years meant peace and growth occurred. Always, eventually, the Spawn would return in greater and greater numbers until men and dwarves either abandoned the fight or died in their homes. Mostly they were forced to flee once more.

As time passed there came incursions of men, seeking to distance themselves from the great evils that sought to overthrow them. Initially, some of these were the few Edain and the dwarves held them in friendship and trust. They were the Elven that left the Garden of Edain. They shared skills and gave many gifts they had developed from the Creator's glorious song, including a virility that allowed many offspring to carry their genes into the lesser men they sought to support through many years.

Their offspring in early generations were often tall, lithe of limb, and many males were over seven feet in height. Even the females were themselves six feet tall. They were powerful and were good allies, keeping the laws of men by which the dwarfkind lived.

They were gatherers like the dwarves and good hunters and fighters when the need arose. They loved one another on merit and many females in their companies bore children, mixing their genes in each generation with lesser men when they mated. They too were prolific of their seed and were born into large family groups, which held together. These were the ancestors of those men who came to live beside the dwarves outside their great halls of stone

By 15,000BC, as you would reckon it, the dwarves had moved from Central Africa and settled their home in the interior of what is now the Middle East on the continent of Asia.

The mountain range which shielded them from assault by their enemies was impenetrable due to great height. The dwarves, as great diggers and delvers, had set warning alarms at all levels to inform them of any diggings that might create an entrance to their halls. The dwarves were 10,000 strong in each of their city strongholds. They were well armed with steel and iron weapons that were superior to any weapon known at that time. The dwarves' confidence was high.

When good and moral men came to the Kingdom of the Dwarves, they welcomed them but were cautious about defences. The dwarves were honoured to allow men to live with them for their protection but kept them in the plains. Here, dwarves could support the men in their care while keeping a wary eye out for any small betrayal. For this reason, dwarves were encouraged by their leaders to move freely among men to get to know them as people and spot any nefarious characters that needed watching. Dwarves honoured the men as equals before the Creator, but even among these the evil had taught dwarves caution against complete trust.

CHAPTER NINE
THE BATTLES OF THE DWARVES

The dwarves were keen planet watchers and believed that the constellations were useful for understanding the world and were a part of creation, there to aid men in their interpretation of signs to teach the dwarves and men, warning them of coming dangers. They were stargazers and knew that when Saturn lined up with Jupiter, which they could see through their magnifying crystals, every 2,000 years these planets align with the Earth and the Sun and this great sign was believed to bring great change to the Earth. Six thousand years later it may have heralded the coming of a celestial saviour born in Bethlehem.

There was great interest and some concern as to what this conjunction heralded. Rumours spread across the dwarf communities and even the men in their care became aware that the conjunction of the planets was of importance to the dwarves. It was about this time that the first reports from men arriving at the dwarf kingdom arrived, reporting that Spawn were not far behind. The dwarves gathered intelligence about the coming threats.

The shooting stars were visible in the sky above the homes of the dwarves. The North Star was pinpointed by the dwarves as coming from the constellation of Draco. The dwarves watched these shooting stars firing across the sky. They noted how they interacted, passing directly through the Great Bear and down towards the Little Bear. Both these constellations were signs of impending change on Earth. The dwarves, in their councils, shared their thoughts and all agreed that this was a portent of great change.

The dwarves' fragile peace was unsettled by the signs and the elders of each tribe felt dangerous times were ahead. With the new incursions of men and their reports of the enemy, the dwarves called a large council. They met in the Great Hall of the first mountain, which housed many thousands. Chieftains from the five great clans came together with their most trusted and wisest supporters.

Lowin had told the story to the dwarves gathered in the Great Hall, which was filled with dwarves from the settlements. She spoke of their recent history and then she paused. The clans loved a story and Lowin told them well, remembering the detail and bravery of each tribe and its heroes past and present. Her audience was convinced by her words. They shook hands with one another and vowed to fight the evil that was coming together.

The dwarves Lowe (The Lion) and Lowin (The Lioness) ruled the oldest of the dwarves' great cities, named Zuerst. Lowe stood with his wife Lowin beside him. They were a mighty pair, both strong of mind, skilled in attack and defence and equal leaders in the eyes of their clan in the first city. The debate in the Great Hall had gone on for many hours.

Lowin continued. "So then, we all agree that war is coming to us and coming soon. There can be no more doubt. Our outlier brothers have said as much. They count the enemy numbers as a lot more than one hundred thousand cursed Spawn and forty thousand traitorous men. We must plan attack and defence in the face of such numbers. We must also give thought to the men on the plains."

A murmur went up from the hall where the onlookers stood.

"I know, I know," said Lowin, "the bad men are not to be trusted, but the vast majority of those who live near us are faithful, as are their families. We have an oath sworn by all dwarves to support all who are against the evil Queen Yonlik, curse her. We need only concern ourselves with those men lately arriving. They are different to the men mixed with the blood of the Edain. These men are not so wise nor good for that matter. Physically they are shorter and less in stature and beauty, but many are true to their families and race. They evidence many fine qualities in how they bond with each other and in time they will mature. Those that are not trustworthy we watch."

Grobest (The Great Heart) and Hammerhurz (The Great Hammer) ruled from the mountain closest to the entrance to the Great Plain, in the dwarf hall named Zweite. Grobest Great Heart was the oldest and latest member of his family to rule Zweite. He was greatly respected by the other chieftains and second to speak at the conclusion of the great debate that had discussed their portents of doom from the stars. Grobest stood tall for a dwarf at five feet five inches.

"My fellow dwarves, I agree with Lowin that we are come to exceedingly dangerous times. We are mighty!" he bellowed. "We are strong and we fear no one in a fight, be they wicked men or Devil's Spawn!"

There were loud shouts of approval in the hall.

"I stand with my wife, The Great Hammer!"

More applause as Hammerhurz came to her feet and added, "We stand with our brethren and will defend our halls while the blood flows in our veins! As for men, well, I tell you this! We have lived closest to men, being near to the plains, and I know for certain that every man I have met has been the sworn enemy of Spawn and Slaver alike. They hate them nearly as much as do we; they will defend the plains when we ask them to!"

"Well said my wife!" shouted Grobest. He was powerfully built, almost as wide as he was tall. His wife smiled at his clear voice of command. She knew the hall would follow him into battle if he marched. She would too. As the noise in the Great Hall abated, Grobest and Hammerhurz sat down.

A great hammer was swung and shattered an empty chair into very small pieces. It had been swung in a great arch by

Blutschläger (Blood Beater) and then retrieved by his wife, Sensmann (Grim Reaper) who passed it casually back to him.

Blutschläger spoke through the silence. "This will be no easy victory against so many enemies."

His rather harsh tone surprised no one. Blutschläger ruled the third great city, named Dritte, a dwelling where the dwarves were more bloodthirsty than their peers. They loved battle, were great fighters and were hardened to it.

"My clan have hunted the Spawn and their Slavers many times over the years. They come in great numbers and die in great numbers. We have let none live. This policy has kept us safe!"

There was much applause. When it died down the Blood Beater spoke once again. "BUT NO MORE! We all knew the day would come when the great war of our times would have to be fought, with tooth and nail and hammer and axe, spending our blood in defence of the Creator's great plan. We will hold true!"

Bär (The Bear) and Barin (She Bear), rulers of the fourth city, called by them Vierte, came to their feet together.

Bär spoke up. "We stand with you, all of us in this hall stand with you, but we must also look to the future of our kind and to the future of those men in our care. It would be an offence to the Creator to suffer them to be murdered, men women and children. Our plans must include these and we can't sit in defence alone. I fear this more than death itself. We will be worn down and walled in at the last if we stay within our halls. These Slavers are clever. They use blasting fire made from oil. They will send a million Spawn against us if we wait. The latest intelligence suggests this assault will only be the first. I am sorry to say that our information as to their numbers has been underplayed. There are nearer 500,000 enemies coming against us!"

The Great Hall, so full of dwarves, fell silent. This was

beyond expectation. Five hundred thousand was more than any of them believed existed in their time.

"Our plans need to be bold, secret and very thorough!" Bär sat down. He was a deep thinker; he watched the stars and knew they faced a holocaust.

The oldest of the dwarves, Lowe, spoke quietly and all awaited the response as he called on the next speaker. Dunkeln (The Dark) and Dunkelherzig (The Dark Hearted) were rulers of the fifth city, Fünfte. They were black haired dwarves, darker of skin than many due to the depths to which they dig. They were the greatest stone masons among the dwarf clans.

Dunkeln stood up slowly, as if for effect. His piercing gaze looked out on the hall. "Our halls are deep. The defences strong. But the first halls in each city will be overrun and taken, I fear, in spite of the bravery of the dwarves. Our enemies are so many that they will pile their dead up upon our axes and eventually the second halls will be taken. All the dwarf cities will be surrounded and confined to fight on in the lower levels of their homes. Food stores will dwindle, become scarce and our mightiest folk still standing will seek to break out to draw the enemies away. Once they are gone, the four Kingdoms of the Dwarves will eventually fall under continuous assault. This is fact. Only the city of Fünfte is impregnable. This is because its halls are a secret known only to the dwarves. It lies not in the mountain but far beneath the mountain. It is dark and difficult to approach even for those that know the way down."

The room was silent. The dwarves sat fascinated to hear of their doom. They looked to their leaders and to each other as they took account of all they had heard. A lone dwarf stood up in the hall. "Are we then beaten before we begin this battle Dunkeln?"

"Fünfte can never fall unless the world itself breaks apart.

Few of you have visited our halls since the early days, except Lowin, who has been a friend and great leader for our kind. She has seen the mighty caverns that sit adjacent to the city. Lowin has lent her expertise and knowledge to light these great caverns forming the liquid rock above the roof. We grow as much food underground as you do on the surface. Our halls are mighty and can house all of our people at a pinch. There is scope for animal husbandry and air comes to the halls from a vast expanse of fresh water that is an underground river. This river drops from the surface of the land far above and pulls fresh air with it from the surface. Our secret city has many secret ways we may use in time to replenish supplies. This is our last and safest hall and city. It must remain secret. It is safe because it is hidden. It must remain so."

Lowe bowed low to his long-time friend, to emphasise the respect he held him in, and spoke to the silent gathering. "We will fight the Spawn and defend our halls. We will make these beasts suffer from our axes and beat them with hammers. We will destroy this first wave of our sworn enemy and this will take place on the plains where men and dwarves will fight the Spawn to a standstill. The enemy will expect this for we always fight this way. It is to our advantage to begin with. We know their weapons and their blasting fire will shake us. We will be forced to retreat or perish unless we find a way to defeat this danger before the main attack."

Lowin stood tall next to Lowe and before her people, unafraid. "My people, we may all go to our doom in this battle. We do have a fighting chance to overcome this enemy, but not in open battle alone."

The dwarves' ears pricked up and their eyes focussed on their leaders.

"Our first action will be to attack the Spawn as they move against us and long before they reach the plains. The risks are high and those that survive will go to the defence of our mountains. Now we must make our plans. I intend that we ambush our enemies at Ten-Mile Gorge. They have to come that way but will expect defence there. As they overcome one barrier of wood, we will make a fighting retreat to the next. Our forces will move through and go onwards. We will seek to kill as many Slavers as we can find, in any way we can. We know they drive the Spawn into a frenzy in battle. Without so many Slavers the frenzy will be lessened and we will be able to kill more Spawn and perhaps at intervals cause them to fear us."

Lowin spoke slowly and carefully to emphasise each point before going on. "We will retreat for a few miles at our best speed and draw the Spawn onwards. When we are about to be caught, we will turn and fight. We plan the ground. We release our forces waiting there upon the Spawn and attack on both flanks. We will kill many Spawn and more Slavers. Our enemies will do as they always do and keep moving forward. We will retreat, fighting as we go, and the Spawn will attempt to outflank us by pure numbers. We will lose some dwarves and others will be injured. The injured and a few brave fighters will allow our brethren some time to get ahead of the battle.

"When we take the fight to the enemy and have to retreat, we will approach the mountains of home and our archers will man the ramparts that block the way into the plains. Our archers will stand their ground. They will fire volley after volley into the enemy, causing their lines to falter. The hardiest dwarves will hold the line. That is their honour. When we are behind the barrier of stone, the entrance will be sealed permanently."

It was now the turn of Lowe. They could do no more for the present. "Other thoughts may come to us over time, but once behind our secure barriers we must have a plan to escape, however that may look."

Lowe sat down and Lowin sat down next to her husband. Both exuded courage from their demeanours.

The hall emptied and the few remaining dwarves went about clearing the area of detritus and collecting the rubbish before polishing the remarkable bejewelled floor that shone with reflected light so that it appeared almost translucent.

The five leaders and their partners moved off into a side chamber where they could get refreshments, food, cooked meats, meads and beers to keep them at their brightest for the next part of their now more private discussions. Once they were settled and everyone had eaten enough to take the edge off their hunger and drunk enough ale to cool one or two temperate issues, The Blood Beater, Blutschläger, was already keen to crack heads, as was his wife Sensmann. They mapped out their plans. Lowe was now clear in his mind.

"We can't take any men into Fünfte at the end of the fight," said Dunkeln.

They all agreed, even Grobest and Hammerhurz, who had spoken up for them in the Great Hall.

Lowe knew the clans would pull together when the great need arose, as it did now.

Grobest looked at his wife when he answered. "My clan will take half of their number for the defence of the plains. We will fight with the trusted men and ensure they know enough of our plans for their own satisfaction. Their king, as we will now name him, will be chosen by them to lead them into battle. I know without asking that they will feel honoured to be fighting with us."

Hammerhurz nodded in agreement.

Lowe spoke again. "It will be our mountain home which will be the first to suffer assault once we have to give way in the plains. To take our halls will be a momentous fight and we must defend it well. For once we lose the first city the enemy will be encouraged. At the last stand, which will be high in the mountain home, we will set the charges below us and blast and block as we climb. Our final act will be to travel the secret way from the mountain top to the next city. The Spawn will try to follow us, but the way is precarious. We can spring the many traps set there. It might even be that they give it up and be content to hold the mountain and take to the field."

Grobest spoke next. "We will hold the field as best we can Lowe. My people, under command of Hammerhurz, will be ready for your arrival. If we come under assault by Spawn upon the mountain, then you, your people and Hammerhurz will have to fight your way down to the secret ways in the second hall and flee that way."

Dunkeln nodded. "We will be waiting," he said.

Bar and Barin agreed that some of their people would go forth and begin the ambush of the Spawn as planned. It would be perilous but they were proud to do their part, they agreed. The Blood Beater and Sensmann would fight on the plain.

"It will be the bloodiest battle of all and much will depend on you if any of the rest of us are to escape once the press comes on," said Lowe.

Blutschläger and Sensmann were filled with passion and they vowed they would hold their ground as long as Lowe needed to defeat the Spawn, Slavers and anything else that ventured into the plains. Blutschläger seemed to grow even bigger as he stretched out his torso, showing the rows of muscle upon muscle that gave him the strength to wield his mighty hammers or axe that a grown man of the plains would struggle to use with two arms.

Their plan was laid down and the array of their forces agreed. Their battle plan looked simple but was quite deadly if it worked. The dwarves would form into the horns of the buffalo, pulling the frenzied Spawn on and into direct conflict with the Blood Beater and his mighty forces. Forming the horns were the forces of Barin on the right side and Grobest on the left. In this formation the Spawn, although very many, would not be able to overwhelm the dwarves in a single charge, at least that was the hope. If the plan faltered, then the dwarves would fight their way back to their mighty homes and give the enemy a battle as they went. Lowe was hoping against hope that the Blood Beater was all that his name suggested.

Sensmann smiled at Lowe across the table as if guessing his thought. The smile was one of surety tinged with sadness for what was to come. Grim determination replaced the smile as she once more focussed on her role in the field. Sensmann would fight behind Barin's forces on the right. The plan was adventurous and unexpected. 'Lowe and Lowin are cunning dwarves. We will need those qualities if we are to survive,' was Sensmann's thought.

The plan was weeks in the making. Stores of food and grain were piled onto great wains, pulled by six oxen. All the mountain strongholds were stored up so that each could fight for a year and yet eat heartily each day. At a pinch they could last three years before their hunger forced them to be entirely reckless in defence of their lives.

The greatest lines of carts carrying food and weaponry were heading into the fortress of Fünfte, where Dunkeln prepared the mountain for the final defence. Meats were salted, whilst beers and spirit of alcohol were brewed in vast quantities in giant butts made of wood.

The men in the plain approved the plan as it was shared with them and they praised the bravery of the dwarves, loud and long, for their willingness to protect men, women and children of both dwarves and man in the final battle of their times against the Spawn.

Everyone worked with a purpose. It was either work hard together, or face extinction, and this focussed everyone's efforts. When the great carts grew few going towards the Dwarf Kingdoms, the training grounds were formed behind and before the Great Wall, which was the first defence of their Dwarf Kingdom home. Dwarves trained men to harden them for the coming battle. Horses were broken and armoured. Although dwarves fight on foot, Lowe knew that men on horses with some armour would be very effective as an assault on Spawn should they be required. With horses the men would be nigh as deadly as a dwarf.

Scouts were sent out, both trusted men and dwarves, to warn travellers of either race that were upon the roads as to what was coming and to offer them the chance to fight within their armies in the coming war. The travelling dwarves were few and some had their own plans, mainly to move on. The men, who were far more prolific on the trails, were not minded to accept the help. These were mostly families with little defence against being enslaved, or worse, by the spreading evil. They preferred to use their time to travel further away from trouble. These families were not fighters but farmers and other trades seeking an escape from evil.

The first attempt to engage the enemy was to take place at a narrow passage between mountainous heights that was the route the Spawn would take to attack the dwarves. The Gorge of Plenty lay between two mighty rivers and funnelled down from a mile at its broadest down to a hundred metres at the narrow end. This was the chosen point to engage the enemy. At the near end was the main force of Barin. He was ready with his dwarves to plug the bottleneck to delay the enemy. All those who were to take part were preparing axes and hammers for the battle. They were serious but relaxed and their spirits high for they knew they were fighting to a good cause and their deaths would have a purpose. Their faith in the Golden Path was unshakable.

CHAPTER TEN
A SURPRISE ENCOUNTER

Lowe and Lowin retired to their chambers. The days had gone quickly since the great debate when the five dwarf leaderships had unveiled the future for their kind. Lowe was pleased with the way all the dwarves had come together to meet the terrible threat to the world. Lowin was dressed in her evening attire. She was a beauty among her kindred. Dwarves measured beauty in terms of feminine qualities. Lowin had remained lithe of limb, yet had powerful muscles. Her strength was natural to her kind and she could match the power of a male body builder in modern times. Her skin was velvet to the touch but with the muscle power of a heavy weightlifter. She wore a scant cover over her frame, which allowed her partner to watch her as she moved to collect a full barrel of the finest dark beer available. Lowe followed her movements with a keen eye as she effortlessly lifted the beer barrel and tucked it under her arm. He watched as the muscles across her shoulders tightened and then how her torso also flexed, showing the strong stomach muscles, as she moved back across the chamber to the table. They sat upon comfortable low chairs with soft armrests, perfect for a dwarf to sit at ease.

Lowin enjoyed such attention from her partner when they were alone. She had been mother to five sons and four daughters, all now grown to adulthood. Although she had no plans for more, it was not beyond the realms of possibility that this could occur, should Lowe and she decide to entwine once more.

Such decisions were important in a dwarf marriage and both parties had equal say on the subject. If a female dwarf decided she did not wish to entwine she would fight fiercely and, if provoked, would call on her sons and daughters to back her. Dwarf males, although stronger than their mates, had to behave themselves if they wished to remain in a dwarf home. Many a dwarf had been ejected by his offspring if he took too many liberties. Respect for one another was of paramount importance in the dwarf home.

Lowin poured Lowe a generous quart of ale. She sat opposite him as was their favoured habit when alone. Lowin like to watch Lowe's eyes, which sparkled with humour and mischievous thoughts, even when he was being quite serious. They sat quietly supping their beer, each watching the other. Lowin noticed for the first time that Lowe had developed a frown line upon his forehead, not too deep, but most definitely visible.

She stroked his forehead and moved to his ears, which she knew would relax him. Once the frown had retreated Lowin removed her hands gently and held his head in her hands. Her finely bearded face and beautiful skin were soft to his touch as he reached forward to stroke her cheek. It had been many years since he had seen her clean shaven. This only happened for a female when she wished to bear a child. Lowe treasured these memories as he helped his partner relax under his firm but gentle touch. Lowin pulled away and Lowe sat back to take a long pull at his tankard, as did she on hers.

"Well," said Lowe, "things are going rather well don't you think?"

Lowin nodded her head in confirmation. "Yes, my husband, we are ready for whatever comes against us. Have you now given thought as to what you will name the great war that we are about to commence?"

Lowe grinned at her, by which she knew he had made up his mind. "We will call the Great War 'Exodus'," he said, with a gleam of battle in his eye.

Lowin liked it, short, to the point, and she guessed the dwarves would like its simplicity. She bent down to her left and picked up a small drum. In her clear voice she began to strike the drum in a war beat and then to sing. "EXODUS! Exodus! Exo – Dus! Exo- Dus!" she repeated as she imagined herself swing her axes to the beat of the drum.

Lowe laughed out loud. "I knew you would like it," he retorted, and then he joined her in the chant.

They giggled and beat the rhythm out on the drum. Lowe danced around the table while Lowin skipped ahead of him. Lowe, being older and full of recently consumed ale, tired after a while and stopped to refresh himself from the jug of ale on the table.

Lowin lowered the drum. "Okay my wise and masterful husband, what does your fine intellect tell you about our chances?"

Lowe was always very frank when speaking about risks and he knew that Lowin would want to hear the truth. He put his now empty flagon down. He always tried to finish his ale in case something prevented him from getting more. It pained him to think of a scenario where unfinished ale was ruining while he was occupied elsewhere.

"Our chances are not good to be honest my beloved. We will of course make a large dent in this army of craven Spawn and Slavers that are approaching but I fear that if we merely hold our ground, then within three years and perhaps a little less, or a little more, we will meet our doom as a race above ground."

This statement of the likely demise of the dwarf folk was a sobering and fearful thought, for them both. Lowin took her seat again, having been in deep thought while Lowe recovered his breath a little. Lowe continued his thoughts out loud as they sat opposite one another. He loved his wife dearly and it pained him to see her face so full of concern for her people. She was a great fighter in her own right but what had sealed Lowe's love for her was her ability to plan battle tactics and think outside the box of known dwarf fighting strategies. She was a fearless fighter in battle and Lowe needed to give her hope and something to build upon for their people.

"I have decided it is not enough to just help our fellow men escape this probable disaster. I have devised a strategy to take the fight to the evil queen in her own lair."

Lowin showed real surprise in her face, then looked very hard into Lowe's face. "How?" she asked. She showed by her body language she was not expecting to like the answer.

Lowe also went entirely serious of face. "The first thing I will say is that I will not fight separately from you. Secondly, our family and our most loyal and closest friends within our own clan will come with us. I will not risk this venture with other clans, for they will need their leaders to keep them alive with their own cunning and skills.

"When our forces first meet the Spawn horde, we will be in the vanguard. I intend for us to be hidden from sight within the gorge itself, until the enemy is all around us. We will let them advance down the gorge where the rest of our forces will await them. We will be decisive and vicious in the assault we launch. We will make the Spawn and their Slavers pay dearly for every step they take towards the dwarf kingdom, just as we have planned.

"We must be in place before the approach of the enemy. Once we are behind the barriers at the foot of the gorge, we split from the main force with fifty of our kin and move away at speed up the gorge. We will take up our hidden position and await the enemy. When we have done as much harm as we can, we will take flight over the great river, which will cover our retreat. As we are made to retreat it will be on our terms and not on the enemy terms at all.

"Once across, we will move upstream until we leave the Spawn forces way behind. We will then take stock of our strength before we trek along the riverbank with all the stealth we can muster. We know roughly where the evil queen hides. I expect her lair to be very deep underground. We will spy out the ground and enter by fair means or foul into the old dwarf ruins in which that evil queen has built her kingdom."

Lowin looked sceptically at her husband. "My, my, my husband, what a strange and rather insane strategy that sounds! Do you realise what the odds are in even getting into her lair? It would take legions of fighters to even give battle."

Lowe spoke in detail for his wife's better understanding and he saw the light of hope replace the sadness there earlier. He smiled, "I know, but it's not suicide to do a desperate thing. It is not an all-out attack. The aim is to put doubt into the mind of the queen and make her pause by attacking her where she feels strongest. In this way we may buy time for others to cause her significant problems.

"We know she has three princesses to lead her forces and I can guess two will come against us here. What I will attempt to do is despatch the other princess if I can. If we can do this, then I do not think the queen will want to expend more of her precious kin and forces that she would have already despatched to finish us off. Even if we fail, we will have sown the seed of doubt in her. She respects the dwarves in the fact that we are resistant and not turned very easily to evil. The names among us, even in death, in her lair will be enough to instil caution in her. If we dwarves can then fight our way into Shimishi's lair, having despatched her to Hell, then those that are left will have done a great deal to aid our fellow fighters defending our homes."

Lowin looked at Lowe long and hard once more. "Alright," she said, "I will support you completely but if you try and leave me and mine at any time in this crazy excursion, I will personally cut off your balls and beard and wear them as a necklace!"

Lowe laughed until he cried and then they both cried at the insanity of what they had planned for themselves and their kin. When they had calmed down and had once more filled their jugs and were happily sipping away, Lowin said, "When are you going to tell the others?"

"Not yet awhile," said Lowe. "Not yet awhile. Maybe I'll write them a letter!"

CHAPTER ELEVEN
THE ANGEL

Deborah moved in the Fifth Dimension on the Golden Path. Deborah was placed there by the Creator for her previous achievements on the Fourth Level of the Golden Path.

She understood her role completely from the instant that Satan began his Great Fall. Deborah had sight upon all the activities on the Golden Path that were below her. She saw how Satan tried to spoil the Fifth Level and then the Fourth Level, how he was able to despatch his evil queen to be Alshaylon Yonlik into the Third Level of the Golden Path. Deborah felt a surge of need within her to despatch this Yonlik back to her master and trap her with the Devil on the First Level on the Golden Path, which would now be called Hell.

As a watcher, Deborah understood her duty was to be the eyes of the Creator on the Fifth Level. Her fate was usually to watch and not to intervene. Although intervening was within her capability, she understood that to do so from the Fifth Level would breach the intended pathways for those below. For although great evil would come from Yonlik, many of those that fought her would benefit with swifter rises onwards and upward on the Golden Path.

Instead, she drifted down to the Fourth Level and there she met with Ruth. Ruth was one of the great and early examples of recognition of the Creator that had once lived on Earth in the Third Level. Ruth progressed her knowledge as she lived and prospered on the Fourth Level, where all was purity. The living spirit never required food or drink, but learned, with those others present, the Creator's purpose for them.

Each level attained gave a new purpose outside of time, starting on Level Four. Deborah was akin to a winged angel and flight meant she could attain Level Six for short periods for renewal of her spiritual strength or fly down to Level Four and below if she chose. Seeing Ruth on Level Four, she alighted near to her. Ruth immediately bowed to show her respect to the winged angel. As Deborah alighted on the ground next to her, she allowed her beautiful bright yellow wings to fold into their natural position upon her back.

Walking forward she took the hands of Ruth who was now standing upright. She saw that Ruth was nearly as tall as Deborah, being two metres tall, lithe of limb with golden brown hair and brown and smooth tanned skin.

"This is a great honour you do me," said Ruth, looking up into the beautiful countenance of the angel. "What can I do for you or help you with?"

Deborah then ushered Ruth to sit upon the grass and she did the same facing her. "Dear Ruth, your intuition is clearly Heaven-sent and that encourages me to ask a great favour of you in the name of the Creator. A dreadful spirit, which we shall call evil, fell to the First Level and is trapped there, fortunately, for his name is Satan and he was powerful even on the Seventh Dimension Level, so that neither I nor you would have dared to challenge him before his fall."

Ruth nodded and responded. "I have seen the influence of evil upon the Earth when I walked there. I have watched it grow in the form of Yonlik who calls herself Queen and who benefits her evil by her link to Satan. I have wondered often whether my role here was to observe this evil and combat it myself. Others here have not shown interest in the evil below, having their eyes and hearts looking upwards."

Deborah smiled at Ruth. "You are quite right Ruth. I see now that the Creator has a purpose for you which will be, err, somewhat distasteful. Many men of the chosen that remained in the Edain have moved up the Golden Path and onwards. As you have observed, those now known as the dwarves fell from the garden but have picked themselves back up and have made themselves guardians of lesser men. Many of those chosen that remain in Edain are reluctant to leave their sanctuary in concern that they also might fall from the Creator's mind and be tarnished with the evil they fight and be unable to get back to Edain.

"This is a fear of men; even the elven, who have been gifted the choices of action or inaction as they choose. They cannot be certain of the impact of evil upon them should they try to intervene upon the Earth. Many roads lead to ascension into the Fourth Level but some Elven will fall if it is their fate. Many if not all in Edain are afraid to be captured. So, you see, the dwarves need someone of certainty as a messenger, to help them in their fight with evil if they choose that path. They are a courageous people."

Ruth listened patiently and understood. She had witnessed for herself how some of the chosen, having left Edain, had been drawn forward by evil and tricked into the presence of Yonlik and their fate was sealed, as far as her vision could tell her. There was a long pause before Ruth spoke once more.

"I wish to serve the Creator in the best way that I can. It is good that you have come to me for this task Deborah, for I will be mighty on Earth and the dwarves will heed what I have to say. This evil upon the Earth will be my mighty battle as well as that of the dwarves, and with your support I will carry the fight against evil with one eye on the Creator and the other on defeating evil. I know it will hold dangers for even me on Earth, but I trust in you Deborah to retrieve me from an ill fate, if I slip."

"I will," said Deborah. "Now, as a reward and also as a part of the plan and for your own protection, I want to take you to the Fifth Level of the Creator's pathway. From here we will see not only into the minds and hearts of evil, but we shall be able to watch matters unfold together before you go forth on your own down to Earth, as the men who live there have named the Third Level of existence."

Ruth was amazed and filled with gratitude for this great honour bestowed upon her. She placed her arms around the neck of Deborah and experienced the weightless flight to the Fifth Level. Of course, this was in reality, at least for Deborah, a spiritual flight of no difficulty, which was rewarded by the gratitude and thanks that poured from Ruth as she flew.

Deborah gently released Ruth. "You will probably feel a little bit faint for a few minutes, Ruth, so sit down while I imagine up a suitable receptacle through which to witness what is occurring on Earth."

Ruth settled down on a grassy knoll that appeared as if out of nowhere and, although this was a novel experience for her, she had at least experienced something similar when she had been granted complete access to the Fourth Level.

Deborah girded herself with a belt, housing a long thin blade that hung now from her waist. Another, slightly shorter, blade appeared next to Ruth on the grass. It was beautiful and smooth, with a silvery hew and white edges which looked very sharp to Ruth's keen eye. In front of Ruth there appeared a window, ten by ten feet across its width and height, through which she espied the whole of the Earth as it spun on its axis. The picture of the Earth began to change and, over a very long period or in no time at all, Ruth watched the fall of Satan, the escape of Yonlik, the birth of the princesses and the arrival of man on the planet, as she now called it. They watched the evil spread across this world. They viewed great bravery in man and extreme courage. Ruth and Deborah felt a close longing to bring the chosen who were the Edain to a safer place and this happened in its right time. The picture narrowed now and followed underground tunnels to a chamber where a single dwarf could be seen.

The window showed Lowe at his bath, lying at ease in the warm soapy water. He wore a small cloth singlet which covered his genitals comfortably. With a rush of water, he jumped to his feet and grabbed for his mighty axe as before him a window opened in the wall and, through this, he saw Ruth and Deborah, both standing with swords in their hands. Deborah, with her full wings displayed beside her, with Ruth before her. Ruth stepped nearer and then, on the brink of stepping through, a gentle hand stayed her. She smiled at Lowe who was open mouthed in amazement, nearly naked and with his axe now at his side.

"Hail to you Lowe, leader of the dwarves of the mountains. My name is Ruth, and I am one of the chosen, being an elf originally from Edain. Will you speak with me?"

Lowe, although still amazed and in shocked surprise, recovered himself and spoke up with a calm tone. "Speak," was all he could yet manage.

Ruth then explained that the Angel Deborah had chosen her for a mission to help attempt to save the dwarves from their imminent complete destruction. Lowe, for his part, told the two beautiful people of his plan that he had outlined to Lowin.

"There will be much grief and sadness whatever the outcome. The plan you have contrived with your fellow dwarves will suffice for now. I want you to mount an assault on the princesses also, but only with a few and probably those nearest to you, for you will not return to the dwarf kingdom thereafter."

"Where will we go if any survive?" asked Lowe.

"What I tell you now is for your ears and the ears of Lowin only. You and your fifty dwarves will come close to destruction. Some of you will be killed. It will be a hard fight that claims the lives of your kin but there is much glory to the dwarves in death as well as in life, in the eyes of our Creator for those that manage to survive. As you already know Lowe, all life is precious. It is important that each fighter defends themselves first and foremost. We do not seek martyrs from the dwarves. We want each to be at peace when they go into battle. The next time you see me you must do exactly as I ask of you. If your faith in me falters at that time, I will not be able to help you. Do you understand?"

Lowe nodded his bearded head in answer and listened now with great interest. Much was bestowed to his trust. Before long he was once more alone, standing in his bath. The portal into his bathroom had closed. Then Lowe laughed out loud for sheer joy and merriment. He had clearly seen an angel and another blonde and beautiful maiden called Ruth (who was alarmingly tall, not to mention the even taller angel) and they had conversed with him as he stood in his bath. He laughed, feeling a little abashed, as he looked down to see his near naked body.

There was no question of doubt in his mind, that these amazing examples of purity were full of grace and goodness. He felt very far removed from their state of grace and beauty himself as he spoke to them. His dwarfish ability to detect falsehood was clear. He sat back down in his bath. A new hope gleamed in his heart as he heard that he would be able to have a chance to not only strike at the heart of evil in the Earth but also save some of his people and the men and women under his protection. Lowe sat there for a few minutes before he was clear in his own mind of how he should tell Lowin what he had seen and agreed.

He called Lowin into the bathroom. She came with towels and, as she reached him, he grabbed her around the waist and hoisted her, fully clothed, into the water. As she took a breath in surprise, they both went under the water. Lowin came up spluttering.

"You are a crazy old dwarf!" she scolded him. She splashed water into his face and came at him head on and he was hard set to keep his feet in the bath. Lowe felt Lowin relax into his arms. He spoke quietly into her ear. "Hush woman. And listen."

They sat in the bath and Lowin's eyes opened wide in

surprise; she looked at him suspiciously to see if he was joking with her. She could not detect humour but was keenly touched by the warmth and grace Lowe was now portraying as she gazed into his gleamingly happy countenance. When Lowe finished speaking, she could not find words, so she got out of the bath, stripped off her wet things and climbed back in with Lowe. They sat there until the bath went cold, while they made the plan for their immediate clan, as described by the lady Ruth and the mighty angel that accompanied her.

Lowe said to his wife, "Lowin, we have been graced with a chance to make a difference in this world. We must not fail!"

"My husband, you have been granted a great honour by these miraculous souls who have chosen you for this task. I too feel the weight of the world on my shoulders. Yet I am also filled with a surety in my heart that I can't explain. We will not fail if we hold true to one another!"

Deborah closed the window onto the world on the Third Level of the Golden Path. They watched the interaction between Lowe and Lowin and sent their joint blessings to aid the dwarves in the challenges before them.

"I need to explain some rules that apply to all of the Golden Path, Ruth. In the first place, only those who are truly pure of heart can move onto the Fourth Level of Creation. Here is where others, not unlike myself, watch over the worlds below. On the Fourth Level we observe and watch how the spirits of men and women are attaining continued growth as the Creator intended. As they grow, they become more talented in the creative ways in which they engage their imaginations. When they are ready, in life or in death, they may seek to attain the Fourth Level. Tell me Ruth, have you tried to conjure yourself armour, weapons or wings?"

Ruth smiled. "No, I haven't tried, mainly because I have been at peace on the Fourth Level and did not wish to engage in weaponry or change my form. I was blessed with beauty and health by the Creator and saw no reason why he would wish me to change myself in these ways."

The Angel Deborah smiled. "That's fine Ruth and it is why your creative spirit has flourished and grown and now you are ready to take up the fight again on behalf of the Creator, as we have discussed. In our own space I can teach you many wonders about the Creator's song and you will see its glory unfold for you, giving you power to create tools you will need in this fight with Satan's forces"

"I have my wits, my sword and my skills learned on the Earth. I am ready to resist the evil that spreads upon the Earth, despite the peril it will place me in. That evil queen Yonlik is more than a match for me, but I will challenge her in spite of this. Without help, all of those dwarves and men and women will be slaughtered except those Yonlik will turn to her evil purposes."

Deborah then laid down the rules. "Where I send you, you must stay. This means being between the Fourth and Third Level for as long as you are guiding the dwarves. You will have all your powers from the Fourth Level of the Golden Path but don't descend physically to the Earth or your powers will fall away and you will be fully human again and in peril.

"You must not harm any men, even evil men, unless you are yourself in danger of being slaughtered. If they kill you, you will return to the Fourth Level and recover there, but your quest to save the dwarves will fail and they will be consumed.

"All men that have been created have been promised salvation, at least those that are deemed worthy. Even evil men, if they repent prior to death, have a hope of being raised up on the Golden Path. Those that fail the test will descend. It is not our part to judge the human spirit; that lies with the Creator, his son and the Creator's majesty and song that incorporates all levels of the Golden Path. When called upon, it comes to protect the good, but at the Creator's intent and decision, and not that of man. For, as you know, the life of men is but a beginning and their fate, including your own, is known only to the Creator in the end.

"Be sure to understand dear Ruth that this request, made by me for your assistance, will not be a guarantee of success. It is my hope you will succeed but it may be our fate to fail. I hope and expect that the Creator will inspire you to use your great goodness and guide mine. We must have love and trust in the Creator and accept the fate he has in store for us.

"Please understand Ruth. Satan is beyond my comprehension. I know the purpose of Yonlik, who was allowed to escape to Earth when she should not have done. There are perhaps other forces of evil that I am myself unaware, so be on your guard. Flee when you have need to and fight when you can't evade it. Most important of all, remain true to yourself, for you may be tested in ways I cannot fathom."

Deborah sighed, "I wish I could go with you, Ruth. I fear I have asked too much now that I have set such boundaries about you."

"No, Deborah, I feel this is a perilous but very needed adventure. Without making this attempt to help those in such need, how can I grow further? Fear not, for I feel just what the dwarf Lowe expressed after we left. I feel hope."

CHAPTER TWELVE
A CHANGE OF PLAN

Lowe called the senior dwarves to council once more. He and Lowin had discussed the arrival of the Angel Deborah and Ruth and decided they had to act. The first order of business was that they needed to sell the ideas from Ruth in a way that did not sound like suicide or insanity, or something deceitful to protect Lowe ahead of others.

Lowe knew well that dwarves are, after all dwarves, and have great hearts and great willingness to keep their promises, but this situation was unlike any other and so had to be handled subtly. Talking about a visit from an angel, never seen on Earth by any of them before, was a challenge even for Lowe. He had not seen the impact upon himself until his wife Lowin drew his attention to it. Lowe accepted he was old in years but something about this meeting with the Angel Deborah and Ruth seemed to have shed a hundred years of his age overnight. He would not have been fit to go to battle as he had been. Now his mind was clear, his energy restored and his fate set. Lowe was a man with faith in the Creator. He did not fear a good death. He taught his children to be the same. Lowe feared sickness and weakness far more and he was happy to know this might now not happen. He would enjoy the adventure and accept his fate.

Lowe spoke quietly to the dwarves gathered at the table where they all sat. "I have received news from an unexpected source. It seems that not all the chosen are unaware of our plight. I ask you to trust me in what I am saying next. One of the fabled Edain came to my quarters via an opening in the bedrock of our bath chamber and, before you ask, it was a woman, very beautiful, fair of hair and skin and over six feet tall."

Around the table there was a mixed response. The males,

Grobest, Bär, Blutschläger and Dunkeln grinned despite attempts to keep straight faces. Blutschläger gave an involuntary giggle, until he received a friendly tap on the back of his head from his beloved Sensmann. She, like the other wives, were studying Lowin's serious face. Lowin looked hard at her partner and he at her. There was no humour in the eyes of either.

It went very quiet, before the Blood Beater breathed out a sigh. "Well, what about that!"

Lowe spoke up. "The lady's name was Ruth. She was speaking to me from the Fourth Level of the Golden Path. Apparently, the Earth and all we know is on the Third Level. With Ruth, through this portal I could see what I can only describe as an angel, who called herself Deborah. She had wings of pure silver and she was magnificent! I wish you could have seen her for yourselves!"

"Is she a god?" asked Dunkelherzig, looking uncomfortably at Lowin, who she could see was taking her husband seriously and clearly worried by the event. All the women saw the change in energy and apparent liveliness in Lowe that was not there at their last encounter. The women looked to one another, not speaking but seeing this beautiful female as equally a threat to their relationships with their men and were now very keen to hear what had been discussed. Lowin was calm and guessed easily what her friends were thinking.

Dunkelherzig spoke again. "You are changed Lowe since I saw you last. You look to me to have been energised and somehow look younger in years than you ought. Lowin, you also appear more relaxed and focused than of late. You seem to have gleaned purpose from this experience. I wish I had met them too."

There was acceptance and full agreement from the others. The men now focused on Lowe, and they saw it too.

"The message is grim," said Lowe. "Unless we can somehow

sow fear into our enemies we are lost. The forces coming against us are very great. Ruth told me that there are already the same number and more coming on behind the foes we already know about. In other words, we will be slaughtered even if we overcome the first wave, which itself is rather unlikely."

Blood Beater looked at Lowe and spoke. "Yet you don't look defeated. In fact, if I didn't know better, I'd say you have more hope now than when you spoke before all our people to bring them to battle readiness."

Lowin spoke on behalf of her husband and Lowe allowed his head to drop just a little as he eyed his wife. His eyes never moved from her face and the others saw the seriousness between them.

"Lowe has devised a plan to take the battle to the enemy," said Lowin.

She looked directly at Lowe, focussing all her attention on his countenance. "The lady Ruth has told him this enterprise will be his last adventure. He has been told also that he will not be returning to our home, whether he achieves the aims of the plan or not. We do not know the fate of others that go with him. We have come to understand that we cannot overcome Yonlik but we are told our future on the Earth depends on delaying the enemy. The only way that can happen is if we can strike fear into the princesses, and so we are going to attack the princesses in their lair. Our guide will be Ruth. She is ready to risk her very soul to prevent our destruction. Lowe and I are prepared to risk ours in the hope that, by doing so, we can buy the dwarves the time they need to revise their plans. We need to split our forces. Some to fight for our homes. Some to attack the enemy upon the road and a few to venture into the heart of the enemy territory and assault the princesses where they will least expect it."

Immediately Blood Beater spoke up. "I want to go with you

Lowe, I am the strongest fighter and with Sensmann, my wife, we will be very hard to kill. We can break through the enemy ranks by our forces driving a wedge into their ranks. I am ready to lay down my life for this purpose if it gives you the distraction you are seeking to confuse the enemy."

"No," said Lowe, "I need you here to protect our homes and hold together the dwarves who will be sorely tested and might very well be overcome. We all know that Sensmann is a great general in her own right and able to plan a better defence than any sitting at this table. No, you must hold the line here, Blutschläger. No one else has a better hope of doing so. This is not a mission with a lot of hope, but it needs to be carried out by a few. I won't allow you or anyone else here present to come with me, except Lowin. I will allow two of your better fighters to join us with our immediate guard. We will number only fifty. Ruth's plan requires stealth, cunning and speed if we are to succeed in even entering the lair of the enemy. We quite possibly go to our deaths but if any survive it will be a great story for the dwarves and our minstrels to sing to the big hall."

"And now we see why you are so energised!" said Dunkeln. "Not only do you give to yourself hope. You also share that hope with us and with your people. You are a noble dwarf and a good leader and a great friend. You will be sadly missed! Get the beer out ladies and dwarves, we have much to share and much to say to one another before Lowe and Lowin leave us!"

The words of Dunkeln lifted the mood of the dwarves sat at the table. Lowin was relieved. She laughed and drank and laughed some more. There was a lot of teasing and questions about blondes in bathrooms and this time there were friendly taps and gesticulations, which friends make when alone. Lowe admitted he was overdressed for what his male colleagues suggested might have happened with the blonde. Lowe politely reminded them that Ruth and the angel had not actually crossed into his bathroom and had stayed on the other side of the window into his world. Of course, the ladies had moved to another table by that time. Lowe took it all in good spirit, but he was glad Lowin had not been there to hear it all.

The women were talking about Ruth. Lowin said with some puzzlement, "I wonder why the heroine is always so pretty, it really does make one feel a bit sick."

Sensmann, who was quite drunk herself by now, replied, "It's obvious to me dear. It is just about the only thing that will get men interested, especially dwarves who, after all, are just so like other men. They think with what's between their legs most of the time, except if there is likely to be a fight or the chance of ale."

There was general merriment at both tables but no further mention of angels on the ladies' table, for which Lowin was particularly grateful. Having one beauty to contend with was bad enough, but add to that beauty and wings, well that was too much. Lowin reminded herself to bed Lowe before they left on the journey, lest he forgot who the true beauty in his life was.

CHAPTER THIRTEEN
LET BATTLE COMMENCE!

"Lowe and Lowin marched with fifty of their kin into the jaws of death!"

This was said loud enough for everyone in the party to hear. The speaker was Lowgrim, The Growler, oldest son of Lowe and Lowin. There was a cheerful sound of giggling from Lowgrim, who was living up to his name. He was hardly ever grim and the most likely of the dwarves to sing a hale and hearty song while still sober. He was encased in tough leather armour, including helmet, as were all the dwarves. A polite knock on the head from his mother was greeted with a ribald display of pleasure. All the dwarves were pleased to see Lowgrim topple forward a step before he regained his balance and turned, grinning to his mother, Lowin.

"Oops! Sorry mother, I did not see you there, I thought you were up the front watching out for the old boy!" he jibed.

Lowin smiled. "Ha! Lowgrim. You are a joy to your mother's heart. It's just a bit of a shame that you inherited your father's weakness in the head area, rather than my charm, wit and good looks!"

"Yes, mother and that's why they call me Lowgrim and not Joygrim! For I am a male dwarf, mother, as you know, with a twinky and so I follow my father. My baby sister is Joygrim, your daughter. She is delightful and a real beauty! I don't see you hitting her on the head." His grin was broad.

"That's because she is much cleverer than you and why she is leading the party up front with your father and I am back here making sure you behave yourself!"

All the dwarves loved the way in which Lowe allowed his family freedom to lead by example. Lowgrim knew his part was occasionally to play the fool and be chastised by his mother. He was a natural and liked by the whole party of dwarves. Lowin knew he would make a great leader in his turn after his father decided to retire from battle.

Lowe began to sing a low beat while they marched and someone near took it up and then the whole party moved to the beat. 'Fast enough to set a good dwarf pace,' thought Lowe at the head of the group and just fast enough to keep the dwarves focused on the speed of the march. Lowe knew, as they all did, that soon they would move with stealth, very quietly (for a dwarf in armour) as they approached the gorge where the enemy was expected. He knew there could be scouts about but he hoped he was marching early enough to evade them. It was important to the plan. Lowe sang along and lifted his tone a notch to impress the beat upon the others. While marching, he was reflecting on battle strategy. He did not know beyond this march just exactly what they would face and when, so the comedy and comradeship from his son was very welcome. He knew dwarves can get a bit mean and growly if they are set for battle. Lowe did not want any heads knocked together seriously until it was the heads of the enemy. Lowgrim's light-hearted nature was ideal for the situation.

Joygrim, Lowe's daughter, liked to spend time with her father, especially on a march. She was second born, a younger dwarfish beauty of a likeness to her mother, slim for a dwarf female and well developed in muscle. A powerful hitter, as many a young dwarf suiter discovered when they requested courtship of her. Dwarf women do not smile and curtsy. Their lives were tough, as tough as the males in the mines. When a dwarf male wanted to get emotional with Joygrim, she immediately resorted to checking out their mettle with a light hammer, which she preferred for speed. Even when she was a teenager the first couple of suitors found themselves sitting on their backsides, rubbing their leather-clad helmeted heads and counting the little stars that were before their eyes, as she despatched them with precise and calculated blows. Others soon learned from this, for they knew Joygrim to be a warrior class like her mother and so future suitors came with soft words (for a dwarf) and full armour.

Joygrim liked to have an audience of her female friends present on such occasions. These battle training-cum-courtship rituals were very popular among the youngsters. They would mark the males on points and discuss their strengths and weaknesses with loud happy laughter, as the male in question protected his life from a hammer that seemed to be able to hit hard from all angles. Of course, all dwarves are good fighters and Joygrim brought the best out in her suitors. The male in question could almost fight with full strength against such as Joygrim and indeed some did. After half an hour or so a good suitor would be invited to sit with her friends and they would gratefully wipe the sweat from the dwarf's head and face, while Joygrim would pour two long flagons of beer.

"Warm work isn't it, all this courting?"

The dwarf would gratefully accept the flagon as evidence he was in the running. Joygrim liked to keep things simple. She could of course play (as she put it) with as many dwarves as she wished until she finally gave her troth. It was possible death to any dwarf who offended either her or her chosen partner once they were bound in the ritual of family. These contacts were serious undertaking.

Dwarves were sensible folk and so contract of marriage was rescinded after twenty years and renegotiated between the parties thereafter. This made sense when you think that some dwarves could live in full health for five hundred cycles of a year. They had learned over generations that the heart grows fondest when both parties have equal status in a marriage contract. It ensured that male dwarves respected their partners if they wished to keep them. Female dwarves could pick and choose if the partner they were with was no longer suitable.

The family contract worked well underground in the more confined spaces families had to live within, where dwarves spent much of their lives. Many a murder had been avoided through patience. Jealousy was kept to a minimum where all were concerned. If there was rejection now, there would be opportunity later, even after dwarf children were conceived. The outgoing father would expect the incoming suitor to respect the children and care for them as they would their own.

All dwarves loved children and they were quite safe until they were old enough to defend their lives in a fair fight. In dwarf language if a fight was fair, there were no recriminations, even from the mother. If it were deemed a spiteful killing, then the mother or her children could bring the victor to battle immediately, once the slight was named and agreed by the elders in conference.

Although men found these arrangements harsh, it was a harsh world they were surviving in. It made the dwarves respectful of skill, strength and talent and it protected those few that were perhaps not so skilled from an early death, for every family had some talented dwarves in such an occasion to fight for the honour of their kin, especially if it was a female. It also meant that in the dangerous world where they lived, many were lost in battle or succumbed to sickness from wounds received.

Joygrim did not require help from her family in relation to courtship. She was a match for most dwarves in battle and there were at least four suitors in the party, quite close to the front of the march, who saw it as their first duty to protect her with their lives. This made Lowe happy, for he watched with interest as they would quietly fall back in line, quite discretely to remain close by, should Joygrim change her position. This went unremarked of course, for it could mean instant offence and battle soon after if someone spoke out of turn.

The dwarves had hatched their plans after much debate with Blutschläger. He was very keen to be involved prior to the entrance to the gorge where he, Lowin and Lowe had planned to pin down the Spawn. There was a small hill and on the side opposite the gorge, a cave, which went nowhere, had been delved into by the dwarves some years previously and covered with grass and moss to hide the entrance. Inside they had dug a tunnel with room for one to travel at a time and which came out in thick trees to the right of Ten Mile Gorge, leading away for many metres. It had been built as a refuge in hard times of attack, should any come. Lowe now intended to use this to spring his surprise on the Spawn.

Lowe hurried his people into the cave and spoke quietly to them. "Listen," he said, "if we get caught in here by the body of the approaching Spawn this will likely be the shortest jolly outing we have ever been on. No one moves until I do. If the plan goes well, the Spawn will be drawn on by the Blood Beater and his archers who will fire and retreat. This will draw the Spawn forward. There are thousands of the scum so don't expect an easy battle or be surprised by the numbers. We are not after the Spawn and they will be facing the archers. It's the Slavers we want to slaughter if we can and they are our only real target. They are craven and stay well behind their Spawn, but when the Spawn pass, then out we come and we pile into them. They are big and they are strong but if our timing is good, we will be on them before they know it. You are ordered to slaughter without thought of self or sympathy. None of us is expendable, so no heroics please," he finished, looking at his daughter's suitors.

They understood. Lowin had explained what would happen to them if her daughter failed to make the cave. She also explained that Lowe was a male and therefore, in this matter, her junior, so they should nod in all the right places and then do as she asked and not what he ordered. The cave was dry and the floor clear of refuse and the dwarves waited there patiently until it was time for the battle to commence.

* * *

Princess Zhuxi had the honour of launching her attack. She was keen to prove to her mother, Alshaylon Yonlik to give her full title, that she, Zhuxi, was more than a match for the dwarves. Not only winning this war against the dwarves and the scum men with them, but that she was better at tactics than her sisters. Zhuxi suspected that her sister Shimishi was favoured by Yonlik rather too much and this little adventure was her chance to prove her worth.

Gashima had been her choice of general. He was a brutal Slaver and did his princess's most important roles in battle. He was arrogant when not in front of Zhuxi and she knew he abused the female Slavers under his command and brutalised the male Slavers that dared to question him. He ruled by fear. Zhuxi was well protected by her elite Slaver, with her Spawn escort of over five thousand, with she in the middle. Zhuxi liked to spread her wings occasionally and would leap into the air and spiral back down to earth. While she was spiralling on her great scaled wings, she could see her general, whips in hand, organising the Slavers, ordering them closer to the Spawn which they commanded.

The Spawn were creatures of small intellect and so were effectively spellbound when the Slavers used their talents to drive them forward through a form of telepathy, inherited from their queen, Yonlik.

The Slavers drove the Spawn into the mouth of the gorge. No sooner had they arrived there, than a large cohort of dwarf archers stood up and fired a rain of arrows down on the leading ranks. There were cries of anguish and pain from the

Spawn and many fell. A second wave of arrows came down and more Spawn fell. The nearest Slavers began to reorganise and the Spawn picked up their dead and, with them held high against the arrows, they moved forward at a slow trot. Even those Spawn who were only wounded were raised high and did not resist but squirmed in pain and death under the third volley of arrows from the dwarves.

Gashima stood on a small hill just inside the gorge. From this point of elevation he could see the dwarves in steady retreat, keeping the distance between themselves and the Spawn. He saw how the gorge narrowed and how easy it would be to defend unless he could overrun the retreating dwarves. He ordered the forward ranks of Slavers onto the small hill. From there, they could see the mouth of the gorge and ordered the Spawn into a frenzy of rage.

The Spawn moved at a fast run, despite more volleys of arrows into their ranks. They began to run down the dwarves. Twenty thousand Spawn raged after the dwarves who now took full flight up the gorge. Twenty thousand more crammed into the gorge behind them. Gashima was brutal but clever. He ordered a halt halfway down the column of craven that were still perhaps a mile behind him.

These were commanded by his second-in-command who felt the order form in his head and halted his horde. This included Princess Zhuxi and her vanguard. She also heard the command in her mind and did her leap into the sky. She could see from about three hundred feet the Spawn chasing down the dwarf archers. She had been warned about these by her general, who was linked to her mind. Zhuxi could see why the general had halted the larger part of her forces. It would be just like those blood thirsty dwarves to stage an ambush.

She looked on her forces as she descended and knew her numbers would overwhelm any force that tried to intercept them. Her general had warned her about Ten Mile Gorge. She knew it would be defended and she was confident her Spawn would very soon overwhelm the wooden defences of the dwarves she had seen from the air at the end of the gorge.

As her feet alighted on the ground once more, she gave the order for Gashima to attack. Gashima called more Slavers to his position and ordered the Slavers already on the hill to move forward with them.

Lowe and the other dwarves pushed aside the boulders, wood and fresh cut grass hiding their entrance and sprang out onto the hill. Lowin, being lithe, ran up behind Gashima and took off his head in a single blow. His blood gushed upwards and outwards and Joygrim slaughtered a surprised Slaver at the same instant. The dwarves swarmed on the Slavers, now fighting for their lives and losing. Those that were in front turned and were met with at least ten dwarf axes burying into their flesh. Lowe and his son were among them and killing out. Some Spawn began to turn in the face of the assault but the death of their Slaver commanders caused confusion and panic among them. The ferocity of the assault was so great that, as a Slaver fell, confusion formed in the minds of the Spawn and some were slaughtered where they stood. Twenty dwarves had run and charged the Slavers coming up the hill. Many went down under the assault and those that avoided the instant massacre fell back into the ranks of Spawn, who attempted to close the gaps and protect them.

The rest of the dwarves on the hill now swept down to join their brethren. After one more quick skirmish, Lowe called a halt and all the dwarves returned in quick order and retreated into the mouth of the cave, where the entrance was now visible to all. Lowe knew this was their chance and that the forces before them would quickly begin a charge. With everyone inside the cave Lowe ordered the liquid spirit firebombs to be lit and these were lobbed into the Spawn ranks as they were rallied by the Slavers that had survived.

Screams went up among the Spawn who were burning. The firebombs had spirit and tar within, which made them sticky as they exploded. The confusion spread once more as a few of the Slavers were engulfed.

Inside the cave the dwarves opened the exit tunnel that had been built as an escape route. Lowin led the way along the tunnel. The dwarves moved fast, almost doubled up in the tunnel, and yet their speed was undiminished for they knew the ground. The noise of the battle faded behind them and at last they began to exit the tunnel in the trees, perhaps a mile from the scene of their recent adventure. Lowgrim was the last dwarf into the tunnel. The dwarves' luck was holding. Lowgrim now set his firebombs in the cave itself and, lighting them, he ran for his very life after his comrades.

The explosion within the cave itself was massive. The Spawn had finally launched into a counter offensive and forty were either in or in front of the entrance when the explosion occurred. It ripped the top of the hillock into the air and stones and debris killed many Spawn caught up in the blast. The fire killed many more Spawn and scorched a few more Slavers. The fire could be seen readily from the wooden barriers, manned by the dwarves. The archers in the meantime had continued to harry the Spawn and many more were killed in the confusion before the dwarves took refuge behind the wooden barriers they had constructed for the defence. Blutschläger and Sensmann were smiling quietly. They had ordered that no cheering should occur when the cave went up. The size of the explosion was a surprise to all of them. The cave had effectively become a sort of cannon, which had sent stones, fire and burning spirit shooting from the entrance. The explosion itself was very destructive and the Spawn bore the brunt of this. The dwarf commanders had ordered silence after the explosion. They wished to keep their enemy guessing while they prepared for battle themselves.

Princess Zhuxi was in a rage, a quiet rage. That fool general had got himself slaughtered and with him forty or more of her Slavers, together with five hundred Spawn. These were less of a loss to her, but still five hundred fewer to throw against her enemy. Zhuxi lifted herself into the air and took stock of the situation. She used mind control once she landed to calm the Spawn and ordered them to leave the gorge. She did not want any more such surprises today. She rearranged her command structure and Slavers once more took up their battle positions with their Spawn. "Feed the troops," she ordered. All the slain and the nearly dead were cut up and cooked in pots brought from the rear. The army sat and ate. There was no mercy in the horde.

Zhuxi now called for Wahushi, a Slaver, and allowed him to approach her in her tents. He was shaking from pure lust for her but cowed by her mental strength, so that he fell on the floor in ecstasy and fear of what was coming next. He both feared and despised Zhuxi but her hormonal impulses made his evil hidden self swell with a dark wish to consume her that was entirely evil and, if discovered, he knew Zhuxi would snuff him out in a second. All of this fear and lust was intoxicating so he chose to show her his fear.

Zhuxi fawned on him and she spoke her words of command for him, checking his mind was fully open to her. 'Hmm, this one has a dark space hidden deep within him. There is heat and lust and something else, but I have no time to delve,' she thought. "We must have order," she said aloud for him to hear. "Wahushi, you are my new general, get up and do as I command you."

"Yes Princess, I will do as you order."

Wahushi went to work and Zhuxi gave commands, looking through his eyes and seeing that all was well. Guards were posted while the horde ate its own. Zhuxi made a mental note to check the mind of Wahushi more thoroughly once she had won this conflict. Zhuxi giggled insanely to herself, which unnerved the human females in her court as well as the few men in attendance. 'The dwarves are tricky. We will have to be much more careful as we approach this next barrier. We do not wish our sisters to hear of another delay to our assault, it wouldn't do at all,' she thought.

Wahushi commanded the evil army of Spawn with the same distain as his predecessor but with more subtlety in his dealings with his fellow Slavers. Many of the Slavers that met their end under General Gashima had been relatively distant from the general, but Wahushi recognised the advantage of allying as many Slavers to his favour as he could. It was not out of kindness that he acted. He was cruel and callous like all Slavers, but he had something warm and dark within him that made him dangerous. His spirit within was pure evil, filled with ambition, driven by lust. This complicated his hatred of all things human and devilish. Wahushi had secret desires that, if discovered, would mean his demise. At his core was an old evil spirit that was pure badness and lust and it had passed from host to host over a millennium of time on Earth. Each time it moved it diminished in power until it was much akin to other Slavers and out of sight and mind of Zhuxi, who had not recognised it, but she was still wary. There had been evil delight in the core of Wahushi when Zhuxi had promoted him to lead her armies.

He now ordered the Slavers as he wished and once Zhuxi was no longer watching his mind so closely, he began to order his affairs. He set strong defences to each side of the horde and allowed them to rest. He brought captured human females to meet the needs of the male Slavers, who pleasured themselves as they wished. Males were brought to female Slavers and they were in turn used and abused with mental torture and exhaustion. Some of the older male slaves died in the experience. Many of the female slaves were impregnated and sent back along the lines to return to Queen Yonlik who nurtured the abominable offspring that would be liveborn. Half human, half Slaver evil. They would be taught to torment their humanity and debase it and in doing so sharpen the ill will and intellect of Yonlik's forces.

Queen Yonlik had always seen the destruction of men as coming from within the race. She used Spawn because she had complete power over them, as did her princesses. This was how she intended to undermine humanity, giving her complete hold of power on Earth. The future for humanity's destruction lay in these creatures' eggs, which she hoarded beneath the earth, deep down, near her stronghold. When Queen Yonlik conquered a dwarf mine and home, she would settle some of the Slavers, male and female, to work on the perfection in evil and integrate the offspring now growing into her ideal warrior. These became strong and were most potent and were called by another name secretly, known only to the queen and her princesses.

Wahushi pleasured himself with both female Slavers and human females. When he had finished in his depravity, he visited the scene of destruction and examined the cave in some detail. He saw for himself the cunning disguise of the cave, the burnt area outside and surmised that the dwarves must have either been slaughtered as martyrs, which was what he would expect of his fellows, or had somehow escaped. He pondered for a long while before re-entering the cave cautiously with other Slavers at his command. The torches showed him how the inner walls had crumbled and cascaded onto the cave floor.

Wahushi was now not in a rush. He ordered Spawn to clear away the debris and this was piled up outside the cave. Once clear, the cave showed signs it had been dwarf constructed. Wahushi found the tunnel. It had of course been collapsed by the retreating dwarfs. He surmised there was no point digging it out and following the dwarf trail, but then changed his mind. He ordered two Slavers, both very junior, to dig out the cave, find the tunnel and follow it and then the dwarves. He was not concerned to send many Spawn and gave the Slavers one hundred Spawn to aid them. He did this to show Zhuxi that he was thorough and to give her confidence in him to find those responsible and report back to him. They would of course report to him first and that might prove useful, as a distraction with Zhuxi, should he need it. This thought only took shape in the dark place in his mind.

Princess Zhuxi and her entourage of Slavers and slaves were holding court in large animal skin tents, made from the skins of dead Spawn and other animals that had gone into the food pots many years previously. The hide of Spawn was thick and suited to such uses. It felt like something approaching rhino skin, but paler in colour and softer in texture. Zhuxi liked the smell of the dead, the slight odour of flesh coming from the fabric. It made her feel at home and was also a good reminder to her Slavers of their own fragile existence should they displease her.

Wahushi came into the tent, feeling pleased. He gave his report and declared he was now ready to move on with the wishes of his princess. Wahushi then made a brave decision and asked what the princess could see of the dwarf defences they were soon to overcome. Princess Zhuxi was pleased that Wahushi was a thorough and devious character and prepared to think for himself in his deviousness. "I think we shall find the dwarves will not be able to hold out long. We should learn from the enemy and use what we have in our favour." She ordered Wahushi to make preparation and he left chuckling at his cleverness and Zhuxi's cunning. The dwarves were not the only ones who could use fire.

CHAPTER FOURTEEN
ZHUXI'S CUNNING

Blutschläger and Sensmann stood upon the barricade. From their point upon the wooden wall, they could see the Spawn were carrying straw, timber and other burnable items, no doubt to burn down the defence wall. Sensmann was unhappy for the first time. She realised that with the wind in the current direction, although only a breeze in the spring, it would mean the smoke would be in the dwarf faces and would hamper their attempts to fight off the Spawn. She and Blutschläger had a long conversation and agreed they would need to adapt their plans due to the smoke. They ordered cloth facemasks to be soaked and shared among those defending the wall.

The Spawn on approach made their first assault as normal and were met with a hail of arrows. Once more the dead were hoisted up and they approached the wall. The bodies took the dwarf arrows. The Spawn began to pile wood against the wall of timber. The dwarves made their plans. Archers continued to harry the Spawn that showed any part of themselves near the wall and others continued to fire volleys at the Spawn in range. The Slavers formed the Spawn into a line under which the fuel was carried to the front.

Blutschläger stayed on the wall while Sensmann organised the dwarves into the woods behind the wall and soon trees, bushes, anything that would burn, was carried forward. The Spawn now withdrew under the command of the Slavers and the pyre was lit. Dead flesh was cooked and the fat oozing from the Spawn slaughtered by the dwarves created a blaze with oily black smoke. The dwarves retreated from the wall and stood well back. Once it was clear nothing was coming over the wall yet, they could relax. The fire burned hot. Sensmann and the dwarves worked hard for five hours while the fire before them grew hotter and larger and began to burn the walls of the barricade.

Blutschläger was most unhappy as he spoke to Sensmann and his senior cohort of leaders who were meeting well away from the raging fire and smoke. "I had not thought that the Spawn scum would have the brains for this nasty trick! I was hoping to hold the scum here for many days and really make them pay for taking the barricade. I fear we have been outwitted for once."

Sensmann knew her partner was keen for battle and was suffering a disappointment that they all felt. Retreating went against the grain with dwarves once they were committed to battle. She looked at the fire wall before her. Even two hundred paces from the wall she could feel the warmth and was thankful there was only a breeze so that the blaze, though hot, was not as fierce as it might have been and that meant it would take longer to burn out.

She spoke to the gathering. "Okay, when we deem the time right, we start to pile our fuel to the fire. Once this is achieved, we will retreat at our best pace and return to home. I know we are unfought here which makes my blood boil, but if we stay then we are going to lose a lot of our kindred and without doubt will be harried all the way home. That prospect means the injured would be slaughtered where they fall and the enemy would claim a victory against us. My feeling is we are better to retreat now while we may and give further thought to how we might better defend our homes. I have sent runners back already and ordered all fuel the enemy might use against us to be brought within our stone barrier and it gives me some thoughts on how we might turn this situation to advantage later."

Blutschläger was indeed angry but also grateful for his partner's clear mind. His thought had been to stay and make them fight once the fire burned away. He was confident they could hold the narrow gorge for a long time, but Sensmann then reminded him that without the wall to protect them, the assault from the Spawn would be frenzied. The Spawn would no doubt have plenty of rock and timber to throw over the fire defences, and it would be a bit chaotic. Retreating over rocks and timber being thrown and fighting Spawn at the same time would give rise to dwarf casualties. Slowly but surely the common sense of the situation hit home and Blutschläger agreed the strategy, albeit begrudging, as the best chance to make these Spawn and Slavers pay for their audacity.

The dwarves prepared as best they could. They set oil caskets against their side of the now hot wall and filled a trench, dug for the defensive retreat earlier, with fuel and oil. This would be lit by a small number of dwarves under the command of the Blood Beater. He was determined to be the last dwarf to leave and there were no shortages of volunteers to stand with him. Sensmann chose females and younger, faster dwarves to stay with her husband. In her mind she smiled, thinking about her secret conversations with her dwarves. She imagined the Blood Beater being hoisted up at a run by the female dwarves and his howl of indignation as their speed doubled even carrying his bulk. She might not be able to beat him in battle, but she was certain she was not going to let him fight his way on foot and lose him before the big fight was begun. 'We will need his strengths far more behind the wall at home,' she thought.

She swore the dwarf males and females to secrecy after she told them what to do. They expressed alarm at what the Blood Beater would do to them. None of them fancied having to explain Sensmann's plan to him while he was holding his axes and ready for battle. "I didn't say it was a safe plan, and I understand your concern, so do as I now ask, and never speak of it again unless we get to tell the tale of the Blood Beater's great victory in some hall or other after our victory." The conspiring dwarves took an oath never to speak of what they planned and Sensmann thought of how she might aid them in this highly unusual strategy.

While the fire was at its peak, Sensmann ordered the dwarf retreat and all but the chosen few moved off at a trot. Sensmann wanted to be sure her people arrived safely and not caught before they reached the wall. The remaining dwarves stoked the fire with long poles, piling up timber laid out across the gorge for this purpose before they left. The fire raged on and the heat intensified. The dwarves drew back behind the now oil-filled trench and Blutschläger and his entourage settled down and rested, ate a little food and drank some beer to quench their thirst.

It was warm work keeping the fire stoked up high. Four hours passed, then six hours and the fuel was now nearly spent. It was only the fire set on the dwarves' side of the blaze that was preventing the Spawn from crossing. The Slavers sent some injured Spawn into the blaze but they fell and burned, intensifying the heat.

Blood Beater was Blutschläger's nickname among the dwarves. He now stood up, paying close attention to the fire. He estimated that another hour would see the blaze passable. He called for the dwarves with him to prepare to light the trench. The trench was about five feet deep and ten feet wide and filled with timber and oil. Blutschläger estimated it would hold back the Spawn for only a couple of hours. The entourage looked towards their illustrious leader. They encouraged him to drink a final toast to Sensmann before the battle that was to come. He took the offered flagon and drained it.

Within a few minutes he was fast asleep. Out came a well prepared, six-handled stretcher, with three each side and into it went the sleeping Blood Beater, none the wiser. Eight dwarves set off with the stretcher and made a good pace, leaving the two fastest dwarves to light the fire. Both were female dwarves, named Janzen and Zenith. They were proud to be given this role to do for their kindred. They sat watching the fire slowly recede until they could make out the Spawn lined up on the other side of the fire. A Spawn suddenly leapt into the fire and very nearly made it across but burned up before he could escape and his screams caused a moan in the Spawn. This was immediately silenced by the Slaver in the front line. Janzen and Zenith moved as one. They lit their torches and threw them into the trench. The blaze was fierce and fast and only took seconds to light right across the gorge. The other fire was still impassable and stayed that way for maybe twenty minutes.

The dwarves assessed their work. The new defence fire was burning hot now. They shook hands, smiled at one another for a job well done and set off after their comrades at a brisk dwarf run.

Wahushi was near the line of fire on his side, now it was burning low. He called for the Spawn to throw stones onto the fire to beat it down and, when he was satisfied, he sent the Spawn and Slavers across this bridge, expecting a fight on the opposite side, for the smoke was still thick enough to blur his vision but he was hot for dwarf blood.

Wahushi shouted out to the Slavers and Spawn. "Charge! Dwarf meat for dinner boys!"

He followed the Spawn over the bed of stone and found the Spawn assault had stalled. At the same moment he saw the second fire and the heat of rage fell from him into a cold stillness. The effect on the Spawn was instant. They sat back on their haunches and waited. When no command came, they settled down in groups and watched the blaze before them. He called the Slavers to him and set them to watch the fire and to call him when it burned low. This was not how he had hoped this day would end.

Princess Zhuxi accepted Wahushi's report in her tent. She was pleased in her malice to see his nervous twitch, as he explained the latest delay in the march through the gorge. Wahushi was dismissed after a pause of about a minute, while he suffered her displeasure, as he saw it. He was grateful to get back to the front of his army. Zhuxi smiled and summoned a human male to her. She used her wiles on him and he fell on his back. Zhuxi pleasured herself until he began to scream in pain. She then tossed him aside. Zhuxi would use the human genetic material to fertilise her eggs, which she would lay aside tomorrow in the creche. She had laid at least five hundred eggs since beginning the journey, the progeny to which she had recently passed her malice would be carried off to a suitable place to grow and then hatch.

A small dwarf dwelling on the surface a few miles to the rear was chosen by her to build her army from. Within a month the new slaves to her army would start to arrive. These would be stronger and a bit smarter than the Spawn, but would need the leadership of the Slavers to make them useful slaves and to organise them. These offspring would be more wilful and would require a heavy hand to focus them. Wahushi had already selected the Slavers for the job. They were mostly females, as the female Slavers had the advantage of using their pheromones to control as well as their minds when dealing with half humans.

Zhuxi slept while the fire burned. Wahushi moved over the trench some four hours after the dwarves left. He was cautious moving forward, suspicious of the lack of fight from the dwarves. He knew them to be fierce fighters and also cunning. "They are becoming worthy opponents, which is all the better when I slay them and increase my standing with the luscious Princess Zhuxi."

Janzen and Zenith had been running steadily for five hours when they sighted their colleagues and sprinted the last half mile, with the intent to catch up to them. They were greeted with a happy shout from the bearers of the stretcher. They shared experiences with Janzen and Zenith and took turns in keeping the stretcher moving at a fast pace. They approached the wall of their home and stopped in a small copse of trees. All the dwarves were a bit nervous about waking Blutschläger but they knew they had to do it now before entering their homeland. They got their story straight in their own minds, the one provided by Sensmann, and gently woke the sleeping Blutschläger. He opened one eye and then the other before leaping to his feet, axe in hand. Janzen and Zenith, the two young females, were tasked with placating the big dwarf. The males were brave enough but likely in Janzen's mind to aggravate the dwarf. With some serious shaking of the shoulders, he became conscious. "What happened to me?" he asked.

Janzen look directly at the Blood Beater with a serious face, ready to defend herself. "You fell into a deep slumber and we couldn't wake you. The fire had burned low so we did the only thing we could do and carried you with us."

Zenith had discretely moved the stretcher from sight and another dwarf laid his axe to it before they had woken Blutschläger.

"Nothing like this ever happened to me before," said Blutschläger. "Still, no harm done I suppose. How far have we come?"

"We have reached home, just beyond these trees," and she gesticulated behind her. "While we are here, I am thinking we might take down these trees?"

Blutschläger agreed and laid his axe to the nearest tree. Once they had cut the timber, each dwarf carried a tree between two and took them towards the great wall defending their home. Sensmann stood upon the wall and was relieved to see her plan had succeeded and she sent dwarves out to collect the rest of the timber. 'I should have thought of that myself,' she scolded herself quietly. The pleasure she had felt in seeing the dwarves return was diminished by this small failure. 'No time to get sloppy,' she thought, 'so buck yourself up.'

Once the dwarves were safe behind the wall, Sensmann met with her partner. He gave her a great hug. They held onto one another until even Blutschläger's arm began to ache a little from the strain. "Well done, husband for not getting yourself killed!" Sensmann had decided an assertive stance from her was going to work better than silence in the coming discussion. Blutschläger smiled at his wife. 'He knows,' she thought.

"A strange thing happened today before the retreat." He told Sensmann all about it. "If you ever make a ploy like that again Sensmann, I will divorce you."

Sensmann lowered her defences and accepted the terrible threat as very real to her. "I am feeling very ashamed for what I did to you now husband. I can see it was wrong and had you been ambushed on the way back you would have been defenceless and ten other dwarves of whom I am very fond would have died before you in your defence. I was concerned that you would delay the enemy's advance by your own strength and courage and I know for a fact that having you retreating with the rear guard was a decision which placed me in the predicament of bad choices. You can see that the enemy is already with us. If you had been any slower getting home, they would have caught you and killed at least some of your party. You are the strength of our people Blutschläger, my husband. Your duty is to face the main charge of our enemies if we are to survive. We needed you here so that our dwarves would fight fiercer and with more venom than they could do without you. I could not risk you. It was a bad plan made in haste in a bad place." Sensmann relented. She had spoken from her heart and Blutschläger looked at her keenly and he could see the truth in her eyes and in her words.

"Very well, my wife, I can see why you did what you did and that those scallywags with you were pressured into what they did. I will take it no further, but I will say this." Sensmann held her breath. "Never again! If you have fears I will listen and if I have fears I will speak of them. You have a fine mind for this campaign, and we need that cunning mind to outwit these Spawn and their Slavers if we are to survive. It has only just sunk in that with Lowe and Lowin gone, you are the brains behind our strategy. We need to be solid and whole. My anger I hold back for the sake of our people and for my love of you. I will use it to motivate me to the coming battle. Now get me some beer before I explode and destroy our lovely home!"

Sensmann had beer ready and immediately poured two flagons of ale. She refilled Blutschläger's flagon several times before he began to calm down and giggle a little at the ridiculous figure he must have cut with those dwarves in the know. Eventually, he asked for the culprits, and Sensmann sent in ten very humble looking dwarves and sat them at the large table in the kitchen, Janzen and Zenith among them. He looked on all their faces as he sat there and they in turn looked a little terrified. Then he broke into peals of laughter and they joined in and tucked into their beer with relief.

Sensmann turned away from the table and thought to herself, 'Thank God that is over and thank goodness he has a sense of humour, even if he needs to be half cut to remember it.' She then refilled flagons and the dwarves told their tale to him and he muttered his approval and even laughed as Zenith described his fall onto the stretcher and how Janzen had been shaking like a leaf in offering to drink the toast that put him out. They all laughed again. Blutschläger then surprised them all by saying that he wished for the whole dwarf kingdom to hear this tale and of his indignation and recovery from surviving the conflict at the gorge. "It will raise spirits," he said. "Now let us drink a toast to the real heroes of the battle!"

And he raised his flagon to his lips and drank to the health of them both and then to his wife. Sensmann smiled and thought to herself, 'And that's why I love him.'

* * *

Princess Zhuxi looked out on her mighty army arrayed outside the dwarf kingdom. Two hundred thousand Spawn, ready for war. The wall in front of her was high and the gateway had been sealed with rock upon heavy rock and it would prove harder to break than the gate of wood that had been there previously. The wall was twenty feet high and had firing points every three steps. She could see the dwarves going about their business on the inside. Zhuxi was careful to stay out of bow shot when she rose on her wings to spy out the land. She spied slingshots on the walls which could send a hail of stones down on her army and men with longer bows than the dwarves, which fired a greater distance, and one or two audacious men had tried to hit her. Zhuxi soared on a parallel with the wall, not getting too close. She could see her enemies in the land beyond. Her keen eyesight told her there were perhaps nine thousand men and horses in the plain. The dwarves were upon the walls and behind it. Zhuxi was keen to get on with destroying the dwarves before her sister could arrive with the second half of her forces.

She took one more sweep across the defences and landed next to her general. All the Spawn moved away without command. It did not pay to be too close to the princess. Wahushi turned to face the princess. "I have seen enough Wahushi. We will go straight in pushing the ramp before us. Make it ready."

Wahushi had used his time when he was delayed to build resources to his advantage. On the way through the gorge, he had prepared two ramps, which they would use to attack the dwarves' stone wall at opposite ends. They used trees just beyond the clearing that had been the first battleground. He was grateful now to see that he had planned well, as the trees locally had been chopped down, no doubt to create a clear line of sight for the dwarves to fire through. Wahushi called up his Slavers and gave them their orders. They lined up ten ranks to the rear of the Spawn. They put their protective shields, roughly fashioned in wood, over themselves to ward off arrows. Wahushi then ordered the front rank to pick up their bundles of timber and ordered them forward. As they came into range, they used the wood to protect their heads. They moved with a frenzied speed and when near enough threw the wood against the centre of wall until it was piled high. Several Spawn fell on the return to the ranks. They made this journey to the wall until the wood was piled ten feet high against the structure.

The dwarves could do nothing about this and they satisfied themselves with picking off any Spawn that they could with their bows. Wahushi ordered the bonfire to be lit. Still there was no sign of concern on the wall. The fire burned hot. The timber had been pre-soaked in oil and black smoke came from it. Wahushi had borrowed this idea for a weapon from the dwarves. It was not lost on Sensmann as she stood upon the wall away from the smoke. Wahushi waited until the fire was at its hottest. He could see the dwarves preparing for an attack. The fire left the centre of the wall clear of dwarves due to the heat. Wahushi ordered his Slavers to release the Spawn. They pushed the wooden ramps through the lines and they charged to each side of the wall, hitting it with some force. The wall stayed strong and the Spawn now sped up the ramps and leapt the last five feet at the dwarves who were standing above them.

The dwarves defended themselves stoutly and then stubbornly using their axes very effectively hitting the Spawn with crippling blows, forcing them to fall upon those behind.

The Spawn were frenzied and clambered over one another to get at the dwarves. The first casualty of the dwarves missed his stroke and was instantly pulled into the Spawn. He disappeared from view. The Spawn were now on the wall and slowly but surely their numbers by pressure and weight from behind pushed the dwarves back and more and more Spawn went forward. Sensmann watched the fight. The dwarves would have been more effective had they been able to man the centre of the wall and use their bows against the ramps and the Spawn climbing them.

Wahushi now saw that the fire was much lower but still sending up smoke. He ordered his Spawn to run at the centre of the wall. Each Spawn had carried a steel hook and a long rope. The Spawn launched their hooks onto the top of the wall and began to climb above the fire, leaping the last eight feet at the base and grasping the ropes and pulling themselves up.

Sensmann saw the danger in time and rallied the dwarves. The fight to hold the top of the wall intensified and several dwarves were launched off and immediately killed if they were not already dead from the fall. Blutschläger now committed his forces and began to fight his way to the front. His arrival rallied the dwarves and Blutschläger swung his heavy hammers from each fist and was impervious to the blows of the Spawn. He crushed them left and right and gained the top of the first ramp that had been on the left. Other heavy dwarves launched their attack from behind him to deal with the Spawn at the centre and the dwarves on the other ramp redoubled their effort and began to maim and step over their opponents. Those dwarves arriving behind them sliced the Spawn and Slavers up before throwing the carrion over the wall.

The blood was thick on the wall and this made it very tricky for the Spawn to keep their balance. Slowly but surely the Blood Beater, now at the front of the Spawn, jumped down on them, swinging his axes. He exploded from under one Spawn and once more his great arms began dispatching Spawn left and right. Other dwarves joined him on the top of the ramp. Now the dwarves were organised in defence. They hurled burning oil over the heads of those on the front line, and when the Spawn were driven back screaming, despite their frenzied attack, and the ramp was well alight, the dwarves climbed back on the wall.

The battle for the centre of the wall continued and Spawn moved to attack on both sides. Wahushi used this brief time to order his Spawn to pull on the lines that they had climbed up. The hooks were now firmly planted at the walkway level and the Spawn below pulled with a terrible strength. The lines went taut and, inch by inch, the top five feet of the centre began to move outwards. The dwarves, seeing this, redoubled their assault and as they killed Spawn, they hewed at the lines.

Despite this, a few blocks on the top of the wall toppled and fell to a great cheer from the Spawn below. The battle now became exceedingly fierce and, with support from the middle where heavy set dwarves had won their ground, they were able to support their colleagues fighting to hold ground. Now the tables turned, and the dwarves began to make progress. Many, many Spawn died on the wall but so did many dwarves. Once more oil was thrown over the Spawn and they burned even as they fell, leaping off the ramp in agony.

The dwarves had held the wall. The centre was five feet lower in height, but the two ramps were both burned to the ground. As the sun rose, the Spawn retreated from arrow shots and made camp. They carried their dead and many dwarf corpses and set fires to the cooking pots. The dwarves on watch on the defence wall were grateful for the break and the fact that the smoke from the fires burning on both sides of the wall was making visibility difficult, so they were spared from seeing the dwarves being cooked. The Spawn had deliberately set up their cooking pots so the dwarves could see what they were doing to their dead kindred, rendering the flesh and relishing in the task. If the dwarves and men behind the wall had any doubts about their future and possible mercy, these thoughts were driven from their minds.

The dwarves moved to their positions on the wall. Shields were placed across the lowered wall in the centre and the dwarves inspected the base of the structure to check the damage. Fortune favoured the dwarves as, thankfully, the heat had not split too much stone, for the barrier was made of finest granite at the base and the blocks weighed several tons. The stone masons reported this to the council in their forward chamber, which had formerly been a farmer's barn before the battle. Bar Lowin and Lowe, the other eight leaders of the dwarves had taken their seats at a sizeable round table made from good oak brought to the field by Sensmann's folk. Janzen, Zenith and the other dwarves from the successful, if short, battle at the gorge were honoured by being allowed to form the guard within the barn, while trusty and sturdy dwarves, selected from all the kingdoms, were honoured to guard the exterior grounds. No one, not even a mouse could get past the perimeter set up as security for their councils.

Grobest spoke first. "What say you Sensmann, of our situation here, since Lowe and Lowin left?"

Sensmann was relaxed in her chair and sat up straight as the question was aimed at her. "We did good work done at the gorge. We surprised ourselves by the destruction that we caused there. I think we can be sure that Lowe and his people got away. The plan was well set and the destruction in the cave must have killed hundreds of Spawn and maimed quite a few. The Spawn would have eaten well, not on dwarf flesh but very much their own. Yes! It was a good start. As to the Blood Beater's decision to retreat once the defence wall at the gorge was burned, that turned out to be wiser than even I thought.

We didn't give the fight or defence there that we could have done so easily, but our losses have been low compared to what they might have been, had we done so. Given the forces arrayed against us I can see now that we will be hard pressed to overcome this enemy. As things stand, to be able to survive this war we will need a bit of luck and very clear heads."

She saw the serious faces looking at her and she smiled. "Don't get me wrong when I say this, but we still have a chance to end the threat from the princesses for at the least a long time. We are going to suffer as all do in war. We dwarves are hardy, strong and resilient and nothing is going to stop us from fulfilling our destiny here."

Zenith looked to Janzen and grinned, for she could see her friend was having the same struggle not to cry out a great shout of approval. It was a great speech. A short speech, just as dwarves preferred it.

Grobest lifted his arm and the noise abated. "Okay! A good start and it seems a lucky one, if the frenzied assault we saw on the wall here had been performed in the field there would have been a bloody outcome. We would have come through that battle, but I am pleased with the result so far." The others round the table murmured their approval. "Shall we now hear from Blutschläger? What say you?"

The Blood Beater stood up. "I, the Blood Beater, was forced by circumstances to leave a battlefield without swinging my axe for the first time ever! The councils of Sensmann and the intelligence of my guard at least allowed me the pleasure of being present for the fight on the wall. We lost some of our kinsmen, which we will mourn later. We now know what we face and can adapt our defence to meet it. Tomorrow the Spawn will come again in greater numbers against the wall. We will hold because the wall is sturdy. Their tactics are limited by the relatively small area of conflict our city wall provides for them. We dwarves know the value of delving and if the Slavers have not begun to excavate in the next day or so, then their general is a half-wit. We can expect tunnelling under the wall to bring it down in about a week. Once that comes down the battle will become much more intense. The dwarves will hold their ground. We are well set to fight the ground battle and, while we can prevent a breach, the Spawn can only come at us from one direction. The good news is that we can better manage our own forces to withstand the pressure of pure numbers on one front, without getting exhausted ourselves and eventually cut down. Even these Spawn and their Slavers will tire and then we will see how things fair."

This was the longest speech ever made by the Blood Beater to his fellow dwarves. They took in every word and even his wife sat back in quiet admiration at his quiet intensity. 'This battle is going to be his finest hour,' she felt sure of it.

Zenith and Janzen were thinking something similar from the looks on their proud faces for it was their cousin twice removed at least, but still a cousin who was leading them to battle. When they left the barn, they spoke to their kin and everyone polished armour, sharpened swords and axes and checked their mighty hammers for new cracks which might open when killing Spawn.

* * *

With the dusk an hour hence, the Spawn were being gathered for another assault. Wahushi was pleased with the first night assault, for he had been able to show his mistress that he was well capable of storming the dwarf homes and kill and eat some of their people. Princess Zhuxi had enjoyed hearing about the fight and was keen for her army to begin the war proper and bring death down on the ranks of the dwarves.

Wahushi ordered his Spawn, through the Slavers, to attack again and this time there were three ramps hastily assembled through the day, by the Spawn at the rear. The Slavers had to work hard to motivate them in the sunlight. The sun was unloved by the forces of evil and the day had been one of sunshine for most of the time. As the sun set, the Slavers cajoled the Spawn forward with the ramps. The Slavers involved in the labour then retreated. New Slavers arrived and ordered them to lift the ramps and take them to the wall.

The dwarves were well prepared and fired volleys of arrows at the ramps while they were still fifty metres from the wall. Fewer Spawn fell but the ramps were soon aflame and one on the left was abandoned even before it reached the wall. The other two hit the wall and Spawn were frenzied by the Slavers and ran through the flames to attack the dwarves. The dwarves threw small axes to wound the Spawn as they approached and then the front ranks of the dwarves began to slay in rhythm to a low beat, which quickened as they warmed to their work.

Blood of Spawn and of dwarves soon put out the fires on the ramps. The Spawn were losing ten to every one of the dwarves injured or killed. As soon as the press of numbers came on, the dwarves once more pushed their lines close behind to prevent the front rank from being overwhelmed. When a dwarf fell to a blow, he was pulled in by his fellows and another took his place. No dwarf wished to be removed from the battle and they proudly stood and fought through the day.

Bar led the left flank and held the middle of the wall with his toughest dwarves. They fought the Spawn to a standstill all through the night. Their deep-chested song rumbled on the wall until it seemed to Sensmann, who was near the second ramp, that the stones themselves were singing and she could feel the vibration under her feet, as their song came back to them from the high walls on either side of the rocky canyon that protected their homes. Grobest had the honour to fight on the right and his dwarves sang along as if they were a choir of baritone singers, their axes moving to the beat of the music.

The Spawn were becoming dismayed near to dawn, for they had made little progress on the wall itself. While the Spawn were fighting on the ramps, Wahushi had ordered others forward with hastily made ladders and Spawn rallied and threw themselves up the ladders to reach the waiting dwarves. Many ladders were smashed and fell from the wall. The ladders were axed and fell and were replaced by more. It was almost dawn when Sensmann sensed, rather than saw, a change in the energy of the dwarves and she ordered her archers once more to burn the ramps if they could. She set other dwarves to light the litter beneath the Spawn where the broken ladders were piled. These burned well and the Spawn were once more driven back by the heat. Wahushi broke off the attack when this turned the battle in favour of the dwarves. Now, all three ramps were once more burning fiercely, and the Spawn retreated, snarling but still retreating.

As the sun came up on a beautiful morning in the world, the dwarves lifted their heads to greet the dawn. The Spawn lowered theirs to hide their eyes from the sun. New ranks of dwarves came onto the wall to replace those that had fought all night long. There were many females among the replacements. They were keen for battle and for the splitting of Spawn heads and proudly stood among their male counterparts. The dwarves had done well. They had fought well, sung well and killed many Spawn. They did not celebrate beyond washing the blood from their limbs and bathing to ease their muscles. Hammerhurz had ordered young dwarves to see to the needs of the warriors and family groups helped each warrior out of his heavy armour before bathing. Even some of the older men and women had offered to care for the injured and did the fetching and carrying of fresh water and beer. They expressed their gratitude to the dwarves as they bound the wounds.

While the dwarves rested in the day, Sensmann, Dunkeln and Hammerhurz met to discuss tactics for the coming night. Sensmann opened the meeting. "We need a better plan to defeat the ramps as they approach. These ramps are going to get more difficult to stop once the wall becomes more damaged and I fear the Slavers are already digging into the rock to destabilise the wall. What say you Dunkeln? You are our best rock master."

"We have perhaps three days before the wall comes down and then the odds turn unless we make a plan to stop it."

The three dwarves spent the next two hours discussing how they could slow the Spawns' progress. They dismissed the idea of defending the wall from the other side because the weight of Spawn that could come against them was too great, and even the strongest dwarves would tire long before the night was out. This would lead to heavy losses on the dwarf side. Sensmann came up with the simplest and, probably, most immediate way to prevent being overwhelmed at the wall. They set men and dwarves to work to carry out her instructions.

* * *

Wahushi had been studying the dwarves' battle tactics for over a month at the wall. He reflected on the dwarf ability to adapt the fight to keep an advantage. He was frustrated that the wall was still standing. His early success at the wall had given him an expectancy that he would have been fighting in the enclosed valley by this time. Wahushi had always been cautious in front of Princess Zhuxi about a quick victory and to this point he had shown himself adept at pleasing her sufficiently to prevent him being replaced. He had been careful to select Slavers that were loyal to him as much as any Slaver could be. He had his own spies among the camp faithful to warn him of activities to replace while he was busy fighting.

Wahushi knew very well that greed and envy nigh as great as his own was within near proximity and he felt the envy reach to him. His spies reported to him very regularly after each break in the battle to see how the Slavers were aligning for opportunities for advancement in the horde. He was particularly interested in a female Slaver named Kayin. She was attractive by her hormone trail, not ugly in her features and she was cautious. She took advantage to be noticed for her cruelty and cunning and had two nights previously challenged a captured, heavily wounded male dwarf that still had some fight in him. Kayin had taunted him for his capture. The male dwarf had cursed her, calling her cowardly scum unworthy to lick his boots. Kayin saw an opportunity to raise her profile and stood against him in single combat.

Wahushi had recognised Kayin was taking a small risk compared to the glory she would gain in torturing the dwarf to his death. He also imagined she would be asked to reiterate her story to Princess Zhuxi when her spies heard about it. Wahushi had not been present of course, but his own spies, led by his most trusted Slaver Tienat Alzur, had gleefully told the tale to Wahushi soon after it ended. Wahushi was gleeful, not only because the torture had been particularly cruel and lengthy, but he had identified Kayin as a Slaver reporting directly to the princess and this would be useful. It turned out that Wahushi needed to use the information the very day he had heard it.

Progress for Wahushi against the dwarves at the wall had been sluggish at best. The dwarves were worthy opponents and fought without fear of their own death for their faith in the Creator and his plan for them was clear in their hearts. The dwarves knew that death was not the end for them. A good death for a dwarf was after a long life or second best a death in battle with evil. In their view, even a badly lived life might be forgiven by the Creator if they died well fighting evil. It was for this reason that the captured dwarf had reviled the Slaver captors. Kayin offered single combat and the fight had been memorable, cruel and a powerful advert for advancement.

After his eventual death the dwarf was cooked. The Slavers present feasted on him and what was left was thrown to the Spawn who were always hungry. That very day in front of the princess Wahushi had seen the hint of anger rising in Zhuxi and he feared what was coming unless he could head it off. He had seen by Zhuxi's reaction to his failure to break the wall that he was finally on a cliff edge. He reported the bravery of his Slavers in driving the Spawn to greater efforts to dislodge the dwarves but this no longer pleased Zhuxi.

Wahushi took his chance and openly praised Kayin to Zhuxi for her cruelty with the captured dwarf. He told her in minute detail how the dwarf had fought with Kayin for over two hours and how the Slaver, through her speed, guile and cunning had constantly cut the dwarf (less his armour of course) until he was sufficiently weakened, he could no longer stand. The dwarf had earned a quick death for his bravery, but Kayin was cruel and sat before him while he bled to death and told him how she would kill all his colleagues and his family once the dwarves were overcome. She told him his blood would tell him which dwarves were his relatives and she would cut every captured dwarf to taste their blood to ensure she did not miss anyone out and they would all die particularly cruel deaths, just like his. Kayin had allowed the dwarf to injure her slightly in the early stages of battle to make it look more even as a fight than it really was.

Princess Zhuxi had shown real pleasure at the telling of the tale and enjoyed it more since Wahushi was unaware that Kayin had already reported the details to her. In her mind this meant Wahushi was unaware of the Slaver spy so close to him for Wahushi had been so enthused himself in the tale that he asked the princess if Kayin might be promoted to his left hand

and help their cause in defeating the dwarves. Princess Zhuxi was not yet prepared to give up on her general as Wahushi had shown complete loyalty to her and was not sparing himself or the Slavers in the battle. Zhuxi therefore approved Wahushi's request and he left the audience with the gratitude of the princess intact. Only when alone later did he allow himself a grin.

Wahushi and Kayin were in conference and were agreeing their latest assault. Kayin had suggested that it was time to switch tactics and Wahushi was pleased with her thoughts on the matter. Their attempts to undermine the wall by burrowing had been hard and dangerous work and very steady but slow progress was made. Their tunnel had got within ten feet of the wall when they hit a powerful underground spring. Water, especially free running water, was the only thing that could break the Slavers' spell over the Spawn. When the breach happened, fifty Spawn trapped underground as the water hit them were drowned. Panic was instant and the survivors scrambled back in the suffocating tunnel now filling with fresh water. As they came above ground their panic spread to the rest of the swarm and even reached those at the wall.

The dwarves had of course rallied and killed many of the panicked beasts that were in reach and the attack had stalled badly. So badly that Wahushi and Kayin, who were at the front, had no choice but to order a full retreat from the wall so that they could re-establish their hold over the Spawn. There had been great celebration on the wall by the dwarves who saw what had happened and made it heard by all how pleased and uplifted they were by this small victory and respite they had won. Kayin was very displeased to have been at the forefront when this misfortune occurred, for she had been forced to order the retreat and Princess Zhuxi would know of it and her life might be forfeit, for Zhuxi did not tolerate defeat in any form easily. Zhuxi, in her fury, had come up with a suicide mission for some of her Slavers and many Spawn, no doubt.

That very night Wahushi, having approved his lieutenant's plan, watched as she set it in motion. A high tower, thirty feet tall, was constructed. It was solid and soaked in water so it would not easily burn. Spawn pushed it to the wall under heavy bombardment, for the dwarves could see what was coming. Once near the wall, the Spawn were driven to climb up and throw themselves on top of the dwarves at the wall. The dwarves defended themselves by raising their shields but even their strong arms were soon tired after more and more Spawn leapt onto the wall. Many were slaughtered but very slowly the Spawn progressed and, had it not been for the dawn and a sunny day, the dwarves would have been pushed right off the wall to terrible losses. Unfortunately, from Wahushi's point of view, the heavyweight dwarves with their powerful muscles led the dwarves for a final assault to push the Spawn back and, because of the sun, the Spawn could not be frenzied sufficiently to hold on. Kayin and Wahushi were satisfied with their cunning. The next night they knew they would take the wall. Nothing could stop them.

Blutschläger and Sensmann hugged as soon as the dwarves had secured the wall. The Spawn had been recalled by the Slavers. There were losses on both sides and Sensmann hugged every dwarf that came off the wall as they came past her. Janzen and Zenith, the female cousins, joined her, to the great enjoyment and pleasure of the dwarves, male and female, when they were grasped very tightly.

Blutschläger was covered in the blood of battle. Most of it was Spawn blood, mixed with a little Slaver blood, when one Slaver made a step to close and lost his head to the Blood Beater's hammer. It had been this stroke that had finally turned the battle in the dwarves' favour. Up until that point, despite their best efforts, the dwarves had been on the back foot. "Killing the Slaver had been the key to unlocking their courage," said Blutschläger. "Once his head came off the Spawn were easy meat and me and the boys and girls gave it to them fair and square! That small victory was very welcome. I thought we had had it this time."

Sensmann hugged him again. "I agree," she said, "and once more you were there to save the day!" Sensmann and the cousins had been getting concerned all afternoon as the Spawn finally came up with a strategy hard for the dwarves to adapt to quickly enough. Sensmann ordered hay bales to be placed at the ready at the base of the wall. They were soaked in oil and would burn hot. She had been prepared to order if the wall had fallen, as she knew she would need to create some space between the Spawn and the retreating dwarves if their losses were not to be high. She also knew the loss of Blutschläger would have been a heavy blow to their courage. To this point, the Blood Beater had lived up to his name and the dwarves chanted it as they slew the Spawn prior to their retreat under the light and heat of the sun. He was the dwarves' talisman in these battles.

Once the dwarves had rested for a few hours the council of the dwarves was held. Bar and Barin had been in the fight, as had Dunkeln. They all had bruises and were a little stiff in the joints. A few beers and a hearty meal had corrected this. Sensmann expressed her concern. "I fear we are about to lose the wall to the enemy unless we come up with something special. I am open to all ideas so speak up. If that ramp comes against the wall again, we will be lost and will have to retreat. What say you?"

The dwarves looked at each other in silent thought. No one spoke for a good while. Then Dunkeln spoke up. "I fear we also need to consider the tunnelling issue again. The waters have been released and the tunnel may have collapsed but they could come that way again. If we are on the wall when it goes it could be a disaster for us."

"Also," put in Barin, "we are now approaching the end of the springtime and the summer is going to be our best chance to keep battling these Spawn. Once we get into the autumn, the days will be shorter and the nights harder to defend due to the extended nights."

Sensmann listened to all the comments before her. They were all thinking about the winter, which would be harder still. She was hoping for a long hot summer. The dwarves had done well up to now and their tactics had been sound.

Sensmann had known all along that they were going to have to face defeat at the wall at some point. "We will fight tonight as usual and the Spawn will press us hard, if we let them. Once the tower is in axe range, we hit it with ropes and pull in on it. The ground is broken before the wall and we will throw heavy logs under the feet of the Spawn carrying the tower. If we are fortunate the tower will go over. We then rain down fire upon it and the Spawn and set a healthy blaze."

"And if it doesn't fall?" asked Bar.

"Well then, my dears, you on the wall will have another chance to show your mettle while we prepare the ground for a hasty retreat!"

The dwarves laughed, a little relieved at Sensmann's abilities as a leader.

"It is much easier to fight than do all that thinking!" Grobest retorted. They all took up their beer and drained the flagons, only to be refilled and empty them again.

Eventually, the Blood Beater yawned. "Time for a kip I think!" and they went to their cots so as to be fresh at dusk.

* * *

Wahushi and Kayin were marshalling the Slavers and giving out instructions for the coming battle. Both were hungry for dwarf blood and both knew that their fate depended on success very soon. Princess Zhuxi was watching every move with her spies and now Kayin was also in the firing line should she fail. As dusk approached, the dwarves could be seen reinforcing the wall. The Spawn were driven to lift the great tower. It had again been soaked to make it hard to burn. The Spawn moved forward, rank upon rank, snarling as they came. Kayin was confident, as was Wahushi, and she made sure she was near to the front with other Slavers as they advanced. Wahushi was just to the rear of her, perhaps four ranks back.

The Slavers brought the Spawn towards a frenzy and they moved quickly forward. Wahushi watched as the first volleys of arrows came raining down upon at the front of the tower. After two volleys more, the dwarves switched tactics and threw heavy logs, which cluttered the ground in front of the tower as it moved forward. At the same time heavy axes were thrown with great accuracy at the top of the tower. Each was attached to a line. Some of the axes appeared to miss but wrapped themselves and the line they carried around the wooden beams. More logs were thrown and now they rained down, making the Spawn slow, as they slipped and slid with their heavy load. They dropped the tower briefly before the Slavers got them and the tower moving again.

At that moment, the lines went taut and sung like piano wire. The dwarves had tons of stone behind the ramparts and when they pushed the stone off the wall the lines pulled the tower too quickly for the Spawn to keep up. The tower tottered forwards and everyone on the wall and the Slavers behind the tower held their breath for an instant, which seemed to last a whole minute before the tower crashed to the ground. Many Spawn were crushed to death instantly. Slavers and Spawn who had already climbed the tower fell to their deaths. At least the Spawn did. The Slavers leapt from the tower as it fell and landed on top of those behind. The Spawn were in a panic; the Slavers were disorganised and had lost control of the front few ranks who, in fear, now turned to run, only to crash into the ranks moving forward.

All was chaos now. Slavers were knocked to the ground and Wahushi lost sight of his lieutenant Kayin, who went down in the front of him. He cursed the dwarves as he reordered the Spawn. All the time dwarf arrows were striking their mark. Now the longer bows of the men began to fire. Their arrows were longer in shaft and went much further back into the Spawn ranks. Wahushi and those around him were now in the firing line. The Slavers, Wahushi included, ordered the Spawn to protect them by taking wounds that would have hit the Slavers. Still some shafts struck home and Wahushi felt a sting, then pain in his shoulder as an arrow hit him. The Spawn around him were riddled with arrows that would have hit him also had he not acted so quickly.

Wahushi was now vexed and dangerous. He snarled at the dwarves and screamed at the wall, that they would pay a thousandfold for his hurt. Wahushi had lost himself in fury and ordered his forces back out of range. He had been humiliated in this assault and he had now to get desperate if he wished to keep his head upon his broad shoulders. He looked for his lieutenant in the mayhem and then he saw her unconscious body being carried back in the retreat.

Two Slavers, who were her trusted allies, had plucked her up before she became a pin cushion for the arrows that would have hit her. Wahushi was thinking hard. How might he dispose of Kayin with other Slavers present unless he killed them too. They were bound to see and might even attack him. No, he would have to act fast to recover the situation. He looked at the lines attached to the tower still and then ordered his Spawn to tighten the lines from his side by pulling on them hard. They then cut the lines free and began to climb the wall using the ropes to pull themselves to the top.

Once the Slavers saw the idea form in the mind of the

Spawn, they moved quickly, using the lines to climb the wall. As one Spawn reached the summit, he was met with a hammer swing. Forty or so lines had Spawn climbing them now and the dwarves were kept busy holding the Spawn off. The Spawn nearest to the top was ordered to stop and the next Spawn climbed over him and jumped at the dwarves in front of him. The Spawn's momentum helped him get a foothold on the wall before axes hit him. Before he fell, he managed to lift a dwarf and throw him backwards over his shoulder. Now two more Spawn leapt over the highest part of the wall and attacked with the same momentum. The tactic then was replicated across the wall and the dwarves now found themselves fighting for their lives. It only took about half a minute for the dwarves to realise their mistake, by which time the frenzied Spawn (Wahushi was incandescent with rage) launched themselves at dwarves, clutched them and pulled them off the wall before dying themselves.

As soon as news reached Sensmann she ordered the lines to be cut. Dwarves leapt to break the lines that were tough and even a heavy stroke with an axe had to be repeated once or twice more to break them. In the meantime, the dwarves battled hard and, within a couple of minutes, the wall was once more their own. Wahushi was feeling better. He ordered a break in the attack as the lines were cut. He at least had some live dwarves to set before Princess Zhuxi. This might stay her hand for a while. Wahushi ordered the fallen dwarves bound and taken to the rear to meet the princess. He then ordered ladders forward and these were then run to the wall and the battle recommenced and the dwarves fought all night on the wall right up to the dawn.

Zhuxi was pleased to see ten dwarves bound hand, foot and finger hauled into her presence by Wahushi. He bowed low and reported that the wall was close to collapse. He related his tale, promoting his part in the battle, before giving explanation of Kayin's accident and therefore absence from the audience with Zhuxi who hardly listened. She felt real excitement as the first of the dwarves was brought to her. She was ready to exude her pheromones on the dwarves but ordered the room clear except for her guard Slavers and Wahushi. "Your reward is to watch my power over these dwarves and know my strength and how I will use this gift."

All the dwarves were then stripped naked. Zhuxi approached them and, even while they cursed, their bodies betrayed them. She took each to climax until they were exhausted. Three of the dwarves died that day from their wounds and from Zhuxi's attention upon them. They were the lucky ones. When Zhuxi was sated, she went to her chambers and began to lay eggs, each fertilised by dwarf sperm. She relished the pain and thought to herself what wonderful weapons these creatures would become very soon, once the entirety of her brood was laid before her. She ordered the human slaves to take the eggs and place them in the nest where they would be safe until she needed them. Zhuxi then gave orders to her guards to feed the surviving dwarves, once the other three were cooked to perfection. Once away from her, the dwarves regained their sanity for a while.

Zhuxi slept through the day and began the torment all over again in the evening, forcing them by her will and pheromones to eat their kin, before once more robbing them of their sperm for her evil ends. Another dwarf died in the night. He went into the pot the next morning to feed his brethren. The dwarves were horrified but powerless.

Wahushi was extremely content with the day, preferring the dark, but as days had gone for him this was one of the better ones and he was pleased with himself. He sought out Kayin and found her lying on a comfortable cot, still unconscious from the battle. As no one was watching out for her he joined her on the cot and ravished her while she was unconscious. He lavished cuts on her back. When he was satisfied, he went back to the battle to accomplish what he must. Destroy the wall and the dwarves upon it.

The dwarves were on the wall in numbers, which was fortunate as Wahushi's assault started before dusk. The Spawn were poorly responsive in the light and not so eager to kill but they soon gained their normal ferocity when the sun had fully set. Once more many ladders were set against the wall. Wahushi's miners had reported that they were almost back to the point where the first tunnel failed. Wahushi had ordered the stream from the first tunnel to be diverted away from the second tunnel. He, like all evil creatures, did not like running water or the sound of it because it contained audible evidence of the Creator's song. They would not cross it if it could possibly be avoided, and the Slavers lost control of their Spawn when in water, which made them disoriented and confused themselves and obviously vulnerable. Wahushi shuddered at the thought. He knew that he would be under the wall by the end of the night and then, with luck, it would fall before dawn so he could gain a foothold and return to the princess with the news. It was going to be a good night for him.

* * *

The dwarves on the wall held firm and the battle raged on for four hours. It was early in the morning before the dawn when the first cracks began to appear in the great barrier wall. The dwarves fought on and the Spawn and Slavers pressed them as hard as they may, but the dwarves kept their footing and the blood of Spawn drenched stone from the top to the bottom of the wall. As dawn approached there were now large cracks appearing in the stone.

Wahushi made his decision just as the sun came up. He called back his forces and ordered all the Spawn to retrieve their dead, together with any dwarf corpses and set the horde to feast on the carnage. The Spawn and their Slavers will be at their best tonight. If we continue to dig and undermine the wall it will come down early in the night and we will all feast on dwarf flesh tomorrow.

He retreated to his personal camp and found a recovered Kayin there to greet him. Wahushi was cordial, as was Kayin. He could see she was unaware of his visit to her earlier in the day. He invited her to join him in feasting. She agreed and was perplexed by this greeting. She ached all over from the battle and was pleased for the rest in the day. Kayin knew her close call with death was a little too close for comfort and she had learned of Wahushi's reception from her spies and was not at all pleased. 'Still, while there's life, there's hope for Wahushi's death.' She smiled at Wahushi and tucked into a dwarf leg, the fat and gristle dripping down her chin. This dwarf was well proportioned with powerful arms, shoulders and legs. "I don't suppose you managed to cook that dwarf chieftain yet? I would like to tuck into his leg and soon!"

"No," replied Wahushi, "that dwarf they call Blood Beater is very hard to kill. He will be for Zhuxi to feast on alone." They both laughed cruelly, imagining what Zhuxi would do to him, if he could be captured alive.

Sensmann leaned over the wall to get a better look at the cracks. 'This comes down tonight,' was her thought. Sensmann set the dwarves to work. They were excellent at stone masonry and were entirely aware of the tunnel being extended along the wall. Their interest was in how far it went. The dwarves had used the day well to this point. They built a defensive barrier from wood that was eight feet high to slow the charge of the Spawn after the wall was breached. The walkway was wide enough for a dwarf to fight in comfort. Behind this wooden structure was a deep ditch filled with fuel and timber and this ringed the expected breach. Behind that were the massed ranks of the dwarves. Before ordering the men in their care to give way on the field and prepare for their long march, she had asked that the men build smaller, manoeuvrable wooden fences. These were light enough for four strong dwarves to lift.

By the coming of the setting sun all was as ready in the defence. The dwarves had no choice but to defend the wall as usual, but all were ready for a swift getaway from the collapse when it came, and the dwarves on the portions of the wall set their trust in the Creator that they would survive intact.

Wahushi was again early, starting the attack before dusk. Once more the Spawn were sluggish but when the sun set they came eager for the fight. For two hours the dwarves battled the Spawn and then the word came to retreat. A great horn echoed its sound and the dwarves leapt from the wall into haywains put there to break their fall. The wall crumbled and Sensmann drew a great breath of relief that the twenty-metre breach in the wall fell outwards as she had predicted. The Spawn fell with the wall and many were killed under the stone.

Wahushi waited for the dust to settle. Kayin was standing next to him. There were screams from crushed and dying Spawn and a few Slavers were killed along with them. Acceptable losses for both Kayin and Wahushi. The dust began to settle and, in a short period of time, where there was little sound, the breach became visible and the horde screamed in triumph. Wahushi turned to Kayin and gave his orders. "You have earned the honour of attacking the breach. You have four hours to set the horde on the other side. I go now to inform Zhuxi that we are progressing well."

Kayin was pleased. She ordered the Spawn to attack and they rushed to advance. The horde threw themselves at the breach, ignoring the arrows from the wall that remained standing. Kayin ignored the dwarves on the wall now and focussed the frenzied Spawn on a headlong charge, with

Slavers in hot pursuit, to see they remained aggressive. Spawn found themselves pelted with arrows, struck down by another hail of arrows and then they were at the barrier and the arrows ceased for the dwarves' fear of hitting their own folk.

The Spawn were met by axes and hammers as they assaulted the barrier. They met it at a great force of numbers and, before long, the dwarves were once more fighting for their very lives. For four hours the dwarves had held the line. Kayin was again close to the frontline and she was desperate to break through but was unable to do so due to the width of the horde forces having to be squeezed through the gap in the wall. This caused the horde to falter and, being cramped by their numbers, made it easier for the dwarves to cut them down at the barrier. As dawn broke, the horde also broke and Kayin ordered their retreat.

Wahushi was waiting for her. "I have reported personally the breach to the wall. Please report to Princess Zhuxi how the night ended." Kayin moved off without a word. She knew Wahushi had outfoxed her and now she would deliver a less than happy result to the princess. A bead of sweat trickled down her neck.

The dwarves had won another reprieve at dawn and they wasted no time in calling for a council of war. They all knew that there was no hope of planning anything once the battle started at dusk.

"Now we come to the crunch," said Sensmann to the others around the council chamber. "We cannot defeat the enemy in the field and so I don't think we should try. I think the dwarves returning with Zuerst, Vierte and Fünfte should now retreat behind the river. Bar and Barin will lead the dwarves of Lowin and Lowe and set up defences on the other side of the river. It is good that the mountains have been fed by the spring rains and that it is running high. We start the movement at first light when the Spawn will be less willing to follow if they get wind of the change. You ought to be able to hold the river for quite a time from the other bank, which is higher and steeper on your side."

Bar and Barin agreed, as did Grobest and Hammerhurz. Grobest asked his wife if she wished to lead the dwarves of Lowe, but she merely looked at him and said, "If you think I am going to the other side of the river and let you have all the fun you can forget it. My axe is as good as yours, my speed is greater across the ground and our halls are long. I will probably end up carrying you to the escape road to Zuerst as it is. Once we get there, I will happily take charge of all the forces, including you dear husband. Now say no more about it!"

Grobest groaned. The other dwarves smiled broadly. "At least our morale is good," said Grobest, with a rueful smile.

Blutschläger looked nearly asleep in his chair. He had been fighting hard all night. He was always visible to other dwarves at the sharp end of the battle, where he liked to give encouragement to those around him and keep the heat of anger and aggression high in the conflict so that his dwarves always had the edge. While he lived the dwarves knew he would be where the dwarves expected him to be. Sensmann filled a flagon of ale to the brim and placed it before him. His eyes widened and he sat up and took a pull at it. Sensmann then carried on. The other dwarves poured drinks for themselves and Hammerhurz filled Sensmann's flagon also. Sensmann then laid her plans out for the others. "With regard to our halls [she nodded to Grobest] our job is to hold the Spawn where they are for as long as we may feel we need to. We are not giving ground!" Her fist hit the table to further rouse the dwarves to full attention. "The men we have released to follow their families will need a good head start. I have high hopes for their escape. Grobest and the Blood Beater will hold their ground and our folk will hold with them."

Both looked sternly at her. They took this as an order of command. They would have happily taken a vow to stand until they were both dead had she but asked. Sensmann went on. "When we feel we are near the end of our strength, I will make the decision to set fire to the barricade that bars the way. If it happens that we are forced off the wall, I will light the barricade and the dwarves will have to get clear as they can. We will have barrels of water standing by to put any dwarves into nice cool water if they get too hot!"

Hammerhurz looked at Barin and their eyes met and sparkled with unspoken joy! They loved the humour Sensmann managed to inject at just the right moment to keep everyone engaged.

"Our retreat will be coordinated by myself and Hammerhurz and our leadership will not be challenged at any point until all the dwarves are behind our gates! I say this because I know there are some rather strong characters among our clans. Hammerhurz and I need you to drill this into all the dwarves, including the females, so that there are no misunderstandings." All agreed to do this.

"If we get overwhelmed and the Spawn are upon us, I will lead the defence for Dritte and you will lead the defence and retreat to the halls of Zweite. I hope that is clear to all and everyone. We could make better use of the time we have together by resting but I am guessing sleep will evade us this night. Do you all agree? Good, now can we please sample more of the beer?"

The party then began and the dwarves acting as their guards with Zenith and Janzen joined them at the table. With beer in hand Sensmann turned to Zenith and said, "Yes Zenith, that last order applies to you and Janzen particularly! Do not think I don't know my kin!" They all laughed as Janzen giggled into her beer and then sneezed loudly as the froth went up her pretty nose.

The Blood Beater howled with laughter. "These dwarf youngsters can't hold their beer it seems!"

Janzen was quick to reply. "It wasn't me that got carried home earlier this spring you know," referring to Sensmann's trick. If he had been laughing before, he was now beside himself, rubbing his extensive belly with pleasure. When he calmed down and the laughter around him subsided, Zenith remarked, "That was an exceptional comeback cousin!" And now she giggled into her flagon. The sounds of the meeting being held drifted out over the vale, where many dwarves stood on duty or were sharpening their weapons. The dwarves were warmed by the confidence and high spirits of their leaders. It boded well for them that the dwarves were so well led. It gave them all heart, no matter which clan they came from.

At dusk, the dwarves' plans were well laid, and Blutschläger the Blood Beater and Grobest took their positions on the wooden defences to await the assault by the horde of Spawn. The horde had been somewhat reduced in their numbers since the battle commenced and the Spawn near the front were driven now by more cautious Slavers, for no Slaver, once out of sight of the generals, was going to sacrifice him or herself on a whim and so the Spawn sensed this and moved more cautiously to the wall.

Battle commenced and archers once more fired down on the Spawn but this time, thanks to Sensmann's creativity, the arrows were aimed just before the wall, about twenty metres or so. In this way, the Spawn were constantly hampered by their dead and dying as they moved forward. The Spawn bodies began to pile up and, although they reached the wall, it gave the dwarves much more time to despatch the Spawn before them.

Wahushi and Kayin stayed out of range from a long bow.

They too were a little more cautious. As the night went on, the battle intensified. The dwarves held on for another night and then a third night. Behind them was ordered chaos as the last of Sensmann's designs and orders had taken fruit. Sensmann went over their plans with Hammerhurz and her cousins Zenith and Janzen, who acted as runners to and from the council table. At last, the council table itself was removed from the field and returned to its rightful place in Dritte, Sensmann's home.

Wahushi heard from his closest spy, Tienat Alzur, that Princess Zhuxi had received word that her sister Yuehan had left their home with her army and was marching towards the battleground to finish off the dwarves. Wahushi knew this meant his head would roll unless he made serious headway and soon.

Kayin was no less displeased herself. Since her promotion to number two in rank to Wahushi, her fate had somehow become entwined with his and she was not at all happy with this. She knew she had to get results or face her own painful death before her princess.

The next night, the dwarves came under constant pressure and the Spawn were frenzied once more to their maximum and the fighting was bitter. The Blood Beater held the centre and Grobest and he were under constant threat of being killed or overrun. Sensmann ordered all the archers she had at her command to release every arrow they possessed. Now a thousand arrows every thirty seconds hit the Spawn. The front ranks of the Spawn were slaughtered by the dwarves and then the dwarves leapt to a man, off the barrier to retreat between the forces guarding Dritte and those guarding Zweite under the charge of Hammerhurz. The barrier was lit and became a fierce and raging fire, too hot to cross by the Spawn. All the dwarves now retreated to their respective halls in orderly fashion as the fire guarded their retreat. Once inside the halls the gates were shut. Firing points within were opened and the dwarves who had manned them prepared for the defence.

When the fire burned low after perhaps an hour, the Spawn attacked over the fire and sought out enemies to kill but there were none. The field was completely cleared. There was no rubbish, no food, no weapons and no dwarves to be seen. Wahushi and Kayin came across the barrier together. Both were relieved to have entered the vale. They set their forces to assault the two dwarf cities of Dritte and Zweite. Wahushi chose Zweite to focus upon and he gave the capture of Dritte to Kayin. She was pleased enough.

It was near dawn when forward defences were placed before the dreaded river. The river was a natural defence in the centre of the plain and the opposite bank was defended by the three chieftains of the dwarf strongholds on that side of the river. With the bridges taken down it would take an all-out assault by the whole horde to breach the dwarves' defence.

Zhuxi's horde was now encamped on the field in a great triangle. In the centre of the triangle was Princess Zhuxi and her entourage. She was mightily pleased with herself for getting into the vale before her sister arrived with reinforcements. Zhuxi had lost one hundred thousand Spawn and Slavers and her forces were showing the signs of fatigue. She ordered the dead and injured Slavers and Spawn into the fire pots and her army fed on this and other, stored, less fresh meat that night. She allowed Wahushi to take his fill of female slaves and Kayin was equally rewarded.

The princess was pleased with Wahushi, but she still harboured a small doubt about the dark place within him, which she could not read when she had last tried. Zhuxi put the job on the back burner of her mind again for a more peaceful time. She needed Wahushi at his best in the war and working into his mind would weaken him. Kayin, on the other hand, was an open book. The princess thought to herself, 'I wonder if she knows she was repeatedly raped, beaten and abused by Wahushi. I'll save that little ditty for the present. It will be interesting to watch Kayin's reaction when I tell her.'

Then Princess Zhuxi remembered that she had two captured dwarves alive and she spent the rest of the night sucking them dry of all their sperm and, when they gave out, she cut them and drank the blood as it came out of their bodies. The pain had been extreme for the dwarves until shock set in, but she had to admire in a sad way how, even unto death, the dwarves stayed true to their kind and went to the Creator with a smile finally on their faces. Princess Zhuxi was annoyed by their deaths being so peaceful. How nauseating it was that their spirits could rise while hers could not. Then a little trickle of fear crept upon her and she shuddered and decided to secretly watch Wahushi as he ravished his female slaves, in order to take her mind off her fear. She felt cold and, while she watched through a spy hole, at one point Wahushi, while finishing off a slave girl, seemed to look straight at her with a terrible lust in his eyes. Zhuxi loved cruelty but, for a second, she felt she was his victim and then the moment passed. She looked on. 'My sister will be here tomorrow night. I had better prepare for her arrival with Wahushi and Kayin in the evening and morning before her forces begin to interfere with mine.'

The arrival of Princess Yuehan was a disappointment to Zhuxi. It was also the same for Yuehan who had hoped that Zhuxi would fail to get into the vale, as her spies had reported as she left their home. Zhuxi had arranged a guard of honour for her sister's arrival in the field and had ordered her Slavers to yield the straight path to the river, where Yuehan's forces now gathered. They kept a respectful distance from the river. Princess Yuehan could see no sign of battle fatigue from Zhuxi's somewhat diminished forces. She realised that there had been hard times for the horde. Now there were four hundred thousand Spawn and Slavers to take the dwarves' cities and eradicate the last stronghold of dwarves and men in the world that they knew.

The princesses met in Zhuxi's now well-established centre of her forces. Both fawned on the other in a sickly show of false concern for each other. Zhuxi for the tiresome journey and battles and Yuehan for the tiring journey and no fun when she arrived. They each dismissed everyone except their personal guards and Wahushi.

Yuehan then introduced her general, who stepped forward. It was a man. "His name is Mazdul. He is a mighty man and great strategist, I am informed by our dear sister Princess Shimishi."

Zhuxi was intrigued. "Now that is a surprise," she said to her sister, "Shimishi does not give such gifts very often. What inspired her to give this man Mazdul to lead your forces?"

Princess Yuehan was pleased with Zhuxi's response. "We had heard you were struggling to bring the battle to the dwarves and that you had been ambushed, outmanoeuvred and then failed to breach the dwarf defensive wall that stands now broken. It seems you have been more successful than we had heard. I must have the messengers who told these falsehoods slaughtered for their misinformed judgements."

Zhuxi smiled and said, "You are too kind sister. In truth we only recently took the wall and stormed the field. We have eaten many dwarves and our taste is for more. If you are happy to watch, I will carry the battle forward with my General Wahushi, who has proven himself in battle." At this point she eyed the man Mazdul with doubt in her eyes. Mazdul was unmoved by the exchanges between the princesses. Zhuxi played her key card against Yuehan. "Perhaps you would like to replace my forces so we can cross the river in force, Wahushi and I."

Princess Yuehan gave a cold smile. "No, I don't think so Zhuxi." (She had dropped the courtesy and smiled in her mind, but her face was all innocent sincerity.) "It is my turn to battle the dwarves in the field. Your forces should be enough to root out the dwarves from their hovels on this side of the river while I take the three over the water." She shuddered at the thought of entering it herself. She had already seen how wide, deep and fast flowing it was. It was more important to Yuehan that she put her sister in the shade for the interim and any new advance would be hers and for her own glory!

Yuehan thought to herself, 'Our sister Shimishi had expected you to have failed already my dear Zhuxi, but you have had some good fortune in choosing your general. He has saved your face and shame for the present. Even so you have lost some of the trust the queen placed in you for your earlier tactics in the field and you have lost more than a third of your forces and that makes you weak in the eyes of our queen.'

Out loud she applauded her sister for winning the battles fought. Zhuxi was happy not to have to front the battle over the water. Had her sister not taken the bait through her jibe, then she would have had to achieve the near impossible quick victory expected by the queen and her sister Shimishi. Now she had time to plan how to enter the cities while her sister was distracted by the river and the dwarves defending the other side. For, while the dwarves held on over the river and in their hovels, she had time to bring the three cities to their knees and kill all the dwarves within. 'These dwarves might be cunning and good fighters, but my Spawn are their equal underground, with their night vision so much better than the dwarves. We will win in the dark. Yes,' she thought to herself. 'I think things have turned out okay.' She withdrew to rest and see out the daylight hours.

* * *

The summer went by slowly for the dwarves, for they held the river through the whole of summer and well into the autumn. Princess Yuehan had tried to cross the river on logs, then by bridge building, but these failed miserably. She then built tall towers and let them fall across the river, not unlike a pontoon. These had also failed because the dwarves could see them coming and merely set to destroy them with fire. Some Spawn reached the other side, but they were confused by the water and could not be frenzied and so the dwarves made short work of mopping them up. Princess Yuehan decided to wait and see what winter would bring. She hoped for cold and lots of it. The river had slowed now and would soon begin to freeze. The dwarves were waiting to see the opposite.

Blutschläger and Sensmann had been pleased to return to the comfort of their mountain home. All the dwarves were feeling safe for now and, although contact was rather limited between the cities and rather slow, every city was secure and each day a young dwarf would come to Dritte via secret passage and update Sensmann on the enemy movement. Sensmann could see much for herself of course, from the high gates of her city but it was reassuring to know the other dwarves were as safe and secure as they could hope to be.

Winter was coming of course and that would bring its own issues. At some point the new forces of the horde would cross the water. It was inevitable. Sensmann sensed her enemies growing more cautious as the year wore on. Gone were the attempts to forge a pathway across the river. All the dwarves knew the weakness of Spawn and their aversion to fresh, clear running water. She blessed the Creator for the gift of water. Without it, the dwarves would already be under dire pressure in the cities. Food would be shorter and, without the crops that had grown this year, next year there might have been a shortage of beer. 'That is one less worry,' thought Sensmann. Dwarf beer was sustaining and rejuvenating, and a dwarf will fight happily with a good few beers to finish the day.

Sensmann filled her husband's glass. "Now that we are all locked up, I have been doing some thinking. Wouldn't it be nice if we dwarves could find all of Princess Zhuxi's egg nests and burn the lot!" Blutschläger thought this an excellent idea.

"Shame you didn't think of it earlier then isn't it," bemoaned Blutschläger, "that would really help mankind in the future and us as well if any of us get to survive the war. Such a shame," he repeated to his half full flagon.

Sensmann innocently put the question to Blutschläger. "Have you seen cousins Zenith and Janzen and their loyal little band lately?"

"No, I haven't, it's been quite a few weeks since they ate with us. Why don't you invite them over? They would love it and so would we."

"I cannot do it I'm afraid," said Sensmann, innocently.

"Why on earth not woman? I'm sure they would come if asked or have you done something to upset them?" Blutschläger was now wanting to know what had occurred and he put his flagon down as if to emphasise his point.

"I haven't upset them," she responded. "The last time they were here dear husband they were really rather excited. We ended the night with quite a party! Yes, it was a good party, wasn't it?"

"So why can't they come?"

Sensmann filled their flagons before replying. "They can't come because I sent them on a mission with their followers, friends and lovers all, to wipe out all the nests they can find between here and the queen's lair."

Blutschläger sat back with a great big grin on his face. "You really are the best of dwarves and I'm so glad you are on our side in this war." He giggled in his beer, which was quite un-dwarf like for an elder like him. "Well, well, she [meaning Zhuxi] is going to be spitting feathers when she finds out."

"Yes, she will be," said Sensmann, smiling at her husband. "That is not the only surprise we have for her."

"What now?" asked Blutschläger.

Sensmann smiled at the Blood Beater and said, "We are going on the offensive dear husband. I want you to lead the charge through the main gates as soon as the sun comes up. It has been too quiet for that Zhuxi and I would like you to put a thorn in her side if you can. When we come out, so will Grobest and Hammerhurz. We will see how they like fighting in the sun!"

The next morning the dwarf clans launched momentously successful assaults on the horde, which was much surprised to be attacked. The sun made them cower as it came up over the mountains and above Dritte. They turned away to avoid the intense light and their vision was somewhat impaired. They did not see the dwarf attack coming but they heard the rustle of running feet and, as they turned, the Spawn and Slavers guarding the gate were slaughtered where they stood. A thousand dwarves launched into the Spawn and there was complete chaos in their ranks.

The dwarves formed a V-shaped wedge and, with Blutschläger and Sensmann at the front, they drove into the enemy with speed and agility. Left and right, Spawn were felled. Sensmann saw the tents of Zhuxi and headed straight for them. There was terrible bloodshed and no quarter given as the dwarves murdered the disorganised Spawn. The sun was bright and although the forces of Zhuxi were far superior to that of the dwarves in numbers, within minutes the dwarves were hacking at Princess Zhuxi's personal guard and then Sensmann saw Zhuxi retreating with her slaves.

Sensmann broke through the ranks of Spawn before her and closed the gap to Zhuxi and immediately launched one of her small axes once she was in range. It flew across the gap between Sensmann and Zhuxi, turning handle over head at a tremendous rate. Sensmann screamed the princess's name after she threw the axe, which made Zhuxi turn her head towards her. The axe hit Zhuxi full in the face and split her skull before the Slaves and Slavers could react. Blood spilled everywhere and Zhuxi screamed in agony, with her forehead split open by the axe that was embedded in her brain. She collapsed onto her slaves, sending them sprawling and did not move again. It was only the dismay in the horde that saved Sensmann from certain death. It gave the other dwarves time to reach her.

"Time to go home, my wife," said Blutschläger at her side. "These Spawn are going to get organised soon by the Slavers, so we better fly back to the city."

The dwarf retreat was organised and nearly as deadly as the advance. There was great cheering in both cities and then in all five cities as the word spread that one of the princesses was mortally wounded.

Wahushi and Kayin had been planning their assault on the dwarf cities when the dwarves attacked. They were effectively caught away from home and rushed back to find the princess. When Wahushi and Kayin saw Zhuxi, blooded and with the axe still in her skull and barely alive, they were both terrified. This failure meant their death and they knew it. Kayin moved close to the cot where Zhuxi lay in a coma.

Wahushi took his chance and stabbed Kayin in the back and, as she fell, he roared that she was a traitor and had abandoned his mistress. Wahushi called all his closest, most loyal Slavers, to him and sent all the princess's guard to report to the Princess Shimishi, who would surely slay every one of them. Wahushi knew that nothing could save him unless he saved himself. He would, of course, have happily given his life for the princess, but he knew she was dying and as good as dead. Once she ceased to exist, all the Spawn that she had brought into existence with her egg laying would die very quickly. Only the unborn would survive her death.

Wahushi gathered his followers. Their number was fifty or so Slavers. He ordered the rest to attack the cities they had laid siege to all these weeks. He knew they would fail but he needed the Princess Shimishi to think he was still in control of the forces. The Slavers not close to him were ordered to take revenge on the dwarves. He did not need to feign his anger, and when one of the Slavers, a small female, questioned him he slaughtered her out of hand. The rest went and assaulted the cities, driving the Spawn to frenzy and getting them to ram the doors with great trees brought from the forests outside the vale. They fought under the sun, knowing that they were in grave peril, and they fought into the night, filled with hatred for the dwarves.

Princess Yuehan saw the assault from afar. Her contact with the mind of her sister was tentative from such a distance but she felt the change. She also saw the assault against the cities begin and assumed all was well and Zhuxi was deliberately making the mental link seem weaker. Yuehan had done this many times herself in the past when she wished her sister not to read any thoughts when they were close by one another. Princess Yuehan went to her rest for the rest of the day, leaving orders to wake her in the night. She had no plan to assault the dwarves over the river and her general had been ordered to oversee the building of yet another bridge made from heavy timber over three days ago. He would not complete it until dawn tomorrow. Princess Yuehan went to her bed.

The guard of Princess Zhuxi arrived at the camp of Princess Yuehan late in the afternoon, some hours after the princess had been mortally wounded. They expected death when confronted with the news, but they were spawned from Zhuxi and so, as Slavers, they knew she lived and, while she lived, they had life too. They were reluctant travellers to Yuehan's camp and once there they sought audience with Yuehan. They were denied access while the princess slept. They had no power to argue and no wish to die and so they waited outside the camp centre. Wahushi used this time to get himself and his followers as far away from the vale as he could. The demon spirit within drove him to the end of his strength. None were granted leave to rest. They all knew what being caught would mean for them.

Princess Zhuxi lasted until the dawn of the next day. She had lain alone on her cot with the body of Kayin set in a kneeling position as if she were listening to the princess. Zhuxi died at dawn. The Spawn and Slaver born of her fell to their knees and began to gasp for breath. They took an hour to die. Thousands upon thousands of bodies lay in the field.

Instantly, Princess Yuehan was awake and raging. She knew her sister was dead and ran and flew to Zhuxi's tent with her entourage flailing behind her. The Slavers that lived retreated into their camp, all plans of battle eradicated from their minds. It was replaced by cold fear. The Spawn were all dead. Princess Yuehan lifted her sister into her arms and set herself to return to her camp. She turned to the Slavers still alive and ordered them to hold their ground. There were perhaps five hundred of them left. She sought out Wahushi with her eyes and with her mind, but he was not there. 'He better hope he is dead for this betrayal,' she thought.

Yuehan was not fooled by the presence of her sister's body and guessed Wahushi knew what was coming to him. Princess Yuehan still had her full army of Spawn and now had the field clear for her glorious victory and her rise in the favour of Queen Yonlik, her mother. She would avenge her sister in the blood of the dwarves.

Her army had enough meat now for weeks. She set the Slavers who had survived their mistress to render the flesh of Slavers and Spawn and cook some and salt down the rest. The

Slavers were demeaned by the task but also still alive and so worked with all the relish their evil spirits could muster. In doing so they might survive to kill dwarves and maybe a few might commend themselves to their new princess.

The great horns in the five cities blew all night long for the dwarves had won their first victory in very unlikely fashion as it turned out and the first aim of their leader Lowe's plan was almost achieved.

When Yuehan calmed down, she felt a tiny sense of fear before she banished the thought. That thought had been, 'If the dwarves could kill Zhuxi, they might get me.' Princess Yuehan called for her general. The princess had had an idea. She spoke to her general. "Use the dead Spawn to feed my army but allow a few thousand to putrefy and bloat with gas. The scum might have been useless in life but we will put them to good use now they are dead. When they are nice and tender, pack them under the bridge you have built. The last bridge wasn't steady enough in the flowing river but this one will float high in the water on the gas of the dead. While you are at it, cut off their arms and legs. We will feed the Spawn and let them use the bones as weapons."

The general was impressed and liked her thinking. He was too astute to ask how Zhuxi had met her end. There was time enough for that later. He set himself and his army to the grim task before them. Princess Yuehan ordered her guard to be doubled immediately. The general had informed her that three of her personal guard had died without known cause. Princess Yuehan was furious. "That bitch was spying on me all the time! Three in my own ranks." She reminded herself to reward the Slavers in her pay that had been in Zhuxi's army, to report to her when she was ready. Yuehan then took herself to her rest.

At dusk there was a lot of movement on the field while the Slavers set to the task of rendering hundreds and then thousands of Spawn corpses to feed the remaining Spawn army. Thousands were hung on hooks on erected beams and blood drained into bowls for their blood wine that Slavers and, indeed Spawn, were so very fond of. Other bodies were covered in salt brought for the very purpose and the cadavers were piled in the shade, away from the sun. Still others were cooked over open fires and the black smoke and stench from burned flesh drifted over the vale until there was a foggy mist across its entirety. Hundreds were placed in piles and their arms and legs ripped off and cooked in fire pits.

After four days the Spawn corpses were dragged to the river and tied in clumps of torso under the bridge, ready for the crossing. The dwarves saw all this happening and they began to plan the defence of the river. They were outnumbered ten to one and the general was very keen to get his army across the river and catch the dwarves before they could retreat to the cities behind them.

Mazdul was mindful of the dwarves that had killed Zhuxi and placed a force of Spawn to attack the cities of Dritte and Zweite, with another fifty thousand Spawn and Slavers drawn from his ranks and he also reprieved the surviving Zhuxi Slavers to assist. They were keen for revenge and filled with a renewed hatred for the dwarves. These Slavers had been from Shimishi's horde on lone to Zhuxi for the battle.

The assault on the dwarves' stone and iron gates on this side of the river was renewed and the great hinges on the gates were grinding and whining under the strain from the intense battering.

While this was in full swing, General Mazdul gave his attention to the assault over the river and ordered the bridge to be pushed into the river. Once there, Spawn were frenzied and sent against the dwarves in their hundreds at a time. Mazdul did not want to damage his bridge with too much top weight.

The dwarves stood their ground and the battle commenced. The dwarves had the early advantage of hitting down on the Spawn and the river ran red with their blood. The whole of the river had to be guarded by the dwarves and this also meant they needed to be grouped in such a way that they could retreat to their cities should they be forced back. Mazdul saw this and pressed his forces across the bridge until numbers were so great the dwarves were forced on to the backfoot.

After three hours the dwarves were pushed away from the bank and fought in three tight formations close to one another. Three quarters of Mazdul's forces were now across the water. He joined them on the other bank. Princess Yuehan was with the Spawn on the far bank, from where she could watch the battle unfold in relative safety. Her guard of five thousand surrounded her. The dwarves fought stubbornly but retreated slowly towards their cities. They were now having losses, one to every four Spawn killed. Mazdul knew they would not be able to sustain the losses as well as he could, and he pressed his armies to break the enemy line, but the dwarves were well disciplined and when one fell, another leapt in the gap and the injured or dead dwarf was placed in the centre. Bar was battling ferociously in the front rank, killing and giving ground.

Things were beginning to look a little bleak for the dwarves, fighting with Bar, Barin and Lowe's dwarves. Their retreat was slowing as the fighting all around them increased. Sensmann could see the battle over the river was turning in favour of Princess Yuehan. She went to meet with Blutschläger near the gate. He had been checking the defences now that their gates were in peril. They met in an offshoot from the main gateway. "Things are looking serious out there," said Sensmann. "I need to understand your mind on this matter. We are following Lowe's plan, which is sound only if we survive it."

At that moment Blutschläger pointed at the wall behind Sensmann and, as she turned, the wall became as a window. There stood Ruth, tall, slim and quite beautiful, just as described by Lowe at their first meeting where they laid plans down in faith to Lowe. Ruth spoke and both dwarves stood their ground in amazement, before Sensmann gave a slight bow and Blutschläger followed with a lower one.

"Well met! Sensmann and Blutschläger. Lowe is alive and making the best of a hard job." Sensmann smiled. "I am Ruth, I am here to give quick council. Quickly, tell me what you face."

Sensmann quickly updated Ruth.

"Right," said Ruth, "there can be no doubt we are at the crux of this current battle. Attack from all sides with everything you have. You may win or you may lose. If it is the Creator's will, I know not, but you dwarves are, I believe, a match for the evil horde you face." Ruth looked to her side. "I must go to Lowe, fare well!"

Blutschläger and Sensmann both reacted immediately and, as they ran for the gates, they called for a message to go by the firing of an arrow to blow blue. This was the signal for attack. Blutschläger ran to the gate and mustered the dwarves there. Sensmann hurried every dwarf who could fight down to the gate. The attack did not wait for those stragglers. Blutschläger ordered the bolt hinges to be shattered. Great hammers swung on his order, even as the dwarves finished their lines for attack. The gates exploded outwards, crushing the Spawn and Slavers that had been hammering at the doors.

Blutschläger sprang over and onto the gates and Sensmann joined him and beat him to the first victim, a bemused looking Slaver. His head left his body, which was rippled with muscle, and blood squirted from his neck in a wave. It seemed to Sensmann she was fighting with time. Before the head hit the floor, another Spawn's head met her axe and the head split down to his neck. Now, the Blood Beater was with her and his hammer sent a Spawn flying backwards with a crushed chest.

The dwarves' blood was boiling and they careered into the ranks of the Spawn, killing left and right. There were two hours to dawn. The Slavers from Zhuxi's army were now in the battle with the dwarves and they were fearful. Their fear spread to the Spawn and what should have been a straightforward even contest became a rout. The Spawn, no longer frenzied, turned and ran in panic, running into Princess Yuehan's horde, who in the confusion could not be frenzied in order to hold off the dwarves. They died in their hundreds and broke.

At that exact moment, the gates of Zweite fell and out stormed Grobest and Hammerhurz to fight the Spawn at their gates. The Slavers facing Grobest and Hammerhurz saw the rout of the Spawn at the other city and doubt was upon them. The battle joined and within thirty seconds it was clear that, despite their much greater numbers, the Slavers were looking at the retreat of their kind, with slaughtering dwarves hot on their heels. The Spawn were broken in spirit and the Slavers fled towards the river.

Bar and Barin now saw some hope. They stood their ground and, while this was occurring, the dwarves from the other three cities marched out to join their brethren. Mazdul was now the one harbouring doubts. The dwarves from Zuerst (those of Lowe's clan) were reinforced and the Spawn forced on the defensive despite their numbers. Lowe's clan fought their way to the bridge and held their end. And the dwarves still had the numbers, just, to press their enemy.

Too late the general saw the trap. It was a fight to the death, win or lose everything. Mazdul made this plain to the Slavers and they tried to renew their efforts over the Spawn and a bloody conflict began with neither side prepared to relinquish another step.

Over the river, Princess Yuehan was for the first time truly afraid. She could not cross the river to her main force other than by abandoning the Slavers with her and she feared to risk the axes she knew would be hurled at her by the dwarves. She ordered her Slavers to defend her at all costs and they took the command and went to do her bidding.

The Spawn were in full flight and the dwarves in hot pursuit, the swift not waiting for the slow. At the head of the dwarves was Sensmann. She signalled to Hammerhurz and Grobest to keep the Spawn running. The Spawn moved one way and then the other, like a herd of wildebeest running from a lion attack. They flowed one way in fear and then the other until they crashed into the organised ranks of the princess's defence force. The front rank's defensive line was thrown into chaos under the impact of the Spawn in full flight.

The Slavers, who had fled now, were sending fear into the ranks and spreading their fear to the Slavers in the horde. Princess Yuehan sent a counter command and ordered her Slavers to kill the Spawn to stop the rout. Now Slaver was fighting Slaver to survive. Into the shambles came the dwarves and they drove deep wedges into the horde. The Spawn were now surrounded by enemies and in confusion. All they could do was move inward on the princess, seeking her protection. They began to be slaughtered by her personal guard, again at her orders.

Blutschläger caught up with Sensmann in the fight. She was bloody with several rake marks on her armour and some of the blood was her own. He shouted for all the dwarves to follow him and he pressed on towards the princess's position, ignoring all else. The Blood Beater lived up to his billing and the Slavers he met were afraid and this made their Spawn easier to kill.

The Slavers retreated, leaving the Spawn to be slaughtered. It was no longer a battle. All the dwarves gave no quarter, and few could escape them. Princess Yuehan saw the possibility of her death before her eyes, as the great brute that was the Blood Beater smashed through the ranks. She went berserk herself and sprang into the battle with a scimitar in each hand. Her Slaver guard were emboldened by her show of courage and order began to assert itself near to her. The dwarves were still heavily outnumbered, but the slaughter continued.

The Blood Beater saw the princess coming. She ran at him at full tilt and rose in the air on her wings, aiming to strike down on him. Sensmann saw the danger to her husband and threw both of her axes, one after the other, at Yuehan as she was still in mid-air. The axes did not hit her body but ripped through one of her wings and the wing collapsed, which put her slightly off course. Sensmann was bowled over by two Spawn together and disappeared from sight.

The Blood Beater focused, moved to one side and avoided the killing blows that would have hit him with full force. The princess hit the ground off balance and stumbled slightly towards the Blood Beater, still snarling. The dwarf reacted quickly and brought his great hammer down on Yuehan's right foot. It smashed the foot to a bloody pulp and Yuehan screamed in pain. She fought to hold off the dwarf with her swords. The Blood Beater came forward, swinging his great hammer. She tried to parry his blows, but the swords were no match for the weighty hammer strokes. Off balance, and in agony, Yuehan tried to flee but her wing was smashed. She was struck a partial blow to her arm as she frantically tried to defend herself. The blow broke her arm. She crumpled in front of the Blood Beater and cried out for mercy. The Blood Beater smashed her skull where she lay. All around them, on both sides of the river, Spawn were now dying. Those few that were left were executed where they stood. The human general Mazdul was despatched by Grobest himself. Not one of their enemies left the vale.

Once the fields of battle were cleared, the dwarves came

together. With the enemy defeated entirely they were free, against all the odds. The clan leaders met during the celebrations in the field.

Sensmann and Blutschläger told their tales of meeting Ruth and of their response to her instruction. Each told their tale and all the dwarves drank toasts to Lowe and Lowin and the others in his entourage and wished them success. Sensmann was still quite sober, and when the males Blood Beater and Grobest, still hot from the battle, suggested they seek out the third princess, she and Dunkeln firmly said no.

Sensmann spoke and said, "Our battle is over for the present, but we know that evil is still strong. Our enemies will seek our destruction in their own good time. No! Our purpose under Lowe's plan was to put fear into the enemy, even at our own expense and lives. We have done that and more. The enemy will soon know of this victory and doubt will have been sown in the mind of the last princess of evil. No, Shimishi will be in doubt. She expected victory, not the death of her kin. The Queen Yonlik will not risk her yet, although they still have the forces capable of our destruction if they chose to give battle. They will lick their wounds. We will do the same. We have many of our folk in this victory and we stand still against the evil pursuit of the men we sent to safety with a few of our own folk. This victory will give them a head start undreamed of and they will thrive, build and multiply as must we if we are to survive in this harsh world.

"We will seek out our kindred sent on their mission to destroy the egg nests of the dead princesses. These may still be under protection from the enemy or they may not. We will have to wait and see. We will drink a toast to my cousins Zenith and Janzen on their quest and let them be victorious!"

The dwarves drank many more toasts that night and well into the next day. Sensmann came to later in the afternoon and the autumn sun shone cool. She breathed deeply before turning over to snuggle into Blutschläger, who was still sleeping and snoring on his back. Her thoughts mulled over how their fortunes had gone. She knew that without the help received and her own good fortune, without the push from Ruth and the immediate trust she had made through her senses that Ruth was all goodness, the dwarves would have missed their opportunity when it had come and that may well have given rise to a different outcome. 'This adventure isn't over yet dear husband, not by a long shot!'

CHAPTER FIFTEEN
LOWE AND LOWIN AND WHAT HAPPENED NEXT

After the battle in Ten-Mile Gorge and once clear of the tunnel, the dwarves marched all day. All fifty dwarves knew very well that they would have to move swiftly away from the battlefield, for there was no doubt that the princess would seek revenge upon them in some form or other. Lowe set a good pace, comfortable for him and the others, and the dwarves beat out a quiet rhythm for each step by tapping their fingers on their thumbs as they walked.

As the night passed into the next day, they kept the same pace and at midday Lowe called a halt for sustenance near to a clean running brook that clearly fed the river some miles behind them now. The dwarves unpacked some bread and fresh water was collected from the stream. A cordial was drawn from a pack and when the fire was built and nice and hot, a large pot of steel, fine and so light, was placed across it to begin to heat water. When the water was boiling it was taken off the heat and meats were now strung above the fire to cook.

A couple of dwarves had during the day gone off hunting and returned with five brace of rabbit, a brace of hares and six ducks. These were added to their provisions and cooked over the fire. The dwarves had with them salted meats but these they would save for when they had less on offer. When the water had cooled in the pot by about ten degrees, the cordial was added to the water and mixed thoroughly in. The alcohol content was adequate and the beer it produced was wholesome and hearty and would allow three flagons for every dwarf present. The dwarves, being such travellers in their past, had invented the cordial for just such occasions as this. They had a taste of home with them which was, as any traveller will tell you, as good as a feast with reminders of happier and safer times.

The dwarves set up watchers outside their camp and took it in turns to eat their fill. When the fire burned low, they leaned against each other, back to back, for comfort and extra warmth, for the cold was the enemy of all that travel in the wild and they would not always have the luxury of a hot fire. Being now well fed and feeling rested after their labours, the dwarves chatted in the happy conversational way that extended family groups tend to do. They talked about the fight they had with the Spawn and how they fared well in not losing a single casualty. There were one or two minor wounds, which had been carefully cleaned with some of the boiling water and bandaged as only dwarves know how. They were used to injury in battle and the importance of hygiene.

Lowgrim held court for a period and teased his sister Joygrim for not banishing more of the enemy with her axes. Joygrim had retorted that she was sure Lowgrim had felled two Spawn and a couple of Slavers with his sharp wit! Lowin was pleased with the morale in the party and, when it was appropriate, she ordered sleep.

The dwarves slept for three hours and, as the sun set once more, they packed up their belongings and cleared the area of refuse. One of the younger dwarves went into a small copse of trees and carefully dug a hole, placed the rubbish into it and then replaced the turf. Two other keen-eyed dwarves inspected the area where the fire had burned and replaced the turf there which had been removed. To a casual passer-by it would not be obvious that a party of fifty dwarves had camped there. In thirty-six hours, there would be little to see (or smell) at all.

The dwarves travelled on like this for seven days, always careful and keeping the river on their right side, until they came to a small open area which had a ford that was crossed with great care. The dwarves had thought the enemy might have set watchers there but when they had explored the area thoroughly before attempting the crossing of the ford, they had found no one. This was not particularly surprising to Lowe or Lowin because the Slavers that ordered the Spawn were careless about traps because they never ventured out in small enough groups to risk assault. At least that had been the case up until then.

"We can expect a change in behaviour I think after our last success," said Lowin to Lowe, who agreed with her. Lowe and Lowin had no clear plan yet as to how they were going to breach the defences of the enemy when they got in proximity.

"I wonder whether Ruth will open another portal or will she come herself. I think we are best to make our own way and plan for ourselves, otherwise we might come unstuck very quickly and get ourselves slaughtered," said Lowe. Or even worse, thought Lowin, get captured!

The next night the dwarves walked until just before the dawn and, as it was early autumn in feel if not in fact, they rested until midday. Lowe guessed that the next march would take them into the range of potential enemies. From the high point they could watch the surrounding lands with ease. Their woodcraft had taught them never to build a fire on a hilltop and so they had settled into a small, enclosed space and built their fire there as soon as they stopped their march that morning. Every dwarf closed in to eat, talk and rest, except for those on guard.

Society of these occasions, especially away from home, gave the dwarves the sense of belonging and trust that each person was valued and so even the less attractive characters could feel the warmth and togetherness so important in life. No dwarf ever grew up in isolation except in extreme cases where sometimes a dwarf family would withdraw from the clan for their own purposes. This was a rare occurrence because it was a dangerous thing to do in this dangerous part of the world. All these dwarves were so close they would happily lay down their lives for one another. Their faith in the Creator and his existence was not in question for them at all. They knew the truth of this. It simplified matters for all of them. If they had any doubts whatsoever they were dispelled by the sight of Ruth and of the Angel Deborah, living proof that their God ruled all, as the greatest man to walk the Earth said many thousands of years later. Even the birds and bees have great value, and a man is far greater in the eyes of his Creator than a bird.

There was nothing to fear from a good death by the dwarves. Lowe and his company had not practised with their weapons for many days now, except the hunters. He called for the circle to be drawn and then began dwarf training with bow, axe and hammer. These were the favoured weapons for they were heavy and lethal for Spawn, whereas swords, preferred by other men, were less effective. It was easier to remove a head with an axe than with a sword. Having said that the dwarves all carried long stout knives in their belts. Some carried sling shots with small iron spiked balls which would pierce a Spawn's thick skull if it hit him squarely on the side of the head. Many Spawn in the last battle had several spikes buried into their skulls but carried on the fight until a lethal blow was given. Sometimes the dwarves used hammers against the spikes that were imbedded in a skull to speed the demise of an opponent.

The dwarves paired off and began to fight at half speed, and over twenty minutes their speed increased until all were working quite hard to stay alive. Lowe and Lowin knew that training was key to winning battles because it brought confidence and fitness to the company, which had to remain high. It also helped the best fighters to improve those less able.

An older, larger-stomached champion knew his strengths were his power in his arms and shoulders, but he had to be tested in his speed in order to survive and, where he was found wanting, he would practise defensive moves against an attack until he was satisfied he could do it in the heat of battle.

The greatest fighter for fifty years had been the Blood Beater and he was the example every dwarf wanted to measure themselves against. Lowe and Lowin were very able fighters, but Lowe lacked the stamina he had at one time and so his defensive practice took much of his time. The lithe females would try to best him with their speed. When he fought Lowin in single combat everyone stopped their own training for there was much they could learn. Lowe was slightly taller than Lowin but he bent low, sticking his bottom out slightly, so that his balance was secure. Feet spread to shoulder width he faced Lowin. She for her part never kept still. She used her light axes to good effect, keeping Lowe in a defensive position. She changed the angle of attack and moved in and out and Lowe was like a shadow of her movement. They fought for twenty, thirty, forty minutes and, as Lowe began to tire, Lowin seemed to find another higher gear. Eventually Lowe was tricked as Lowin feigned left and went right. Lowe was a tad slow in adjusting and, before he could do anything, she used her boot to the rear of his bottom and over he went. He hit the ground and forced his body into a roll and came up on his legs. Before he could react, Lowin had jumped at his neck, wrapped her legs around it and sent him falling backwards. Lowe hit the ground so hard the wind left his lungs. A cry of victory came from the rest of the company.

Lowin sat where she was, smiling and breathing heavily. Lowe began to breathe normally and then gave a false scowl. "What a way to lose a fight! Get off me woman!"

Lowe sat happily giggling while Lowin demonstrated the end of the fight again with a willing volunteer male dwarf.

Training recommenced and when they had all worked hard enough, they rested again, drank some of the ale prepared earlier and settled down for a catnap. The sun was setting when they broke camp. Once more they cleared the area as best as they could to hide their passing, making a mental note of this place should they ever pass this way again.

The company moved silently through a wooded area. The trees were mighty in stature and related to the great oak trees. These were taller, broad and clearly old. They had lichen growing up into the lower branches, which were as thick as Lowe's waistline and some even thicker. Lowgrim took pleasure of informing his father about these as they passed underneath. Joygrim, his sister, was leading the group when she suddenly stopped and crouched down. All the dwarves now did the same.

Joygrim gave the signal that she could see men before them. Lowe signalled her to query, good or bad, and Joygrim put her finger across her neck to indicate bad. The sun was shining and a slight breeze moved the leaves, making a pleasant rustling sound, and the light from the sun, which was high in the sky, caused shadows to move and sway over the dwarves who were all perfectly still. Joygrim crept forward a little and then crouched again. Now the other dwarves could see a band of maybe twenty men, rugged and bearded and not at all clean, cut across their path at an angle of forty-five degrees from left to right. They were noisy and, as they went on their way, Joygrim waited until they were well past the company before signalling the company to move on.

Once they had moved on a mile, they came together to wait for Lowgrim, who had tracked the men to ensure they had not been seen just in case the men had picked up their trail. Lowgrim re-joined the company and reported to Lowe, Lowin and Lowgrim's sister, Joygrim.

"We are safe for now," said Lowgrim. "It seems these men

had sacked a family group, robbing them of everything before returning to their base camp which is about two miles away by the river. They didn't notice us, but we were fortunate that the sun was quite so bright, so we were shielded by the shadows of the trees and downwind!" The dwarves ignored this last remark, but Lowgrim still smiled inwardly at his jest.

Lowin spoke to Joygrim. "You did well daughter to spot the men before they saw you. We will need your eyes and ears from here on in, I fear. You will lead us on, and we need to find a relatively safe place to camp tonight, if we can find one. Lowgrim, I want you to drop behind the company to see that we are not surprised from behind. I know we are fifty dwarves, but we are not here to fight with bands of scoundrels, but Princess Shimishi if we can find her."

The company moved off at a slower pace and tried hard not to make too much noise. Lowgrim dropped back with another dwarf to cover their rear. Joygrim showed her worth as a guide when she ordered a halt just after dark in an area thick with bushes that were twenty feet tall. At the centre was enough space for the company to stretch out, which they did. No fire was lit that night. Lowgrim came into the camp last, with his colleague. No one was following them. It was a dark night for the moon and stars were hidden from view by high clouds driven by a powerful wind whereas at ground level it was no more than a gentle breath.

The dwarves huddled together for warmth. In the centre were the females and younger dwarves with the older folk on the outside. This was fair because the younger dwarves worked as guides and did a lot of the fetching and carrying and needed as safe and warm sleep as could be arranged. They were also important as a guide to the general mood and confidence in the group. The youngsters (anyone under sixty cycles) tended to chat more and socialised at these times, whether it was a happy light chat or a more serious matter of settling who was next to be given the role of fetching water. The older dwarves were happier on the outside of the throng for they could glean the warmth and comfort of the group at their backs and listen with amusement to all that was said.

It is said of the dwarves that they were a fearsome enemy and moody and a bit dark compared to other men. The truth is that they were and probably are happier than most people today for they were measured against the Edain and almost sin-free men who harboured an innocence and longing for the sheer joy of being alive. There was certainty in their world.

In the morning, the dawn was lit with a red skyline and the dwarves knew the weather was changing. They packed up and moved at a slower pace even than that of the day before, for Lowe, being cautious and wise, reminded the group that it is never wise to run towards trouble, but rather walk, for you never know, the battle might be won easier later rather than sooner.

Joygrim took the lead once more with her mother, Lowin. They spoke quietly to one another about their hopes for the day. Lowe led the company and once more Lowgrim dropped back with a young dwarf to watch their rear. The ground was undulating now and Joygrim led the march over the rolling ground and, wherever possible, avoided the exposed ridges where their forms could be easily spotted. Although the Slavers hated the sun, their vision was good. They never looked up for long periods though as this light was pain to them. The Spawn rarely looked up for more than a glance.

Lowgrim and his companion were watchful. They had climbed a long slope and were near the summit when they saw about half a mile behind them the unmistakable movement of a large group of creatures, which could only be Spawn. There were five hundred with Slavers following the trail of the dwarves. Lowgrim filled his lungs and blew out a breath of relief. If these Spawn had caught them at camp, then many of the dwarves would now be making their way up the Golden Path, wondering what hit them. Lowgrim sent his companion in pursuit of the dwarf company, and he settled to watch them for a while to see what they would do when they reached the spot where the dwarves had last set camp.

The Spawn reached the thicket of bushes and stopped. Lowgrim could see they were carrying some unfortunate bundles, which he guessed to be the men that had crossed the path of the dwarves so recently. He crept nearer and then a cry, followed by a gleeful evil taunt, arose from the Spawn and Lowgrim guessed the poor souls were being readied for the pot. The Spawn lit a fire and two Slavers looked up to where Lowgrim was hidden. Lowgrim watched in still silence until the two returned to the thicket. It became clear that the Spawn were going to cook their prey in the day and run at night. He could see the greasy black smoke lift into the air and guessed at the unmistakeable smells of cooking flesh, such as he had witnessed on previous encounters with Spawn. His expression spoke for him, hoping that they choked on the bones. He wondered how these men would be judged by the Creator and then left the thought at that. It was not his part to judge others, only live as well as he could, following the Creator's clear intentions.

Lowgrim left the Spawn and Slavers to their grim feast and moved at a steady run to catch up with his own folk. He could see his sister Joygrim watching for him with his mother Lowin. He guessed the main company had kept moving for that would have been his instruction in his father's position as leader.

"We have a problem mother dear," said Lowgrim. "These Spawn are close behind and they will be onto us before the next day sets unless we can throw them off the scent."

The dwarves ran after their company, moving with all haste. Lowin might have been the mother of the two younger dwarves but she was at her peak of health and fitness, as she had demonstrated with her fight with the Slavers at the explosion site and again with Lowe in training. Within the hour they were back with the company and were greeted by all. Without stopping, the three runners took the lead and forged a steady pace that the others, even the older dwarves would find bearable. Now they headed towards the great river that had run through their mountain homes. As they approached the river, they came across streams running towards it. They walked through these carefully when they found them, making false trails from its bed occasionally to confuse the followers. All the time Joygrim and her mother Lowin were searching for a safe place to hold up for the night.

Late in the day Lowe and Lowin walked arm in arm under the light of the moon, stopping on occasions to gently kiss one another before they reached the company's camp. All were relieved to hear that they had foiled the Spawn for now.

Lowe spoke quietly to his children and Lowin so only they could hear him. "We have been lucky today, for another few hours and the Spawn would have been on top of us in the dark and with no escape for us but to fight or die."

"Yes, we have been fortunate but let us praise the Creator for the blessing of a moon tonight and his support in helping us make that river crossing without loss."

The four of them quietly gave praise before settling down. The other dwarves listened to Lowe as he said a prayer of thankfulness to the Creator as he settled down to sleep. There were a few mouthed amens and a few audible and every dwarf was pleased to have avoided battle today.

In the dawn, Lowe and Lowin had a conference alone, speaking to one another where they lay facing each other. Lowin smiled at Lowe. "We have done well under your leadership Lowe, but I want to consider using today as a last chance to rest. I fear we will have to fight very soon whether we wish to or not."

Lowe looked serious. "Yes, Lowin, I have been pondering whether we should go on this morning. We are perhaps only one day's travel away from the entrance to the Queen Yonlik's lair. I could see the mountain range over the trees from the riverbank. I think we will have a rest day and now only travel at night and without fires at all after today. We will have one hot meal and let the dwarves have a few beers before we put all thought of comfort away."

Lowin smiled and nodded her agreement. She was particularly pleased that Lowe was considering the older dwarves, which included him of course. For she knew that the dwarves would eat well, drink well and sleep well and be ready for the hard labour that was to come for them all.

CHAPTER SIXTEEN
OF YONLIK'S LAIR

That night the dwarves began their approach to Yonlik's lair. They made the approach near to the riverbank under the cover of small trees, once more led by Joygrim and Lowin. This proved impossible, for no sooner had the trees ended than the dwarves could see Spawn activity at the riverside. There was a wooden structure across the water which allowed two Spawn to cross side by side and there was a long line of Spawn heading over the river. The dwarves withdrew back along the way they had come and moved further inland.

Lowin spoke to the group once they were well away from the Spawn. "It seems likely that the remaining princess and the foul Yonlik have got wind of our journey from across the river and that's why they are sending so many Spawn to search for us. The numbers going won't make much difference when we are detected but it gives me hope that we might find a route into the lair that is less well guarded."

"I like the idea of a back door if it means avoiding getting massacred at the front door," put in Lowgrim.

"Oh Lowgrim!" chortled his sister, "you really are a wit and I'm so glad we are all together because we are going to need your sense of humour before this is all done with."

"Sentimentalist!" said Lowgrim. He got a kick in the shin for his trouble.

Lowe spoke on. "Okay, my friends, cousins and children, we are going to enter that lair by whatever means we can and inflict as much damage when we get in as we possibly can. I do not want to see or expect any independent actions. We all fight, or we all run until we have no choice but to fight. This is not the time to have any doubt or harbour thoughts of saving one another by giving up your own lives. Everyone needs to be clear on this. If it is our destiny to fall in battle here, whoever that is, will have had a good death. No dwarf can ask for more, nor can he be more certain of his spirit moving up the Golden Path, if it be the Creator's will. I tell you all that the lives of others are not of my gift to give or to save on this adventure. Not one of you is bound to another at the expense of your life. No one can rely on another in relation to the battle that is to come, and which may take all of our lives. Anyone who wishes to leave may do so in peace and honour and will have my respect and the respect of everyone here, if they feel their destiny lies not with us alone."

No one spoke. All the dwarves were sombre and all the dwarves expected to fight for their lives. This speech had been made many times before over their lifetimes and it was drilled into dwarves that each dwarf, no matter who, had the responsibility to keep himself alive in a battle and that was his sole and only responsibility. The only time self-sacrifice was tolerated was if children could be saved from slaughter by an enemy. There were no children here.

Lowe continued when he felt his words had had time to sink in. "We have all heard and seen many atrocities during our time together and I know from personal experience that when one hears about these atrocities you feel sorry for those that have been persecuted. If you once witness an atrocity you become in your heart the brother or sister of that person being wronged. We have seen already so much death and endings of life cut short by the evil of the princesses and now we have a chance to play our part in trying to inflict as much harm and fear upon our enemy. Let us go in with courage and strong hearts and give what we have, to aid the Creator. This is our task. If we live, we live. If we die, then we will die well!"

All the dwarves embraced silently. Some spoke love for another through their eyes. All had the same hope and the same courage. They all knew that they shared a love which no evil could break.

Lowin spoke and said, "Blood of my blood and kin of my kin." All the dwarves repeated this and then Lowe set to planning with Lowin what they would do next. Lowe ordered the dwarves into pairs and sent them out to get a good lay of the land. Lowe knew that this mountain entrance had once been a dwarf dwelling, taken by the queen many years before and Lowe knew that no dwarf worth his salt would trap himself with only one avenue of escape. Lowe ordered the best with stone craft to seek out any signs of a hidden dwarf exit on this side of the mountain. He did not wish to risk his people crossing the river again to seek out the opposite side unless there was no choice, for they had been lucky thus far, but he knew it could not last.

The dwarves left their camp at night and returned the next night. It was the safest way to move around. There were guards around the perimeter and that told Lowe that there was something to guard other than rock. It was not until Lowgrim returned near to dawn that they had any new information.

Lowgrim spoke to his parents and Joygrim, who had returned earlier. "We had some difficulty getting close to the guards so that we could inspect the mountain side and then we saw it. A small dark hole about ten feet off the ground. It looks as though it is a short tunnel into the mountain, cut at an angle so that it is hard to spot. You can't see the tunnel at all looking straight at it, because the rock above casts a shadow over the area all day. There are Spawn guards that move past the spot, but none seem to be aware of what is above them. I don't think it could have been cut as a shaft to give access to light for the reasons I have given, so it could be what we are looking for."

The next two dwarves in reported they had found a side door further round the base of rock which Lowgrim had discovered. This was a true back door and there were guards aplenty and Spawn and the odd Slaver directing activities towards a trash heap, where Spawn waste, bones and other fouled meat were thrown. The stench downwind was awful.

Lowe thanked everyone for their energy and focus. He made his decision to move in the next night and all rested up except those on guard for the camp. They carefully cleaned and wrapped their weapons in cloth to prevent them clanging on a rock and tied lengths of fabric around their war boots for the same reason. Each dwarf took charcoal from the last fire out from their packs and darkened their faces and hands. Only bright teeth shone when someone grinned. One or two giggles were set off by Lowgrim who was grinning inanely at his fellows. "I look as old as my father!" he whispered loud enough for everyone to hear. Even Lowe gave a slight smile at this remark at his expense.

"Okay, we go in without being seen if that is at all possible," said Lowe. "We will post twenty dwarves outside, hidden near the entrance. They are only to show themselves once we exit. If the alarm goes off the twenty will leave if they need and return to our homes the best route they can choose. If we get trapped in the lair we will surely not need their support. You can be sure we will give our lives as expensively as we can."

Lowe made choices for the guards and all were younger males and females of the band. Lowe did not spare his closest kin, being Lowin, Lowgrim and Joygrim. He knew they would not be separated from him at this most perilous time for all of them. The ten chosen to act as an impact force were settled upon and each was given instruction as to what to expect once the alarm went off. They were told to give the area where they were to enter a wide birth, so that it might not draw the attention of Spawn or Slavers, if they as guards were spotted before the alarm went off. Once the alarm sounded they were to make straight for the back door and kill any enemy found there.

The ten moved off at dusk, strung out in a silent line, with the moon waning and giving partial vision on the trail. The remaining twenty, including Lowe and Joygrim, who were leading, with Lowgrim and his mother behind them, approached the perimeter. While still under cover Lowgrim silently moved past them and signalled to where the hidden entrance could be seen. Lowgrim and Joygrim counted the seconds between when the guards walked past. It was almost a minute generally between one and the next. With rope over his shoulder Lowgrim and Joygrim moved to the rock and Lowgrim climbed easily onto Joygrim's shoulders and jumped up a few inches. His hands found purchase on the rim of the hole. He pulled himself up with his strength and then lowered a portion of thick line and hauled Joygrim into the hole effortlessly. They both sat one behind the other quietly, until the next Spawn guard had crossed beneath them.

Two by two, the rest of the troop entered the hole. It was completely black inside, but they dared not show a light. They worked by moonlight at the edge of the entrance until all twenty dwarves were safely inside. Lowgrim worked his way forwards, feeling with his fingers and senses, listening to the muffled noises from the dwarves' physical efforts behind him. The air had a clean feel and he knew when the last dwarf was in the hole for Joygrim gave a double tap on his ankle, which was their agreed signal for 'Let us go!'

Lowgrim led the others along the tunnel, which was to his senses moving straight ahead. Once they had moved perhaps forty metres, Lowgrim felt, rather than saw, that the tunnel widened suddenly. He veered to his left and then to his right and decided it was time to risk a little light. In total darkness he found his flint and small torch, which smelled of alcohol drenched cord and struck a spark. Immediately the light showed Joygrim still behind him and a small dark chamber with no opening at first glance. Joygrim and the others joined

Lowgrim in the small chamber and were standing all together, patiently, to see what Lowgrim and Joygrim would do next.

Lowgrim spotted the catch to a secret door cut neatly into the rock. He spoke for the others to hear. "There is good stonework around this door father. It is definitively of dwarf construction. I think we are safe enough to try some real light and prepare for battle."

The dwarves unwrapped their weapons and stowed the rags. They left their boots covered. When all was ready, Lowe took the lead and opened the locked door. It was heavy and moved slowly, making not a sound. 'Good stonework indeed,' thought Lowe. He moved into a larger tunnel which seemed to lead down from the door, which was very normal for a dwarf escape route for it meant that an enemy could not get to the door before you when you were on this path. Lowe called for dark once more and the dwarves moved forward slowly and patiently, feeling the way with their feet and heightened senses. The tunnel was long and headed steadily down into the mountain. Each dwarf was thinking something similar as himself, which was that the kin who had built this route were following dwarf secret construction rules. Only wide enough for one dwarf to move up or down. High enough for comfort and clean edged and clean floor to reduce noise.

On the went gradually. After perhaps 1,200 metres, by dwarf steps, Lowe detected a slight hint of light before him. He approached the glint of what was torchlight showing the end of the tunnel and a concealed door, he guessed from the other side into a lit chamber. He sniffed at the air at the tiny hole and a slight odour of grease was detected. He then listened for any sound beyond the door, but all was silent. Lowe located the lock and turned it and stepped out into a walkway which led down to a kitchen area, he guessed. As quickly as they could the dwarves exited the passageway. They checked the lock so they could reopen the door again, then closed it silently until it clicked quietly into place. Lowe placed some dry dust over the small hole to make it invisible again and they moved down to a room empty of Spawn, but with evidence of cooking not very many hours ago. There were signs of a recent fire and a grate and above it a chimney, small and discrete, which was drawing air from the room.

'A clever and quite ingenious dwarf invention and so low in the dwelling,' thought Lowe. He guessed the princess's quarters would be below where they stood. The dwarves moved on, posting a guard out of sight in the kitchen. They would return the way they had come if they got the chance. Down the dwarves went. It got warmer and then noise began to reach them. Spawn growls and Slaver commands could be heard. Miserable screams then reached their ears. It was obvious that a slave was being punished for some infraction. Hands gripped weapons firmly.

CHAPTER SEVENTEEN
A NASTY SURPRISE

Zenith and Janzen and their party of eight were huddled in the secret back door of the stronghold. Chosen by the group as the least likely to be noticed and approved by Sensmann in their last discussion before the battle for the wall. Prior to its fall, Zenith had watched two enemy camps from high on the mountain from a secret ledge and had seen the Spawn and Slavers leave with Zhuxi's latest brood of eggs. It was in her mind to destroy them if she could, and she reported the same plan to Sensmann who saw the sense in this. Sensmann was happy to approve anything that would bring fear and loss to the enemy.

Zenith had immediately called her group from the battle line and they gathered what they needed for the road. Zenith opened the door and they went down the rope one after the other until they were all on the very edge of the mountain only a few feet from the ground. Moving steadfastly, they jumped down the last six feet and made a wide arch away from the enemy, who were preparing for the final push against the wall. Without looking back the dwarves moved off at a steady run and, within an hour, had managed to put six miles between themselves and the enemy without being seen, as far as they could tell.

On they went after dark and they kept on the march until the dawn, before taking a long-earned break. Janzen, Zenith and the group had talked quietly over the last mile and all agreed they would go further for a rest. They also believed the enemy would feel quite safe away from the battle with the dwarves and would not move so quickly as could the dwarves. Their first task was to pick up the enemy trail as soon as they could.

Zenith had been given this task to lead, due to the courage

and fortitude she had shown in the recent battles with the Spawn. All very keen, the dwarves knew that they would die trying to destroy at least some of the brood of Princess Zhuxi. All were keen to leave their mark on the enemy. The dwarves moved quickly with the daylight and covered several more miles when it was dark. Zenith had discussed with the others whether they should risk a night march and possibly lose the trail in the darkness. It was agreed by all that the Spawn had moved in the same direction all day and it was a fair bet they would continue with this through the night They seemed to be heading for the gorge which led back to Princess Zhuxi's lair.

It was dawn when they caught up with the enemy. Slavers were resting and the Spawn were protecting the brood with the eggs in the centre of the camp. Janzen went forward alone to check out the camp for lookouts and any other unseen threats but came back quickly to report there seemed to be only two guards posted, one at each end of the camp. Janzen spoke quietly. "The enemy seem to think they are completely safe from attack. Only two guards are posted and all the Slavers, numbering six, are eating a hearty meal on the other side of their campfire. They are just finishing their meal of meats." She shuddered to think what the meats they were eating might be and the others didn't ask.

"Okay," said Zenith after sitting in thought for a while. "We attack from two sides, all at once. Janzen, is there light enough for bows?" Janzen nodded. "Okay then, let's go!"

The dwarves moved into position quickly and without undue delay. They took aim, each with a bow, to be sure they made the best of the opportunity and fired as one. They reloaded their bows and fired again from twenty yards and five out of six Slavers slumped to the ground after the first salvo. One Slaver, although shocked, survived the attack. The Slaver raised the alarm and did her best to frenzy the nearest Spawn and about twenty responded quickly. The dwarves moved onto the attack and axes and hammers met rage and claws of the Spawn. The fury of the Spawn was met with stiff resistance from the dwarves. The single Slaver, a female, began to organise the assault now that she felt safer with the Spawn ordered for her protection. The dwarves gave battle and then, on Zenith's command, retreated fifty yards, before turning together and holding their ground once more.

The Spawn came on towards the retreating dwarves but then stopped as one. The Slaver, who was now alone, became distracted by the need to protect Princess Zhuxi's eggs. The Spawn were not so driven to kill under these conditions and the dwarves fought them, killing five before once more retreating twenty yards. This was enough for the Slaver, who recalled the surviving Spawn.

The dwarves retreated further into the trees that skirted the path to the gorge. The light was now only a glimmer through the trees as they retreated. The pale moon flicked the edges of leaves and the shadows were an almost perfect deception for the dwarves to be concealed. The dwarves halted and stood under cover of a tall old oak tree. Its boughs spread above and over the dwarves, as if to protect them. Zenith had a sense of it embracing them in the arc of its branches while a slight breeze rustled the great leaves, providing enough natural sound to cover the voice of Zenith as she spoke to her companions. One or two of the dwarves reported injuries, which were immediately cleaned and dressed using balms and covered in bandages carried for this purpose. The wounds were deep scratches to one dwarf's face while the other had suffered claw marks like tiny daggers that had pierced the leather protecting the forearm. The claw nails had detached themselves in the skin and the dwarves spent some time cleaning and searching the wound for the claw ends in the flesh. One had to be dug out using a blade. The dwarf, whose name was Dwaylin, sweated profusely before they had finished. Dwaylin was then given a draft of beer and he counted himself most fortunate as it took effect.

Janzen then spoke. "We have started well. Eighty and five of the Spawn left, I think! We will watch over the Spawn through the night, taking it in terms to harry them with arrows and retreating. If they follow into the trees, then we turn and hold our ground. I do not think the surviving Slaver will favour leaving the cargo of eggs unguarded. My thought is to tire the Slaver and attack again in the light of day, which will be much to our advantage and little to their liking."

So, while Janzen rested the injured, the other eight went forward as a group and harried the enemy. The Slaver was now in fear for her life. She ordered the Spawn to surround the precious eggs and set the Spawn to ring themselves on an outward spiral shape with she at the centre.

There were always Spawn in insufficient numbers to protect each point. The Spawn lit no fires and sat in the dark like stone grotesques, unmoving but ever watchful. The dwarves began their torment of the Spawn. When the moon went behind a cloud the darkness swallowed up everything but when the moon came out a volley of arrows sought out the still and silent forms of the Spawn. The Slaver was ready for this and, using her control over the Spawn, she ordered the Spawn to remain silent through pain, even unto death. In this way the Slaver hoped the arrows would strike the already injured or dead. The dwarves did not meet the hopes of the Slaver's strategy and picked out new targets for arrows. By dawn there were another ten Spawn dead or mortally wounded.

The Spawn dipped their heads with the rising of the sun despite the Slaver's instructions and the dwarves, now ten in number, attacked as a unit, covering the open ground in twenty strides, launching a lethal hand to hand battle upon the Spawn. The Slaver was now panicked herself, her orders to fight and defend the eggs clogging the minds of the Spawn. They fought without frenzy and fell to axe and hammer easily. With fewer than fifty Spawn left the Slaver ordered a retreat, with the eggs in the centre.

Twenty Spawn were required to lift the cradles that carried the eggs and with only twenty-eight Spawn, in the light of day, they were either killed outright or turned to flee in the direction in which they had come. The dwarves focused on the Slaver now and she fought out of fear and her thoughts became clear. The Spawn frenzied and leapt at the dwarves with a rabid hunger for dwarf flesh. The dwarves were now needing to fight as a group, more closely as an efficient unit, and they did so with great expertise. Zenith, while killing the Spawn before, had her calf raked by the dying efforts of the Spawn. She was bleeding but unbowed and carried the fight without flinching with the next Spawn that came in range.

Now the dwarves moved, with Zenith at the centre. She loaded an arrow to her bow and sought out her target. The Slaver was close, perhaps twenty paces away, urging the Spawn on with desperation in her features. Zenith let fly her arrow and it speeded to its mark, hitting the Slaver squarely into its chest, going through the heart. As the pain struck, the Slaver gasped in pain. The Spawn faltered, which cost another five to immediately perish, before the Slaver, with fear and anger, re-frenzied the Spawn. The dwarves now went on the offensive as the Slaver ordered the Spawn closer in her defence. The Spawn held their ground. The fight was intense for several more minutes with injuries on both sides.

Finally, the Slaver lost her focus through her failing strength, with loss of blood pumping from the wound in her heart. She slipped to one knee almost as if to honour the bravery of the dwarves. The Spawn broke and ran once more. There were perhaps twenty left, some of them wounded. Janzen moved swiftly to follow, firing the last of their arrows and killing several before the Spawn fled. Zenith cut the head from the shoulders of the Slaver who was kneeling before her. Blood splayed out and the head sailed through the air. The battle was over.

The dwarves set about destroying the clutch of eggs singly with hammer and axe. The eggs were the size of ostrich eggs and strangely opaque. Inside each egg was a small, crumpled shape of a princess demon, wings furled. The dwarves continued to destroy the clutch and, when they were done, they moved off the road and into the woods. They used the afternoon to rest after their labours.

Dwaylin developed a fever that night and his arm began to enflame, but apart from this they were left in peace. Janzen spoke for the group and expressed her concern about the eggs they had just destroyed. "I wonder how often small queens are produced. This is the first evidence we have seen of winged young. It cannot be often because we would have been fighting the things long before now. If we are lucky, we just killed Zhuxi's line of succession, but if there are other clutches like this and they grow into demon princesses, then we are all in serious trouble." All the dwarves agreed with this.

"I think we need to move out tonight and try to lose our trail in the deep woods past the gorge if we can. Those Spawn not killed are not bright or a threat to us now other than by trailing us until they stumble onto a Slaver. The Slaver will read their thoughts, such as they are, and be on our trail seeking revenge and thereby gaining great favour with the Princess Zhuxi."

It was dusk when they packed up in their normal manner and headed for the gorge just off the main trail. They reached the mouth of the gorge at dawn the next day and scouted around for signs of the enemy. There was nothing to see. They moved through the entrance to the gorge and made camp under the small hillock which had been the site of the first success in battle for the dwarves that seemed now to be so long ago. The ground was black and cinders ringing the edges of the destructive fire showed singed blades of grass struggling to keep their colour. They formed tufts of brown and green, marking the natural growth from the devastation.

Upon entering the once secret and hidden cave, it was clear that the Spawn and Slavers had dug through the collapse in the tunnel and were pursuing those that survived the battle here. Zenith and Janzen and the rest were all delighted to see this development for it was comforting to know that at least some of their brethren were carrying on the fight.

The group took a decision to celebrate their own success and that of their brethren and lit a fire in the hearth. The smoke was drawn down the tunnel and that was pleasing. Nothing could come along it while the fire was burning due to the smoke. The company set guards to watch. Outside they had good vision of events and would at least see an enemy coming if they were followed and have time to react. The dwarves cooked up a brew of beer and fresh meat caught on the previous march. A deer had been hunted down, which was now turning on a spit for their pleasure. They stayed the night, warmed by the fire and stories of their adventures so far and the successes they had been a part of. Every member of the company, at one time or another that evening, offered up a silent prayer for their kin who were fighting Princess Zhuxi and the horde of Spawn.

Three hours before dawn they discussed what to do next. It was agreed to follow the path towards the enemy indirectly and investigate anything that drew its attention to them. At dawn they left the cave and moved at a steady pace for dwarves along the now smoke free tunnel. Had they known it, they would have been pleased that Lowe and his company had gone this way on their escape from the Spawn.

The first sign of trouble came at dusk when they heard

Spawn screaming at night. The screaming carried by the wind for their ears to hear was some miles behind them. Zenith and Janzen spoke together. "That will bring every Spawn and Slaver on our trail without a doubt," said Janzen. "We had better go cautiously forward from here." Zenith showed by her face that she agreed.

"We ought to check on our wounded as well. I do not like the idea of infection from the Spawn claws but at least it is less deadly than the Spawn bite. A bite could mean you lose an arm, or more," said Janzen.

"Okay," Zenith agreed, and they moved on, focusing on the terrain around them. For the rest of that night, they were spared the howls behind them from Spawn, which suggested they had at the very least put some distance between themselves and the Spawn that had survived the last battle. They guessed rightly that the Spawn would not travel by day for fear of the sun, unless driven by a Slaver. This was some comfort in the circumstances and so they walked until it was dark before making camp in a small hollow in the trees with the main trail on their right side. Once more the dwarves tried their luck and lit a fire.

The camp was resting in the second hour of the day when one of the guards came back into the camp and woke each dwarf quietly. He had seen a company of Spawn, numbering over five hundred. They were moving down the riverbank on this side of the river. Fortunately, the fire had burned low and only small red embers were visible and there was no smoke. The dwarf on watch had waited until the unit of Spawn had gone past them, onwards towards the gorge, before he dared move himself to report what he had seen.

The dwarves wasted no time. When the Spawn that survived report to the Slavers there would be an immediate hunt for the dwarves responsible for the destruction of Princess Zhuxi's brood. Breaking camp was done with dwarf efficiency, and they took their usual precautions, clearing the site, replacing the turfs lifted to cover the fire. Dwaylin's arm was swollen and sore and Zenith was limping a little as the wound on her thigh complained about the activity it was having to perform on little rest. Zenith did not complain or raise it as an issue, but Janzen made a mental note to check the wound at their next stop.

Zenith led the dwarves further from the river they had been tracking. She knew the Spawn would follow their trail wherever it led. Although Lowe and Lowin had covered this ground weeks before, she did not want to bring this hunt down upon them without warning. The dwarves now showed their stamina. They walked all day, crossing open country with caution, and Zenith found herself thinking how very pleasant it was to walk with the sun at your back. She followed her shadow, which grew unerringly longer and thinner. Zenith found that this was pleasant also. In more peaceful times, she would have savoured this walk in the company of her girlfriends while they chatted happily about plans for their future and what they would achieve in their lives. Of course, Janzen would be among them for they had been great friends all their lives and a friendship that is forty years old already will probably last a lot longer into the future if they were spared. Zenith felt a little light-headed and felt the warmth of the sun less and she began to shiver. She walked on as if in a daze of pleasantness, trying to think what it was that she was trying to escape from. Then she came to herself with a shudder.

She found Janzen looking into her eyes and she could recognise concern on her pretty features. "Okay, so now I have a fever along with Dwaylin. We will rest up after a few more hours." There was nothing said between them, but both knew Zenith was not well. She put these thoughts of self-care behind her and with Janzen beside her they walked long into the evening before stopping. The dwarves ate a cold supper and rested for an hour. Janzen insisted on checking Zenith's wound and was unsurprised when it was showing inflammation.

"It isn't painful, it is just an inflammation due to the activity. It will be fine when I have a chance to rest the leg properly," explained Zenith.

Janzen looked at her and scrutinised her face. There were signs of fever in Zenith's face but the lost look in her eyes had not returned and this at least was good news. Dwaylin on the other hand was getting sick and needed rest. The group rested for two further hours on Zenith's word so that Dwaylin could use the break to rest up for a while.

They moved off and began to climb up through trees and they kept going until dawn. They took an hour's break just after dawn and then moved on once more. They reached the top of the hill and were surprised to find that there was a hidden dell just over the hilltop. It was a good spot to camp. A lookout scanned the valley floor from which they had ascended, looking for evidence that they were being followed. A fallen tree just beyond the dell on the slope was dragged forward and it was just the right height for a dwarf to sit comfortably upon. Janzen had made the decision without discussion. It was unusual for dwarves to move something so big, which would be hard to replace, without others knowing that dwarves had passed that way. They would make their best effort to disguise its movement when they left. Janzen saw it as a way to allow Zenith to put her legs up to help reduce the swelling to her thigh. Janzen searched the wound carefully, as she suspected that part of a claw might still be in the wound.

Despite her best efforts, Janzen could see nothing in the wound, so she bathed the wound again with cooling boiled water and rebandaged the area. Dwaylin, the other injured dwarf, seemed to be rallying with the extra breaks in the day and Janzen guessed it might also prove the same for Zenith with a few hours of rest and sleep. The daylight was failing when the lookout reported that there were an awful lot of Spawn coming out of the trees along the route they had taken prior to their current camp. Spawn were seemingly, hot on the trail of the dwarves, despite the daylight.

Janzen bemoaned their situation. "That means Slavers and Spawn. What rotten luck! We can't move on without knowing what is before us."

Zenith made her decision without pause. "Okay, we stay and fight here unless a chance to escape presents itself. Does everyone agree?" All agreed and began to prepare themselves for the battle of their lives.

The Spawn were moving around the hill rather than going straight up it and soon there was movement below the hidden dell also. Zenith was pleased that her decision to stay put had been correct. It was clear now that the Spawn had not come out of the trees, until their Slavers had set an ambush for their likely escape route. As night closed in, the dwarves put out the fire except for a few embers which showed little light. They did not wish to be silhouetted against the light from the fire. They formed lines of arrows to fire, with burning ribbons of dry grass to allow them to see where the Spawn were. Janzen looked down the hill and all around them the noise of their enemy could be heard. The evil whining of the Spawn sounded akin to the whining that jackals make when they are under attack from a higher ranked animal. The noise was loud and frightening.

All ten dwarves moved to the summit of the hill, having first brought the fallen tree with them for it would place an obstacle before the Spawn. It was some small defence which they would have to come over and any advantage that was with Zenith and the others was needed now. The dwarves stood with their backs to the dell wall behind them. This was the only quarter that the Spawn could not easily attack them on due to the steep nature of the ground forming a protective wall of grass at the dwarves' backs.

The dwarves were indeed fortunate that neither Spawn nor Slavers had ever developed any need for bows and arrows. Zenith and Janzen had often discussed the enemy's weaknesses. They were certain that the Spawn did not have the intelligence to become proficient with such weapons and the Slavers were far too self-indulgent and lazy to try. The dwarves sent their prayers up to the Creator to witness and help them to extinguish as much evil, as their axes and hammers could unleash upon the enemy. There were tears streaming down the cheeks of many of the dwarves as they faced certain death at the hands of the enemy. The concern was for each of the others trapped in this place, rather than for themselves.

As the Spawn began to climb the hill, Zenith wiped her tears from her eyes and reminded all that their lives had been well lived, if rather shortened by their fate today. She gave an assurance that they all shared for one another, that they were certain of a kind hearing from the Creator when the time came to walk the Golden Path.

Once in range, the dwarves made good use of their flaming arrows. They aimed high and while two dwarves sent these towards the heavens the other eight picked out their targets as they came into range. As the Spawn came closer there were more casualties and the Slavers became the target. There were ten Slavers on the slopes before the dwarves and two fell to arrows. The hilltop was small in circumference. The Spawn screamed with rage as they charged into the ranks of the waiting dwarves. The greeting was fierce with the dwarves now battling hand to hand and fighting for their very lives. Zenith and Janzen were battling hard against the Spawn they faced. As soon as any dwarf felled a Spawn, another took its place.

One dwarf fell to be clawed by several Spawn and then another and then another. Now there were seven, including the girls, fighting up to ten Spawn at a time. The blood on the slopes was hampering the Spawn now and Zenith was able to make a snap decision. Calling for the others to follow her she leapt over the grass wall at their backs into the dell. The others followed and they landed on a Slaver and many Spawn, who were moving in the dell. Six dwarves had jumped and the other fell, trying to give the rest a few moments of respite. It was Dwaylin that made this sacrifice, for he was weakened by his wound and felt his core strength leaving him. He bravely twirled his mighty axe, wounding his foes, cutting off arms and claws. Even when he felt himself lifted from his feet by the Spawn, he continued to savagely strike at the arms that held him. Claws ripped into his flesh and still he fought. It was a Slaver that finally cut his throat and he gurgled his life blood away and darkness came upon him. He died a hero's death, although not one of his kindred saw his heroics. Unless it be that Ruth was espying his courage from above.

The six dwarves leapt to their feet after rolling upon landing. They lashed out left and right, lopping off any appendages that were in range. The Spawn were momentarily thrown off balance by this unexpected assault from above. Janzen and Zenith and the four surviving males slashed and fought their way down the slope. Claws, arms, heads fell from Spawn bodies. A surprised Slaver went down under an axe stroke from one of the males. The Spawn were at a disadvantage due to the speed of the dwarves' downhill charge. The dark hid most of their movement and they made good progress in the confusion all around them.

On and on they fought through the confused Spawn. The Slavers were struggling to see the dwarves progress as the moon had kindly nipped behind heavy cloud and so the Spawn were easier to confront and kill. Zenith headed straight down the hill and her dwarves followed in hot pursuit. She was in the heat of battle and had suffered no injury to that point, which she was finding quite astounding. The six reached the trees, a small copse of perhaps two hundred saplings, still in full leaf. It was sufficient to hide them from eyes above them. Zenith saw her chance and stopped abruptly and hit the ground, dragging Janzen with her. The four males charged on and hit Spawn on the other side of the trees. Zenith tried to rise and follow but she was held firmly by Janzen. It was too late.

The few seconds it took for the girls to react meant the time to follow had passed. They lay silently in the trees, while listening to the battle moving away from them. Slavers and Spawn skirted their trees for they were eager to be in on the kill. The dwarves ran on over flat ground, the four breathing heavily. One of the four tripped due to tired limbs and a slight injury to his thigh. He hit the ground hard. The three stopped and, as he came to his feet, the Spawn overtook them and, within thirty seconds, they were surrounded by at least a hundred Spawn, with more arriving all the time. The moon came out and the four could be seen having formed a square, each with battle axe at the ready.

The eldest dwarf spoke to the other three as they faced down the enemy on all sides. He was gasping for breath. "Today is a good day to meet the Creator if it be our fate boys."

The Spawn were growling and keen to rip into the dwarves, but were being held back by the Slavers who were arriving just as the dwarf spoke. The senior Slaver shouted out. "Six came down the slope. There are only four here! Kill these and then we will hunt down the other two enemies!"

The Spawn attacked as the command came to their minds and frenzy gripped them as they launched themselves upon the dwarves. Axes were swung, mighty blows pounded flesh and bone. The dwarves' desperate movements were so quick it was hard to see them and many Spawn fell, injured or dead. The defence required all four to achieve the impossible. The first seriously injured dwarf went down and was sliced up on the ground even as he lashed out with his dying breath. The three bravely battled on. The next to fall was a young dwarf. His throat was slashed, he fell dead to his knees as if he were at prayer. The last two dwarves were now back-to-back, desperately swinging their axes and shouting the dwarf chant of "Exodus!" in memory of their fallen comrades. The battle ended with Spawn piling on top of the dwarves who were soon dead. The Spawn clawed at each other to be in at the kill. They were so aggressive that the Spawn could not prevent themselves from slashing the dwarves to death despite a command from a Slaver not to kill.

It took a few minutes for the Spawn to calm down and the Slavers brought them to order. There were still hours of darkness to hunt in. The Spawn made their plan to search the ground for signs of the two missing dwarves. All the Slavers were pleased with the outcome so far, for they had taken revenge for their Princess Zhuxi, for the destruction of her brood. It meant they would be rewarded upon their return to Shimishi.

"Now there are just the two of us," Zenith sobbed, along with Janzen, as they moved away from the sounds of battle. Zenith was feeling ashamed. As the leader in the battle she had hoped the six would have a chance to confuse the enemy by staying in the copse and then charge out down the hill together. It had been a brave attempt to try and save her comrades, but she now realised the males used it as a chance to save her and Janzen. Janzen had seen it that way also. The two moved away and followed a stream, using it to hide their scent. They marched until dawn into the wilds, keeping to the trees wherever they could, until the hill behind them was no longer visible in daylight.

It was two hours after noon when Janzen suddenly fainted dead away. Zenith caught her as she fell. She held her in her arms and upon her knees. It was only then, that Zenith saw the trail of blood from Janzen dripping down her right side. The claws of the enemy had stabbed deep into her side. A long claw could be seen in the wound. Zenith pulled it out carefully and inspected the wound while Janzen was unconscious. Zenith started a fire when Janzen had fallen and began to heat water as soon as the fire was hot. She bathed the wound and bound it. She then checked her own wound, which was inflamed after all the fighting. Both were pretty much covered in blood from their victims in the battle. The shock that occurs after such slaughter began to take hold and Zenith knew that they might not have very long before they had company from the Spawn once more.

Zenith picked up the sound of water moving parallel to their course. It was at this point that Janzen woke and both went cautiously to the stream. There was no sign of the enemy yet and so they bathed in the shallow stream and washed the grime and blood from their bodies from tip to toe. They also decided to wash the clothes and battle garments as best they could before turning to the fire to start the drying process. Neither dwarf cared at all for the risks in lighting the fire. They were too exhausted from the activity and injuries for that.

Zenith made a brew of beer from their supplies and they munched on cold rations, as neither had the strength or interest in cooking. Once the girls had drunk a couple of flagons of dwarf ale, they began to recover themselves. Janzen looked very pale still but had the strength to stay awake for an hour, while Zenith talked through the choices they faced. "These are the options as I see it. We can run away from the Spawn until we are caught and, looking at you, I don't really think running anywhere is a good idea. We can stay where we are and meet the Spawn and their Slavers here. Neither of these choices appeal to me, so I offer you a third choice, which is to circle around and go on the offensive. If we double back, we might still be able to do damage to the enemy and take revenge on the Spawn for the loss of our fallen comrades. What do you think Janzen?"

"I think we avoid a fight until we are stronger, so it's the third choice for me."

The girls sat and discussed the fall of their brave comrades and both marvelled at the courage and valiant fight they had all managed to put up during the battle. Janzen was moved to speak. "It is such a shame that having created the world and us in his image, the Creator doesn't follow closely the ways in which his people suffer in his name. It might be that all the suffering of the dwarves could be stopped with a sweep of his arm."

Zenith looked at her dearest friend and spoke lovingly to her. "We are warriors and so expect a violent death. The hardest deaths are those captured and ruined by evil. I wonder myself why such things are allowed to happen. I even asked Lowe once, to explain why we suffer as we do. His answer was quite simple. He said that the Creator did not wish for evil as we now know it, to enter unto the world. In the beginning of creation evil was in the heavens and not upon the Earth. This world was exploded into existence by the Creator. Once the song of the Creator was already enacted in forming our universe, only then did Satan, the evil one, escape the angels and come crashing through time and space on his way to his prison, beyond our reach. It was just like Lowe to have that answer ready for a young dwarf. I bet he said it many times over to others."

"He said something quite similar to me, you know," said Janzen. "Yet, our holy men and women tell stories of how the first humans were not subjected to evil and they lived in

Edain, which is lost to us. The Elven it was, that sought out the dwarves to protect them and other good men from the evil that came to the Earth. Ruth is likely one of these and I would rather fight evil where I find it in the name of all things good, than allow it to spread through mankind to the ruin of us all. Our lives are going to be short-lived Zenith but still so worth it. Just think about the glorious experiences we have had in just fifty years of life. We have loved, been heartbroken, loved once again and seen so much beauty that is in the world. We will not have brought shame upon our ancestors. These are the treasures to send to the Creator of our memories when we are judged on that special day. I think we can go to our deaths with our heads held high, don't you?"

"Yes!" said Zenith, "we are blessed indeed to be allowed to strike a blow against the enemy. I would not swap my life for anyone else's, even if it has been shortened by my fate. We are indeed fortunate to know the enemy is evil incarnate. It would be so less certain if we were fighting other men in battle. That takes a great deal of faith to undertake and a certainty that we would be right to do so. We have both been spared at the least those hard choices."

The dwarves rested then for two hours before once more packing up. They left a clear trail onwards to the brook and then beyond it, before doubling back then, taking a trail to circle widely the Spawn that they suspected were behind them. As they walked, the sky above turned dark and a localised storm began to boil up in the clouds. Darker and darker the day grew, as sometimes happens in late summer, and as it grew more threatening above, it seemed to warm up at ground level. Zenith and Janzen moved slowly on their wide circle. They were pleased to see that heavy rain was likely to make the trail hard for the Spawn to follow.

It was evening before the dwarves were ready to stop. They found a cave tucked under the brow of a hill on the edge of the stream and decided this would be a good place to rest the night. They had fresh water in abundance and the cave was surprisingly dry. It might have been home to a large bear at some point, as there were scraps of broken bones of discarded small creatures, also fish skeletons cast about the cave. Both were too tired to have a care for what followed them, and the danger seemed remote in this very pleasant setting. There was a preponderance of dried lichen in the cave and the dwarves used this as a base for their fire, which was soon blazing nicely.

While Janzen created the fire, Zenith left her to gather firewood, which was dry, so that they had sufficient timber as fuel to last them through the night and into the next day. Zenith found an old, dry ash tree that had succumbed to the wind in some past adventure in a storm. She made three trips with battle axe, which made short work of the chosen stump. It dulled the blade somewhat and Zenith made a mental note to sharpen it before they departed this place.

The fire was set within the confines of the cave's ceiling just inside and under cover. They were fortunate that the wind direction came from behind, so that air would be drawn from the fire and the smoke billow away from the cave entrance, and when it rained the water would not reach the fire. Janzen was quickly exhausted and lit the fire. She set a pot above the flames with the skill of one used to such tasks, so that the fire was soon bringing the water to a boil. Zenith tended to Janzen's wound and then to her own. Both were feeling unwell and cold, which was not the normal experience for either and so they both were aware they were suffering from a fever.

Their labours finished and with more water boiling to make a soup of their rations, which contained vegetation and dried meats from their packs, they settled down and gave each other the comfort of their arms so as to be as warm as possible. They drank a prepared jug of ale, making it as strong as the supplies left would allow and both consumed more than enough for comfort. The rain began to fall as the wind also picked up and there was a fury in the storm which lashed at the trees and bushes opposite the cave. The smoke from the blazing fire was drawn away from the couple, but the heat was soon creeping into their bones and they grew warm and drowsy. Janzen was soon fast asleep in Zenith's arms. Zenith, for her part, knew that to sleep might be deadly, but within the hour her eyes were closed. She was lost in unconsciousness. Neither moved from the spot all night long.

They woke up at first light together, both feeling a bit startled by their surroundings. Zenith cursed herself for sleeping as she searched for enemies before her. There was nothing to be seen, just bushes, trees and the stream. "Sorry Janzen, I dropped off and slept all night it seems."

Janzen merely giggled. "A fine scout leader and watchout you are!" She scolded Zenith with false anger, before leaning back and stretching, as one waking in a warm bed after a good long sleep. Both chatted quite happily now that they were dry and rested. The food and ale had done their work on them both and the strength was returning to Zenith, who felt her fever had lifted in the night. Janzen still had a fevered brow but reported herself to be fit to travel when they were ready. Neither showed any urgency to leave the cave, which had become, in their minds, something of a haven. They sat together and ate a good breakfast of food cooked the evening before. As they ate, they looked out onto the stream, across the rebuilt fire which burned with little smoke.

The clouds had blown away and neither felt the wind blowing above them thanks to the cave and fire. The sun was out and the sky blue, with birds fleeting across their view on the wind, or held up in their flight as they turned, before tumbling gracefully into flight once more. The girls were subjected to their own air show and commented to one another how glorious it would be to fly off from danger and return home. The stream before them was now swollen beyond all recognition and flowed like a river past their door. The dwarves listened to the music from the stream as it glittered in its fast flow across the myriad of pebbles of all colours and hues. In the music of the stream, the notes played out in concert with the large ash and oak trees rustling in the background to the song of the flowing water, each playing its own part in the communion of nature. The dwarf girls sat in awe as the full vibrancy of the Creator's song for nature dawned in their minds and on their faces. All trace of grief and fear left them in that moment as they were drawn into the full glory of the natural world singing out just for them. Their senses were now entirely open to the deep feeling of warmth that touched their hearts as their senses gave them this wonderful gift straight from the Creator's song, working on their souls in their hour of need.

After a long time, while still comforting one another with their bodies, they smiled at each other and blessed the Creator for this most wonderful gift in a prayer they said together in recognition of his glory. Then they were Janzen and Zenith once more and packed the camp away and began their trek along the bank of the stream. With Janzen leading, they walked away from the last camp, still filled with the warmth of their experience. By the end of the day, they had turned almost full circle and were approaching the hill where they had first encountered the Spawn. Quietly and very carefully they moved forward, axes at the ready. Janzen stayed in the bushes out of sight, while Zenith crept up the slope in the failing light. She crouched low so that her form was almost completely covered by the fern growing on the slope. She reached the top of the hill and peered over into the dell behind the crest.

There was no sign of the enemy. Zenith signalled for Janzen to move to her position. It took Janzen longer to climb due to her physical frailty caused by her wound but soon she joined Zenith in the dell. All the bodies from the battle were gone. The rain had cleansed the hill from evil. No doubt the Spawn dealt with their own losses and the enemies in the usual way. Neither dwarf needed to say anything to one another about that.

Janzen tugged at Zenith's arm to get her attention. "I have changed my mind about revenge Zenith. I think we were caught up in grief and anger when we made the plan to attack those who killed our friends. Our bonds to one another are very powerful, as were our bonds to those who have died already on this mission. While you were on the hill, I had a revelation of sorts which makes me question our motives. Wisdom comes to me rarely as you know dear Zenith. I want you to consider what came to me and then I will follow your council with a clear conscience and a certain purpose." Zenith smiled back at Janzen and nodded her agreement for her to continue.

"Okay, Zenith this is it. We have fought two battles, one at our home which we survived thanks to our skill and the skill of our brethren. We undertook a mission to destroy the foul nest of our enemies. All would have been females, possibly not unlike the princess herself. Can you imagine the challenge of fighting and killing hundreds, or even thousands, of these winged creatures? We dwarves are a hardy folk, yet we have struggled to destroy the Spawn, which are mindless and need the Slavers to make them effective. What if this is evil's intention all along? Our home may already be burning for all we know, stuck out here in the wild, but if they are still standing then we need to warn them about this new threat. The Queen Yonlik is wholly capable of sending her masses of slaves against us without a single thought to the consequences for her brood. What if we dwarves are all that stand now between humanity and annihilation? We dwarves are the best fighters in the world and if it is left to other man tribes to defend themselves, they will surely fail. Human men have not developed enough to see through the wiles of the enemy as we have. They lost the power to determine good from evil and we alone in the world have this skill now. Unless the elves from Edain walk the Earth still. I fear they have abandoned the Earth or passed on like the visionary Ruth who advised Lowe. If I am right in this thought process, then our duty is very clear. Lowe's plan was initially to give battle and survive. Then it changed to put fear into our enemies. Lowe may have succeeded in his mission to that extent but if he doesn't destroy Yonlik, and I don't think he can. Then we are, at best, buying ourselves a little time before that foul creature sets free an enemy we won't have any chance to defeat. I do not trust myself in this state of mind to be sure, but I think we need to warn our folk against the possibility that we may soon face a very different threat. It is not worth both our lives to kill these few Slavers and Spawn, even if they don't kill us first. Let us head back to our mountain home and see for ourselves what goes on there. If the dwarves stand then we can join them and get our revenge later."

Zenith looked hard into the face of her friend and saw her love shining back at her. Zenith was quiet for a long time as she weighed up the argument put to her. It seemed to her that Janzen might be feverish. She might be wounded, careworn from the death of their friends. She herself was suffering nigh as much as Janzen, although her fever had left her for the moment.

Eventually Zenith gave her answer. "Well! This is a new turn of events! I think it is you who should be leading from now on! Whether you are quite mad I can't be sure, but it seems you may have stumbled onto a scenario which will need to be discussed broadly with our folk if they still live. What you describe is truly a terrifying scenario and one that I hope is not true. The evidence is there though, in the nest we dwarves destroyed. If what you propose is true, then you and I must warn our kin and the rest of mankind about what is coming. It now makes more sense as to why an angel and an elf have gone to all the trouble of sending their dire warning to us. We would be fools indeed to ignore it. So okay I agree. We go home!"

Janzen hugged Zenith and the warmth between them was stronger than ever. They moved back down the hill in stealth mode and disappeared into the copse of trees at the base of the hill. Where before they moved with caution and anxiety, now they moved with clear intention and their pace was faster and both felt strength return to their bodies. Little did they know that only a mile behind them and hot on their trail were the vengeful Spawn, who had been tracking them bent on their destruction. Zenith spoke to Janzen with a whole newfound respect, as she had shown great wisdom in how she had portrayed their situation and that was to be admired. She thought to herself that Janzen was a person in balance between logic and emotion despite the situation she found herself in and to have been capable of unravelling the challenges evil might be setting was indeed a sign of great wisdom. She loved her for it.

CHAPTER EIGHTEEN
IN THE LAIR OF YONLIK

Lowe and the dwarves moved down the tunnel with caution as the noise of the screaming slave came to an end. The Slaver was obviously content that punishment could cease. Lowe peered around a rocky bend and saw he was at the entrance to a rocky chamber that was a holding pen for slave servants. The Slavers were still there but with their backs to Lowe as they left the room. Lowe watched their muscled backs go through a doorway opposite to his position. He signalled the dwarves to follow. They crossed the hall in single file, ignoring the slaves. The last thing they needed was to organise an escape with terrified and damaged slaves before they had engaged the enemy. All the slaves looked frightened as the dwarves passed by. Lowe continued down the passage where the Slavers had gone. The passage went sharply downhill and around, almost like a helter-skelter. Lowe saw the Slaver's back and hit the Slaver through his neck, taking the head off in one swipe.

Another Slaver, just in front, turned to see what the noise had been and his head left its shoulders with a look of surprise mixed with pain. The dwarves sprang over the bodies and charged into the chamber at the base of the twisting tunnel. The next opening was onto a large hall which housed fifty Slavers. Lowe and the others leapt at the Slavers. A few fell quickly but then the rest rallied and carried the fight to the dwarves. They screamed as they attacked the dwarves. These were strong Slavers and they fought hard, and true battle was commenced.

Lowe moved to the right with Joygrim at his side and Lowin moved left behind Lowgrim. The rest followed to support their leaders. Lowgrim saw the entrance into the hall that was on his left. He could not prevent two Slavers from retreating that way. He split the head of a third Slaver who tried to leave the hall and was then faced with a fight for his life, fending off Slavers left and right. Lowin moved with him and the dwarves formed a circle around the doorway, preventing any more Slavers escaping.

With all the dwarves now fighting, it was Lowe who continued to press the enemy back until they had either fallen or were cramped with their backs against the Spawn facing Lowgrim and Lowe and the others. In the ten minutes that had felt like an hour, the hall was theirs. Lowin motioned to Lowe to carry on down into the lair for she knew they had to make a bigger impact on the enemy than that which they had managed to do so far. Lowe led the way once more and as he and Lowgrim led the others, the passage widened so they could move two abreast. Behind them the sounds of pursuit could now be heard. Obviously, those Slavers that escaped death rallied their Spawn and set off the alarm to warn the rest of the lair that they were under attack.

The next hall was great in size and was Shimishi's audience room. The enemy was coming up from the deeps of the lair. They charged into the audience room. The dwarves met the assault of the Slavers and Spawn head on once more. The Slavers were savage, the Spawn frenzied, but they were in the minority. Only eighteen, including four Slavers and for once the dwarves outnumbered the enemy. This made it simple enough for the dwarves to despatch them quickly and head on further down into the lair.

Shimishi had been in the audience room when the clarion call sounded in her mind. She ordered her Slavers and servants immediately to hold their ground while she left to descend further into her chambers, for she guessed that she might be at risk if she remained with so few of her Slavers about her. As she moved, she became all too aware of the battle cries and screams behind her. She heard the clarion calls from the dwarves. She listened as they slaughtered all before them. Her anger and her fear were awakened. In her chambers Princess Shimishi mentally summoned her forces to come to her with all haste. She knew that much of her personal guard was based above her and she could only call on perhaps a hundred Slavers to aid her in her own defence.

Fifty Slavers awaited her as she entered her chamber and she instructed them to stand at the entrance from which she had just arrived. Her intention was to delay the dwarves if they sought her, until the forces above could descend to attack them. Lowe and the dwarves crashed into the Slavers and pushed them back several paces by the ferocity of their assault, prior to the Slavers managing to hold them. Several Slavers fell to the axes of the dwarves and these were replaced as more of Shimishi's forces arrived from below her chambers. Blood was being shed close to Shimishi and she sent out another call to arms in a state of alarm as the dwarves continued to slaughter her best fighters. Lowe was fighting like a dwarf half his age and Lowgrim was fighting hard to match his father's efforts. It was Joygrim who spotted Shimishi and called to her mother Lowin that the enemy was before them. She in turn called for throwing axes. Courage began to return to Shimishi for she counted eighty of her Slavers in the defence. She began to prowl at the rear, urging her Slavers on and they responded as best they could.

Joygrim and Lowin judged the distance between them and their enemy to be thirty paces. In quick succession they threw two axes each over the Spawn and aimed at the Princess Shimishi. Shimishi could not use her wings to gain elevation and so she did the only other possible option and crouched with her wings wrapped about her, attempting to ward off the incoming missiles. Fear had frozen her to the spot and in that second the fate of the whole campaign rested on the accuracy of the throws. The first axe hit Shimishi high on her wings and embedded into her left shoulder. The second axe hit a tenth of a second later and pierced her wing and embedded in her thigh. She screamed in pain and awoke Queen Yonlik in her terror.

Yonlik was far beneath her but her message to the lair was angry and powerful. "They wound the princess, kill them all!"

The third axe thrown glanced off the enclosing wings, cutting through the fibres that gave the wings strength. The fourth axe buried itself in the right shoulder and she fell, crumpled and bloody to the floor in a faint. Sixty Slavers were still standing. Three dwarves had died since entering the room. A few late arriving Slavers saw the princess on the floor and quickly ran to her and began to carry her out of the chamber and further down into the lair. Two more axes struck home, but these hit the Slavers rather than Shimishi and she was carried away, unconscious of everything around her.

The senior Slaver in the defence now ordered a steady retreat toward the entrance where Shimishi had left. The dwarves pushed home their assault and were able to kill another ten of the retreating Slavers before they reached what was another tunnel. The senior Slaver then called on all Slavers to stand their ground. Lowe could see that it would take too much time to kill the enemy. He knew the enemy would soon have them trapped. He called a halt and the dwarves retreated, back to the entrance from which they had come. The Slavers did not move from the entrance. The instruction came from a higher source now than the Slaver and it was very clear for every Slaver in the lair. Move and you die...

Lowe and the rest of his kin that were still standing retreated up the tunnel. They moved as quickly as they could back through the audience chamber which now had Spawn and Slavers aplenty to prevent them reaching the kitchen, but nothing was moving at all. The Spawn and Slavers merely watched with their eyes fixed on the dwarves as they moved through the room and into the tunnel leading to the kitchen. A trail of dwarf blood followed them wherever they went, as several dwarves were carrying quite deep wounds and there was no time to rest. A dwarf fainted in the kitchen from loss of blood and was picked up by his fellows. The dwarves could not believe their luck as the only thing that they heard was their own footsteps. As time went on, they became fearful of the silence itself and worked hard not to create noise. Lowe was sweating hard by the time he reached the secret passage leading outside. Lowin was behind him with her children following. The last dwarf was dragging the unconscious one behind him. The miracle had happened. seventeen dwarves leapt out of the secret door and were met by their kin who were still on watch. When the last man was out of the secret door, Lowgrim set a firebomb to oil they carried for such a purpose and set it alight. The dwarves retreated into the woods back to the base they had made prior to the day of the attack.

The mighty Yonlik left her hiding place deep in the earth and ascended to save her daughter. Her rage was plain to see to every servant of evil. Any slave or servant in her way was swatted like a fly and sent crashing against a wall, receiving multiple injuries, and left unconscious. All was perfectly still for her order held firm and no living thing could deny her, at least not her own servants. When Yonlik saw her daughter's wounds she was sent into a cruel and violent temper. She crushed the life from three Slavers in her fury where they stood. Yonlik was grown in her anger and no longer small. She could not follow whoever had committed these acts in her home even if she wished to, for she was far too big to leave her lair unless the mountain itself was split in two.

Had the Slavers not moved to deliver Shimishi to their mistress, then Yonlik would have been powerless to help, but fortunately for Shimishi the tunnel from her quarters was large enough to admit the queen. Shimishi came back to consciousness and was in great pain. Yonlik removed the axes which was all the evidence she needed that it was dwarves who had dared to attack her lair. Yonlik poured her poisonous hatred into Shimishi and Shimishi screamed in pure agony. These screams were heard all over the lair and even outside. Eight hundred thousand Spawn and Slavers alike fell on their knees, cowering in terror of what this would mean for them. They stayed still and awaited a command from their queen.

Slowly, Shimishi began to respond to her mother's evil. She too began to expand in size, even as her wounds were closing, to leave cold white scars on her body and wings. When her eyes opened, they were blood red. Yonlik spoke to her daughter. "Your sisters have betrayed us! They have paid with their lives and will suffer endlessly at the hands of Satan who assures me he has already begun their torment! Alas that he cannot personally slay those who have hurt thee so!" Her voice was rasping and cruel but like melted butter to Shimishi.

"Fear not mother. I will take my revenge on these dwarves as soon as I may, for you have healed me and removed any doubt and fear from my mind. Your essence is a great gift to me!"

Queen Yonlik was still angry and spoke again. "Silence Shimishi! I am weakened by this foolishness. In order to save your precious hide, I have had to pour some of my life's essence into your puny body. Had your sisters not failed me I would have slaughtered you where you stand! Don't look so shocked! You, who were to be a powerful force for my battle, have allowed yourself to be mortally wounded by a handful of dwarf scum in my own home. As soon as you are fit you will leave my lair! You will take the halls of the dwarves to live in, or you will live nowhere."

Shimishi herself was now squirming like a coiled snake,

filled with anger and equally in hatred for the queen but her most clear sign was of fear. Yonlik began to laugh at her daughter. "I did not cure you to then murder you Shimishi, although it is tempting as I see what a craven creature I have spawned! You are brighter than your sisters, I will admit, but they were more purposeful than you will ever be. You want power without paying the price! Well now you will pay the price to me! It seems your sister Zhuxi has spawned some queen eggs which are in my keeping. I want thousands more from you, before you leave, so I suggest you start seducing every male in this lair until you succeed. Only when you have achieved this will I forgive your carelessness."

Yonlik left her daughter and returned to her deep home. She was ruminating what this event meant for her plans. It was not entirely clear to her that she needed Shimishi, but now that she was weakened, she needed to rest for a long time and draw on the link with Satan, her spouse, to recover her former strength and consider her own rise to power that had been her only plan since the dawn of her arrival on the Earth. 'Yes,' she thought. 'If Shimishi creates daughter eggs then my plan may change for the better. I will feed on the essence of men until the world only knows my offspring. When I am fully recovered I will open the pestilence from its housing deep in the Earth and take it unto myself. I will be invincible, and in the end, I will be victorious!' Yonlik was quite insane.

Shimishi began to recover from her fear too quickly for her own good. She was swollen with fury, but it was a good reminder that she had been given by Yonlik. Shimishi would do as commanded of course. Shimishi smiled to herself. She had been granted another chance to live out her life as a queen! Gone were the challenges of her sisters for power sharing. She also knew her mother's only weakness. 'Mother can't lay eggs. She has grown too old! Oh, how very glorious! Yonlik needs me more than I need her now.' A sadistic warmth spread across her body as she called for all her human slaves to be summoned to her quarters to receive her services. 'Thousands of eggs mother,' she thought to herself. 'I will give you a million!'

Shimishi now turned her thoughts to the dwarves who had come so close to killing her. "They must pay with their very souls," she told her generals. They already had twenty hours head start and Shimishi immediately ordered two thousand Spawn and Slavers to track them and kill them. Shimishi then sent five hundred Spawn on the trail from the dwarves' last camp, which had very quickly been discovered after her forces were released by Queen Yonlik.

Fifteen hundred were despatched over the river, for Shimishi guessed they would seek their homes for safety. The orders were clear, for once the enemy was destroyed utterly for the attack on her person, the troops were to return. Shimishi knew the war with the dwarves would have to wait until she had fulfilled Yonlik's requirements and she wanted to have her forces about her to ensure her safety, for fear had not left her entirely.

CHAPTER NINETEEN
THE DWARVES RUN

Lowe was encouraged by his wife and children to take the lead in the dwarves' retreat after the attack upon Shimishi. His pace was one all the younger dwarves could follow. He worked hard to keep his dwarf trot constant. The exhilaration they had all felt when they managed to leave the lair of Yonlik was leaving him. He was feeling his vulnerability to normal anxiety tinged with fear for those who followed him. Initially, his flight with the others was fuelled by adrenalin, which pumped through his veins, giving aid to his speed. He was now running on reserves of energy common to all dwarves. His stamina was good for his age and he moved still with confidence after five hours without a break. He hoped to run for another three hours until late in the afternoon.

The day was cool, with a breeze which brought the relief of a light shower of rain which had helped him to stay cool. Lowe knew this first day was crucial if they were to escape. He could not understand why the Slavers and Spawn had not killed them, or why they had suddenly frozen. He knew something important had happened, but he didn't understand what it was, so while he ran, with his wife Lowin beside him, he talked to her at intervals. What happened was unexpected and Lowe wondered if Ruth had intervened, or even the Angel Deborah. Lowin and he dismissed this thought and concluded that Queen Yonlik had been summoned after the successful attack on Shimishi. He guessed it had something to do with her injury. He also knew that they had not killed her outright. Had they succeeded in this, then her Spawn and Slavers would have perished.

Lowe did not know for certain that they were being chased but his sixth sense told him they were in grave danger, and he always listened to this sense within himself, for it had always served him well. The main group of dwarves halted for an hour, some two hours before sunset. Lowe gave Lowgrim and Joygrim and five of the fittest dwarves the task of going before them. His thought was to arrange the river crossing with urgency so that they could spend the night on the opposite bank of the river. It was then a dash for home, assuming the dwarf stronghold still stood. Cold meats and berries were the order of the day, washed down with the last of the dwarf ale.

Lowgrim and Joygrim went ahead willingly, for they knew the danger was very real for them now. Seven dwarves ran at the same pace as set by Lowe earlier that day. They could have gone quicker but they knew they might meet foes at any time and so wished to be able to offer battle if they needed to. They reached the river before dark and immediately set about launching axes with lines attached as they had done before. Lowgrim was across the river, setting and fixing extra lines to ease the crossing for those following. They did not have long to wait for Lowe and the rest to catch them up. The dwarves fell to the bank of the river, all fairly gasping for air. Lowe was close to collapse but had not spared himself in his attempt to stay ahead of an enemy he feared but could not see.

As the dwarves recovered, they were pulled across the river supported by tight lines on both banks. Lowin and Lowe went over near the vanguard who were securing the ropes. Lowin had to support her husband by being pulled while holding on to him. The race to the river had taken everything that Lowe had in the tank. Once across, the others followed and pulled the axes out, leaving only the marks in the ground. This was on Lowe's orders. Only one hour later, as the dwarves sat in the dark in their wet clothes, all snug together for warmth, they saw lights on the opposite bank. "Torches of the enemy," said Joygrim. "It's time to go mother."

Lowin and Lowgrim helped Lowe to his feet and they began the march away from the enemy. Lowin spoke to Lowe in the darkness, telling him how proud she was with his effort today. Lowe was too tired to comment much. He ached from head to toe and was concentrating on moving one foot in front of the other. Joygrim was the last to leave the river. She waited to see what the enemy were going to do before setting off after her company.

The dwarves had been forced to rest after another two hours to allow those most effected to recover some more. Joygrim arrived in camp an hour later and reported to Lowe and the others. "Good news," she said, "the Spawn can't cross the river in the dark it seems. They made half a chain of linked Spawn out into the main channel but could not maintain the links and at least ten Spawn were swept away with screams of terror. We can thank the Creator for their fear of water, or they would have been right on our tails by now. The Slavers made the decision to camp it seems and so we have some breathing space."

Now Lowin took command for Lowe, who was fast asleep. She ordered a blazing fire to be lit, so that they could get dry and warm. They all needed to eat something hot, with the added opportunity of making a brew of ale. This would remove the cold chill from their bones and help them recover from the horrors and stress of the battle. "If we are caught cold by Spawn on this side of the river then so be it! It will be our fate. I think it will take the Spawn at least another five hours to catch up with us on this bank so we may as well use the time to prepare for battle as best we can."

Everyone was cold, except Joygrim who was hot from her recent run. She fell to sleep while the others worked on the camp. Lowe awoke to a warm fire and a nearly cool pot of ale. He made no comment about the decisions made, for he had been out cold when Lowin had taken over his leading role. The company was fed, watered and dry of body when they broke camp five hours later and that was all that mattered.

Lowgrim was concerned. The wind was blowing their scent down the river and he guessed that not only the fire's scent would reach the Spawn before long. The dwarves had been moving for four hours and were under the morning clouds, making their way directly to the hill where they had camped previously. The very same hill that had seen Janzen, Zenith and the others trapped upon.

Lowgrim dropped back from the marching dwarves by half a mile or so. He listened carefully for a few minutes and, upon hearing nothing other than the natural sounds around him, carried on tracking his own company. After another two miles he stopped to listen once more. At first, he could only discern the noises of nature, but after a few minutes he became aware that the birds were quiet, where before they had been singing. This was enough to tell him that the enemy was drawing near. He wasted no more time and sprinted after the company to close the gap. Joygrim was in his sight after ten minutes. She was waiting for him on the trail and as soon as Lowgrim caught sight of her sent a cut-throat sign to her using his axe. Joygrim turned and sped after the company, leaving Lowgrim to his lonely, now slower dwarf run now that his sister could deliver the message.

Lowgrim found Joygrim waiting for him. "Well met Lowgrim!" she called out as he came up to her. "We are making for the high ground we found earlier. The summit will be as good a defence position we can hope for in the circumstances."

Lowgrim looked serious. "We will be in a fight by midnight I fear," he said as he jogged along.

Joygrim grinned back at him and replied, "I hope you kept your axes and hammer dry brother mine. It would be shameful to have them slip off the necks of the enemy!" Lowgrim was buoyed by her youthful high spirits in such grim circumstances and grinned back at her, saving his breath for the dash to catch up with the dwarf company.

Lowin was pleased to see her children catch up with the party. Lowe was engaged in discussion with all the dwarves around them as they walked now at a fast pace. All the dwarves were feeling uncomfortable, as if they were being watched in the early evening setting sun. The wilderness had gone quiet around them when normally they would be hearing lots of birds and other animals that live in the great woods. Wolves and bears were common enough in the land as were deer and cattle, which were mostly wild. These were wary of dwarves in large numbers for good reason, but many other species should have been audible to their hearing now. Lowin ordered an occasional halt, mostly to listen to the forest around them.

Lowgrim, who was well versed in the wild, spoke to Joygrim and shared with her his thought that they were being overtaken by the enemy. Where they stopped tonight would be crucial to their survival. Joygrim spoke to her mother and Lowe as they walked. Lowe accepted what was said without question and ordered all the dwarves into a steady dwarf trot. They ran for two hours and came to the hill where they had camped before. Lowe did not waste time checking the surroundings but ran straight for the summit. The others followed.

All thirty-seven dwarves were tasked with making their camp on the summit with the walls of the dell at their rear. Lowe saw the recent marks of other dwarves and Spawn tracks all over the summit. Lowgrim reported to Lowe that there were dwarf tracks up to the hill and a few heading down the slope from which they had just climbed. Lowgrim spoke up. "It appears to me that a band of dwarves was attacked on the hill by hundreds of Spawn. There is old blood staining the grass below where the recent storm hasn't completely washed it away. I guess that some escaped, at least from the summit. They could not have run far before the Spawn would have been on them. I think they must have come from home for some purpose not known to us. Or perhaps they were a nomad family group just escaping the battle." In any event it seems that the dwarves did not survive.

Lowe thanked his son who returned to his labours. Lowe hoped it was the former and not evidence of the fall of the dwarf kingdom. In any event they were alone and vulnerable on this hill but there was little choice in where to camp. Lowe guessed the enemy was all around them, waiting for dark to make an assault on the hill.

Joygrim and the others were busy preparing fires one hundred metres from the summit. They set the dry wood they had carried up the hill into as big a pile of timber as they could collect. As it grew dark, they poured oil from a few oil bombs onto the timbers. These would be lit if the Spawn attacked to aid shooting. It was going to be a cloudy night, unfortunately for the dwarves, which would make aiming and hitting targets harder without moonlight.

As the night closed in, the sound of Spawn groaning could be heard from all four quarters. Fires were lit at the base of the hill so as not to light the slopes but so the enemy could eat before the coming battle. Lowe and the others prepared their weapons. Lowin sat with her children and Lowe. "It looks as though our luck has run out husband! Still, I can't complain, for we have done some serious damage to the enemy."

Lowe looked at her and smiled. "That is true Lowin, we have done well, but I would have preferred to have killed the princess rather than merely incapacitate her. I would have enjoyed the destruction of that lair with all its Spawn. I fear our cousins at home have a short period of respite before the evil hordes once more attack them, if indeed they still live."

Lowin was clear. "I believe the dwarves live and they fight on and of that much I am certain. We must do the same." Lowin raised her voice for all to hear. "Dear kindred all. We have a fierce battle on our hands and one I fear we will not survive! Be in no doubt that our lives have been well lived and if fate should save you by some chance, then take it and carry word back to our kin. Tell them of our feats against the enemy."

A chorus of approval came from every dwarf. Lowe stood up. "They are coming!" he cried.

The dwarves fired at the timber collected earlier and five blazes went up. Instantly, with the aid of the fires, they saw Spawn already climbing towards them. They used their bows and arrows, killing many of the enemy as they laboured up the slope. There could be no escape and all the dwarves said their goodbyes to one another while the enemy came on. The last few arrows were spent and then the hand to claw contest commenced. The dwarves were fierce in defence. They slew Spawn and Slaver alike, as they came into range. The Spawn were frenzied and would have quickly overrun the dwarves by sheer volume of numbers had they been on the flat, but on the high ground with nowhere to go to the dwarves stood and killed out. Three hours came and went. Ten dwarves had fallen and had been ripped to pieces by the Spawn. The dwarves continued to battle on until the dawn came and the Spawn stopped the assault. They dragged their own dead off the hill and the dwarves took the respite gratefully. Lowin asked Lowe why they had stopped.

"I don't know," said Lowe, "I don't think it is the dawn that has made them retreat, but something has taken priority over killing us, at least for a while." He slipped to the floor and let his axe rest on his knees. His hammer was at his side. Lowin and the others joined him. They were now twenty-seven.

General Wahushi, the Spawn general and escapee, had watched the battle from below. His fellow Slavers had suddenly dropped to the ground, dead as stone, two days previously. He knew instantly that Princess Zhuxi was dead. He thanked the devil he was a Shimishi bred slave, or he would have joined them. He was surprised to feel quite so confident with the loss of his fellow Slavers and he examined his emotions and found once more that the darkness within him had no sense of personal loss and no concern at all for Zhuxi, now she was dead. A thought deep within his cruel and evil will, came to mind and told him he was meant for greater things, even greater than the princesses. This selfish, spiteful thought, together with his hatred for his past allies, who were now dead, aided his sense of superior confidence.

Wahushi came upon the vengeful Spawn that were chasing some poor prey. He made himself scarce while he looked upon the horde, which seemed to number about fifteen hundred. He sighted a female Slaver who was with a score of Spawn on a scouting party away from the main group. It was in the middle of the day and the Spawn were huddled in the shade while the Slaver sat and ate her meal. She was keeping her Spawn hungry. She knew that not feeding them would make them more aggressive and she wished to feed them when the enemy was trapped.

Wahushi crept into the camp and hit the Slaver unconscious from behind. He was so efficient at rape from practice that the Spawn never moved. Wahushi pleasured himself on the Slaver's unconscious form and took pleasure in digging his claws into her flesh. As he carried out this hideous form of torture, he linked his mind with hers. She was unconscious and so unaware of the intrusion, but he used his superior evil powers to absorb her thoughts and, with it, her control over the Spawn in her keeping.

Wahushi finished with the Slaver. He ordered the Spawn to sleep, and they fell to the ground instantly. Wahushi knew he would have to deal with his victim when she woke up. A cruel thought came to him deep within his mind when she began to stir. He pinned her body under his full weight as she came into consciousness. Wahushi waited until she was aware of him and then proceeded to strangle her. She lost consciousness again. When she came around, he repeated his cruelty until her neck broke. The evil within him was pleased with the sensations of hatred Wahushi had put into his appalling act against the Slaver. He woke the Spawn, ordered a fire to be lit, and he and the Spawn feasted on her corpse until it grew dark once more. Wahushi and the Spawn moved off to join the ranks of the horde.

Wahushi waited to see how the enemy dwarves, who were trapped on the hill, would fare against insurmountable odds against them. He enjoyed watching the battle unwind and cared not at all for the losses and enjoyed the report from a Spawn that ten dwarves had fallen. When he was ready, he approached the senior Slavers who were safe at the bottom of the hill. Wahushi introduced himself as the general to Zhuxi. He told them his princess was dead at the hands of dwarves and he had barely escaped with his life after her fall. They queried how he had survived. He told them he was born of Shimishi and had been ordered by her to lead Zhuxi's forces. He explained that his second-in-command, appointed in the field by Zhuxi, failed to protect the princess., Wahushi, had killed her outright in his rage.

"I have important news for the queen's ears and the ears of Shimishi only. You will obey my orders!" said Wahushi. The Slavers were intimidated by this senior Slaver and so capitulated and agreed he was now in command. No mention was made of the missing Slaver female. The Slavers saw his control over the Spawn that were with him. They knew that he must have met the female Slaver and taken her control to be his own. Wahushi ordered a halt to the attack and the Spawn and Slavers withdrew. Wahushi had his own priority, and the death of the dwarves was not his first one. Their deaths would come soon enough. Wahushi ordered all the females Slavers to his tent and ravished each one until he was confident he had full control over all the Spawn. He ordered a feast with all the Slavers and Spawn and the dead were cooked. Spawn ate Spawn and Slavers ate dwarf. He let the day pass, while keeping a secure circle around the dwarves at the base of the hill. When they died that night, it would be Wahushi's victory to carry back to the queen.

In the interim, the dwarves were using the respite to recover arrows and prepare for another battle. Their situation was hopeless, but they were proud and prepared themselves once more for a long battle. There were now twenty-seven dwarves to face the original horde, whose numbers had been depleted by them killing two hundred Spawn and Slavers. As the evening light began to fade the dwarves watched as another five hundred Spawn joined the battle ranks of the enemy. Lowe grimaced, as did the others. They guessed rightly that these were the Spawn who had tracked them to the river. It seemed a long time ago now. Lowgrim spoke for all present when he said that their luck had finally run out. They said their goodbyes again and thanked the Creator for the respite of another day and then girded their loins to face their final battle. The Spawn attacked in renewed frenzy as soon as it grew dark.

Lowe and the rest retained the advantage of height. All the dwarves were skilled and brave fighters. They held the high ground with twenty-seven dwarves, side by side, at the most advantageous point they could find. As the killing of Spawn commenced, Lowin stood in the centre with seven of her kin and their role was to plug the gaps if a dwarf was thrown off balance or knocked off their feet. This enabled Lowin to support her kin and save injured dwarves from certain death. She knew that they could not win this battle, but they could still hold together. Her thought was to hold until morning and then see what came next. The others knew the stakes were stacked against them. Once more the dwarves lit fires on the hill and used their arrows to best effect. The enemy pressed them hard. The Spawn were hungry for dwarf blood. The fighting was desperate and Lowin and the seven dwarves swapped with the dwarves in the frontline whenever they were disadvantaged.

As the night went on the twenty-seven became twenty-three. Lowe was knocked down twice and pulled to safety, while one of the two dwarves left in the centre replaced him in the line. Lowin dressed wounds as the dwarves fought on. She took her turn in the line. The dead hampered the assault on the hill for the Spawn could not always pull their dead away to reach the dwarves.

For the dwarves' part, they used the extra time to ensure each stroke of axe or hammer was a killing stroke as often as they could make it so. They sang battle songs and beat a rhythm as they fought. There was no better way to die for a dwarf in those times than to do so in defence of the clan. Lowin shed tears for the bravery of her kin. All the dwarves cried during the battle. Lowin knew that if they had been fighting on the flat, they would have been swept away hours ago by sheer weight of numbers. Lowin was also aware that the Slavers were not committing themselves to the battle. Slavers were much stronger than the Spawn and harder to kill, but in this fight, they did not commit their numbers to the battle.

During his rest period Lowe shouted encouragement to his kin. "The Slavers still fear death at our hands!" This and other encouraging words were mixed with compliments on particularly good offensive strokes. Joygrim fought next to Lowgrim and their banter could be heard across the lines as they battled to stay alive. Adrenalin was keeping the dwarves alive. Anxiety for each other, mixed with fear of the evil they faced, kept them on their feet and fighting.

As the dawn came up, the Spawn slowed and withdrew with the rising of the sun. Another two hundred Spawn had died and as many again injured. They pulled many of the dead behind them as they retreated down the hill. All the dwarves that had survived the night stood in silence as the Spawn moved down the hill. They were too tired for much else. All the dwarves carried injuries, and some were quite deep cuts to fore-arms and legs. Lowin set herself to dress wounds with Joygrim. Lowgrim and others collected the few arrows left on the hill. A fire was built up once more and the company cared for itself.

Lowe was feeling his age again. He was very stiff of limb, more so than the younger dwarves. He needed help to get to his feet and walked around the camp to ward off the ache in his muscles. He complimented every dwarf and listened to the tales told of the battle as he did so, with one eye on the enemy at the base of the hill. By noon all the chores that could be done to prepare for the coming night, were completed.

Lowin spoke for all as she addressed her kin. "We have done well to live this long, but unless unseen help arrives, I fear we will die tonight. It will be a good death and I know you will all be on the march along the Golden Path with me when we are defeated. Fear no ill! We are the Creator's servants and our duty has been met and we have all held true to our purpose."

As they sat looking out down the hill, a window from another world opened. A female voice called out to Lowe. All the dwarves turned their heads to see Ruth standing in the frame, casting a shadow into the dell despite the height of the sun. "It's time to go from this place Lowe. Bring your kin through the window. Fear not! For you are to be messengers to the future of mankind." Lowe stood up stiffly and without saying a word walked through the window. The others followed him with amazement etched on their faces.

Ruth stood tall in front of the dwarves as they came through the portal. She asked the dwarves to sit upon the grass. All the dwarves were grateful for being able to get comfortable once more. The ground was spongy in texture and comfortable for all. Ruth offered refreshments of fruit and water and all the dwarves accepted this gratefully. All were in awe at meeting Ruth in the flesh. Lowgrim and the young dwarves were wide eyed at her beauty. Joygrim and Lowin were also totally occupied by Ruth's presence. The dwarves soon found that their wounds and injuries from the battles they had been fighting were healed. Their minds were free of the constant fear they had lived with for so long. It was as if the memories remained, but the pain attached to them had been resolved entirely. They each enjoyed a sense of purity that they marvelled at given the amount of killing they had endured.

Ruth explained to them that they were in a place between the Third and Fourth Levels of the Golden Path and that here no evil or bad experience could come. She told them of her hopes for them and what was required of them. It seemed that they talked for days on end in this place while Ruth schooled them on what they would find on the Third Level of Earth in the Year Twenty Twenty-One. Ruth told them where they would go and what they would find there and taught them their mission. Lowe, Lowin and the others felt neither tired nor hungry during this time and were filled with love for one another. Their children and kin were also experiencing pure love in the light of this place. It was not a hormone driven love but a deep, spiritual experience. They were all content. The losses they had experienced were remembered but the grief and pain were washed clean from them. They talked among themselves and agreed that they felt reborn in this place.

When Ruth was certain that they were ready for the challenges of the twenty first century, she sent them through the portal. Lowe gave his thanks to Ruth, as did all the others. He stepped through the portal and found himself in a walled garden of a large building. The others followed him and once all the dwarves were through, Ruth's figure filled the space in the window, now casting a brightness on a cloudy day into the garden where the dwarves were stood. They looked back at the window into her world. Ruth wished them good fortune and the portal closed. They were alone once more on Earth.

"Come on," said Lowe. "let's go and wake this twenty first century up!"

* * *

Wahushi was furious when his Spawn attacked the hill at dusk. His enemies and the victory he had sought had been stolen from him. He could not fathom what had happened. He took his anger out on the Slavers with his usual cruelty before turning the Spawn to return to the lair of Princess Shimishi and the queen. He was less certain of his welcome there with the loss of a victory, but he had no choice but to roll the dice and take his chances that they wouldn't murder him on first sight.

CHAPTER TWENTY
QUEEN ELIZABETH II COUNCIL

Queen Elizabeth sat in her private rooms and listened to her wisest counsellors as they tried to sum up the circumstances that had buried the truths about the Spawn and the evil that had been forgotten. The bishop had been summoned and now spoke to the queen. The bishop had been shocked by the revelations that the queen had shared with him and had wondered whether age and duty had finally overcome her mind. That was until he was introduced to the dwarves and listened to their rather clear understanding of his world.

The bishop spoke quietly to the queen. "Portals to another world of God's creation it seems, has now become the focus for man in his search beyond this mortal plane. I must admit, your Majesty, that the myths and legends over the history of the Earth seem to have given rise to many forgotten truths, now called myths by modern man. These have similarity to the realities we find on Earth but there are subtle differences and it is clear to me now that life moves in many different forms across the Cosmos. I never expected to meet dwarves in this, or any other reality. It seems man in his wisdom and his creative zeal has for the past many hundred years sought to lengthen his life force by defeating some of the ills caused by different plagues over his time of dominance. He has come to value time and the Earth as his own at the expense of all else. He dreams to reach out into the heavens, while leaving a decimated Earth behind. This is not a false conclusion to reach and does not give cause for man alone to be blamed, for he works as a species with the knowledge given to him. Many of his attempts to see a future through creative imagination on film depicts man in his glory colonising other worlds and creating a new future for mankind. It gives a view of what might happen to the Earth in man's haste to leave.

"Some wise minds have imagined the worm holes in this universe to be pathways to other solar systems. This may be true. Using the pathways or even finding their openings is fraught with danger for such a fragile species. The wisest among humanity know that our understanding of the Cosmos is only a paltry four per cent of the whole of God's creation. The scientists have espoused their own view on our world's history and this has caused a rift in the spiritual protection offered by the religious beliefs in the past. Many sacrifices of the great and the good achieved great things in promoting healthy living and kindness to all, through faith. Many believed we were approaching the apocalypse of our own making and now fiction has become fact. Which sane person could have expected men from the very roots of humanity would arrive in our time from the deep past? How could we expect, after a millennium, that what was once called stories in the scriptures, would be proven by these dwarves, through them sharing their old knowledge of the Song of the Creator?

"What is very clear to the faithful is that the creation of life is a mystery still to all. Man knows something of its past and examines his history for clues to existence and makes many mistakes with no ill intent.

"Some of these seem ridiculous now. That the world is flat and a disc which we could fall off. Others that come to mind are the destruction of machinery invented to improve the life of men. On many occasions a man has conceived that he is a god among men. This is also not true. What the faithful understand comes from the wisdom over many, many, years. We are a part of creation of God through his Holy Song, which we may call today the Holy Spirit. It is all around us and is our protection against evil. Even now, if we stick to our faith and live in the world with our eyes open to the new truth. We have long known from the great and the good from the past that the world is become a battleground between good and evil and that being good and humble and caring for a fellow person was the right way to behave. It is this truth which has helped us to build greater and greater societies and great cultures have grown up over time."

The bishop was beginning to sweat under his collar. He took a breath and requested a drink of water. Once he had taken on some water he said pardon to the queen and continued. "Your Majesty, I am at a loss to understand all that is happening before my eyes today. I had thought perhaps you were (by your pardon) either quite psychotic or playing a joke upon me. You have asked for my view on a serious matter, which to me seems to mark the end of days." Beads of sweat were now evident on his brow. "I fear that if this message is true and the dwarves have come to aid us in battle against evil, we may well have anarchy. The Church of England has been on its knees in terms of popularity lately, as are the Catholics and others within our dominion. We are can no longer call ourselves a Christian country. We are now a secular culture. In the past we might have committed all we have to support the fight, but in-fighting has been at no small expense in terms of lost humanity to wars and other disasters. Secularism is now the major belief. Even among the church there are strong voices that appear to have ditched following the words of Christ, favouring a popularist view to retain membership."

The Queen smiled and gestured to the dwarf to come forward and take his place beside her. The old sofa creaked as he sat down and a bearded, slightly built personage of dwarf proportions, a female, giggled. Lowe gestured to her. "My wife [she bowed] has humour on her mind today." Lowin bowed low in apology.

Lowe explained then to the bishop that the history and the great religions were evident upon themselves to show that they are true for the believers in the one Creator. "It is not for us to make judgement on you although you have moved far from the path of goodness in our sense of the word." He spoke to the queen for a moment then accepted her judgement that the bishop was on the side of good. "No dwarf will tell you of your future or of your past. It has been forbidden by the Lady Ruth, the one who sent us here. We are come to aid your queen who has chosen faith over power, good over evil, and maintained her headship of the religious order, in what you deem England. She is most honourable and we will fight for her, for she is too old now to take the field. I warn you now bishop that any politics or plots against the queen will see the demise of that person." Lowe lifted his great hammer to further explain what he meant, without speaking again to the bishop, who looked very pale as though he might faint on the spot. The bishop looked scared.

Queen Elizabeth smiled and intervened on behalf of her bishop. "My dear Lowe, you are incredibly kind to be so protective of my honour. I only wish you had arrived sooner in my reign. It would have saved a lot of pain in the realm if I had access to such loyalty. It is true, sadly, what the bishop has said today. However, our saving grace is the fact that there are millions of good people who understand that there is probably a creator, as they were taught. Your arrival and our near future will aid them in this belief. I must say I am delighted that dwarf women are so respected by their husbands and have such good sense of humour in the manner which they support their husbandmen!" At this point every female in the room giggled.

Lowe laughed out loud. "Yes! My queen, we are indeed fortunate to have the love and respect from our wives and you won't be surprised to hear that it was my wife that laid many of the plans with me that brought us to your door." Lowe gestured to Lowin and she smiled once more.

The Queen had sat patiently while the bishop finished his rather rambling history lesson. She felt sorry for him for much of what he thought was solid evidence of his Creator was laid bare in front of him. His own faults (and there were many) had been recognised and all of this happened before the queen. Finally, the queen turned to Lowe, as Lowin moved to join them on the sofa. She smiled at them and said quietly, "It seems we shall be needing those millions of good people in a way unexpected."

The bishop was dismissed after receiving a long list of contacts he needed to make around the world.

The scientists were next. Their whole understanding of science was thrown into confusion. The atheist scientists were sceptical right up to the point where Ruth and the Angel Deborah appeared within a portal before them. All were amazed and sent away under strictest security to get over the shock of what they had been exposed to and assimilate this new knowledge. The Queen gave them a simple question to answer. What does the new truth mean to the future of mankind?

CHAPTER TWENTY-ONE
LOWE MEETS THE DELEGATES

The dwarves spent many hours with The Queen and her close servants. They listened to The Queen and together they laid out their plans. Invitations went out around the world to every head of state and every religious denomination, and they were invited to a secret congress to be held in Scotland, where it would be easier to maintain security. No one turned down the invitations. All could see the world was changing and wanted to understand what they were in store for.

The great auditorium chosen for the event held within it every leader in the world, good or bad. The speaker was the Prime Minister of Australia, who had been given the honour to address the world leaders on the matters in hand. This honour had come to her after her own experiences in Australia where she first encountered the Spawn and Slavers. Her speech was a harsh lesson for many there, whatever their belief systems had told them and what they thought they knew of the history of the planet. The Prime Minister was looking at her best for the occasion of her speech. She stood tall and was composed and thorough as she relayed her experiences with the Spawn and how they had succeeded in suppressing the knowledge reaching the public.

Carol Shaw moved an imaginary strand of hair slowly from her forehead. The audience was completely silent as people had their interpreters working hard to keep up with her. They, at least, were grateful for any pause. The auditorium had had many speakers previously and similar occurrences had either already happened in eastern Europe, North America, South America and in the heart of Africa. They now knew they were dealing with a global catastrophe in the making.

Carol spoke seriously and quietly. "We are not alone in this battle to come. I would like to now introduce our ally from the past." ('This is what they have been waiting for,' she thought to herself.) Carol walked off the platform and there was an expectant buzz in the room. The leaders had been warned about their new allies and they were eager now to see them.

Lowin and Lowe walked onto the stage. With them came all their surviving dwarves. They were all in their battle gear and were a fearsome sight. No one was unmoved by their entrance. Lowe stood before the microphones, which were quickly adjusted to suit him. Lowe and his warriors looked lethally at the audience. He began to speak slowly in English but with real force of his personality. "Do not be afraid my people. I can see that many of you are generally good people. Some of you are not. Those of you that have been wicked, you must stop now. The wicked who coerced the weak-minded to undermine society are all equally guilty and will pay the ultimate price on the day of reckoning. That is not far off for any of you here. Those that kill innocent people and sell weapons, deal in drugs and allow atrocities to occur when they have the power to act, will also face judgement. Those that start unjust wars will be punished. They will never prosper and their petty evils will fall on the heads of their children and only the Creator can save them.

"A terrible battle is coming, one that will cover the globe. The enemy has spread to every corner of the globe and this evil is set to begin the greatest and possibly final battle for the souls of men. I advise you all to keep your eyes and ears wide open, do good to your fellow man, love one another, for you will need each other if you are to avoid the pit!" Lowe ended his speech with a smile. "Of course, that last bit comes from the heart of dwarves and is one of the reasons why we have come to be with you in your hour of need.

"Now that we understand one another I will tell you why we are here. I will tell you where we have come from. I will tell you what we are going to do together." Lowe settled into his tale, his hammer resting in his hand. The rest of the dwarves stood behind him and seemed ready to take their axes to anyone who came near.

"In the first instant, I ask for your understanding of my predicament in being here. We dwarves are closer to the Creator than are you because you have all been born much later in the Creator's use of time. We dwarves retain the ability to see the evil in men and for this reason it is difficult for us to understand your reticence in faith or indeed tolerate it. Our gifts as early examples of humanity place us at odds with many of you in respect of faith. Rest assured, that all will be forgiven if you are able from this point on to keep your minds open to the truth. We could read men's hearts in our own time. You are all easy for us read and some of you are extremely far from the Golden Path set for man to travel upon."

The hall was silent now, you could hear a pin drop. Lowe looked all the leaders in the eye as his eyes swept the gathering. One or two heads went down but most looked straight back at him. "I am told you are either warriors or leaders, which means politics. These we understand. Some of you will die quite shortly, for our enemy is exceedingly powerful. You cannot rely on your rockets and bombs to defeat this enemy. Even as we speak there is a giant sunburst heading for the planet. There was little time to warn you and for that we are sorry. Our time of arrival was not by our design and many of my folk were lost in battle and paid the price. The sunburst will hit the planet tomorrow or the next day. Your astronomers will already have told you this."

There were nods in the room.

"When the sunburst hits the planet, there will be a blackout over the entire world. The blackout will take out every missile on the planet. There will be no electricity to power your cities and you will be at the mercy of your enemies. There will be a levelling of the playing field. Before you leave here, my dwarves will speak to you of the Spawn, as we call them. They will tell you about the Slavers and of the evil men already under her sway. Yonlik the queen intends to conquer you all. She has no interest in your wellbeing and will convert or slaughter everyone that comes against her. Each of you has just enough time to hear what we say before you head home. Please do not be on one of your marvellous creations in the air after thirty-six hours or you will perish by plunging to the Earth."

Lowe now spoke sweetly to his audience. "Some of you are not good men and do not treat your people that you govern well. I mean what I say when I tell you we dwarves are not seeking to replace your regimes or make judgement upon you. We are sent as envoys to save you all from the evil that is coming from within the Earth. It is old and deadly."

Some of the despotic leaders in the world were brooding in silence. The meeting was deemed closed and all moved into the debating chamber so that there was room to debate what to do next. Some were remonstrating with each other. Many present, who looked concerned, gave signals to their envoys and security men. Lowe could see they were not listening, so he gave a counter signal to the dwarves and they dashed forward and smashed their hammers and axes into the floor. The noise was alarming. Hands covered ears and security men entered the hall on all sides. These men were handpicked and had been vetted by Lowe and Lowin and knew their duty. There was silence again in the room.

"I will not keep you long," said Lowe, "but you need to hear all the bad news today. We have a chance of surviving what is coming. Indeed, many of you already know and fear the Spawn. Be in no doubt. There is no mercy in this battle and men who side with the enemy are indeed doomed to Hell. Your best weapons that are hand-held will suffice while you have ammunition. You cannot rely on anything that runs by electricity. We dwarves fight with hammer and axe and we are hard set at times to overcome our enemies. We are physically far stronger than you. Soon you will appreciate that you will need to get your young men into armour, your soldiers will have to become leaders of the population armies in each of your countries and together you will face an enemy like no other. My dwarves will now come onto the floor. Do not be afraid of my dwarves. They come to save you all if they can. The dwarves are gracious and understanding and you are safe unless you offend them. They will tell you what there is to know about defeating the Spawn from Hell. FINALLY!" Lowe shouted out before lowering his voice. "You will face something we have not yet given battle too! You will face a third and deadly beast. They are winged and feature beautiful females. They are six feet in height and completely deadly. If they approach, beware. My dwarves will now tell you why."

CHAPTER TWENTY-TWO
LOWIN AND THE RELIGIOUS DELEGATES

The discussions went on for several more hours. Once the politicians had departed for home, The Queen and Carol Shaw felt that the female dwarves would be less intimidating to the audience that the males. It had been difficult to brief the politicians due to their lack of moral fibre. Lowe explained that he would have expelled a third of the politicians from the start if it had been his choice, for there were some very bad men in the room. Lowin took on the role assigned to her. This was to talk to the heads of the major religions. They gathered in a smaller venue but just as well equipped. Lowin and the female dwarves were pleased to meet the holy men from throughout the globe. Lowin explained that she would give a brief outline of man's history from her perspective.

"With the death by fire of the dinosaur by colossal devastation, by an asteroid from outside our sun's influence, past the asteroid belt, the original order planned by God reasserted itself. Man came into existence and began to grow in numbers before Satan and Yonlik were aware. For Yonlik had slept for aeons but her recovery was incomplete and, because of this most fortunate circumstance, Satan was confounded. I have spoken briefly about Despite on the Second Level of the Golden Path." There were nods around the room.

"The evil one called Despite, in his every sinew, sought ways to corrupt humanity. When the species called Man rose above the other animals, as intended, the Song of Creation resonated in his ears. He was the first sentient species on Earth aware of God. For this was before the evil Yonlik could influence events of those that walked the Earth. The Creator did not name the five human species. It is true that they lived in a place of complete safety and were untouched by evil. Nature placed them in the security of the Garden of Edain, a land of plenty and a place to learn and grow in the Creator's image. They, with their offspring, were gifted with the wonders of imagination and of knowing much more than they could see with their eyes. Innocence reigned over an aeon of their time. They became the Older Race and were known to us as, simply, The Edain."

Lowin could see there was great interest from these men and, now that they had seen the proofs and knew of the threat, they were keen to understand more. She continued with her tale.

"A minority of men were content to accept the glory to themselves from their colleagues and these grew in number with the rest of mankind. Some were successful. Some coveted the attention they received and began to covet their neighbour's goods and achievements and conspired with each other to topple the person and claim their successes. Over many generations the majority, being good men, saw this as evil and those who were guilty were rejected and sent away into the wilderness. The story of these events, handed down father to son, are well told through similar writings of your older testaments. The Creator's goodness saved men from the devil Satan by the sacrifices made on their behalf by the greatest examples of God's Embassy, in his continued dealings to protect Man. The relief for mankind came in many forms. There are examples in each of your belief systems of the sacrifices made by the great and the good in leading their people towards the light. Many of you that are Christians follow your Lord Jesus, who positioned Man to be absolved all previous faults. Others follow Allah, Judaism, Hinduism; and there are others of course. What you all share in common is that all good men seek to do good and recognise evil and fight against it. The dwarves can see goodness in men. We see goodness in all of you. It does not matter to the dwarves how you achieve this, it only matters that you do." Lowin smiled at her delegates and all smiled back. She held them with her own honesty and goodness and they could see the truth in her eyes.

"We have a duty to humanity to prepare everyone that we can in the coming days. We have no time to argue or debate. The people of the world must be warned now to arm themselves against evil. They cannot prevent what is coming and they cannot rely on others to fight for them. The armies of each land will face their own battles and win or lose. The only thing that matters is that they fight!

"Those that understood this and hold true to the teachings of the word will be saved whether on Earth or beyond. Those that continue to seek power and dominance and who break the laws of good society will once more be a fair target for Satan's cohorts.

"Before our time," said Lowin, "the devils were in full retreat for they had no power before the Creator's great angels who were so glorious! The senior devil Despite withdrew for that time and sought solace with his master trapped, we hope forever, beneath him. Despite, under the orders of his master then began to grow in malice and resentment, against the good in the world. Man became creative once more, learned through the gifts given from God and built upon the seeds of their learning from the Eternal Song. They built bigger and better societies and nations rose, fell, and rose again over the next two thousand years. The evil of Despite made impacts with wars and even world wars and grew in strength and confidence, so that even in defeat of their greatest human atrocities, there arose other evil machinations among the nations. Their greatest advocate was distrust in man for one another. Your First World War caused great death among nations; a generation of inspirational youth lost to the world. Sadly, goodwill was soon replaced by fear once more.

"Satan, through his spirits, has been working and waiting.

Their influence on Level Three of the Golden Path to Heaven's gates took a serious knock when the First World War, then the Second World War was lost to good. Yet we have heard how some of these men were cosseted by evil spirits, roaming the Earth as spirits, seeking places where they could settle and affect the activity on Earth. Man is a perfect host for them to overtake. Man's emotions are something that the devils can always target."

Lowin sighed. "It has always been so. The spirits continued by merely influencing thoughts, giving comfort to the strong, rewarding anger, rewarding greed with devilish heat and, slowly but surely, they encouraged men who were coming under their sway to get comfortable, lazy and use the energy of others. Satan, through his allies, has warped some humans to such an extent that they become something no longer truly human inside. They look human to you, but we dwarves can see the evil inside. We have spoken of the Slavers, who hide their malice in the dark places of the world, hating the sun's glorious light, but enduring it. They serve Yonlik and her offspring princesses, two of whom we dispatched to Hell in our own time. They will hunt at night when their powers are stronger and quickly became a force of evil to challenge Man."

Lowin's audience listened with rapt attention to her words as she described the early existence of men, bringing them to the present time.

CHAPTER TWENTY-THREE
LOWIN DESCRIBES THE DWARVES

Lowin then spoke of her own people. "Not all those who were lost to the Creator had not yet committed murder. They still had goodness and links to the Creator. These men retreated and when they saw the evil at work, they hid themselves in deep caves, creating their own cultures. They changed in strength, and shape, becoming shorter, but stronger, and great diggers and tunnel builders. They became the dwarves and we were many beneath the earth. We honoured our parentage and the past and focussed on the strong bonds of love we held for one another as outcasts hiding from evil."

Lowin spoke of her people next with some emotion in her voice for she was reminded of all her kin prior to the intervention from Ruth and of the Angel Deborah, who had set the dwarves on their path.

"Happily, we dwarves were organised and moved to one purpose, which was to escape the evil by putting great distance between us and them. The Spawn and their masters were content to move slowly, build little and feed upon those they fought. They would eat crops, animals, men and dwarves that they fought and killed. The further away from the She Devil's original hiding place, the less organised the Spawn became. The Slavers had to coerce the Spawn into battle, especially where it was cold and hard land to traverse or where there were rivers to cross. This gave hope to those who battled them. Some victories lasted years and peace and growth occurred. Always, eventually, the Spawn would return in greater and greater numbers until men and dwarves either abandoned the fight or died in their homes. Either this or they were forced to flee once more.

"As time passed there came incursions of men, seeking to distance themselves from the great evils that sought to overthrow them. Initially, these were the first born and the dwarves held them in friendship and trust. They had many gifts they had developed from God's glorious song. They were tall, lithe of limb and many were over seven feet in height. They were powerful and were good allies, keeping the laws by which they lived. They were gatherers like the dwarves and good hunters and fighters when the need arose. They were prolific of their seed and were born into large family groups, which held together. These were the men who came to live beside the dwarves outside our great halls of stone.

"We had settled and made homes in the heart of what is now the continent of Africa. The mountain range which shielded us from assault by our enemies was impenetrable due to their great height. The dwarves were 10,000 strong in each of our city strongholds. We were well armed with stone, wood and iron weapons that were superior to any weapon known at that time. The dwarves' confidence was high."

Lowin then told them of the battles that had brought them to the future to aid modern man. She drew her audience in with her tale. The holy men were all overwhelmed by her honesty and goodness and knew in their hearts that this was her truthful testament. The men of great learning saw the future for themselves. They sat with Lowin and together with the other dwarves made plans to save mankind from evil.

Lowin and Lowe concluded this debate and planning session together. Lowe explained to the holy men of all faiths that this coming battle was for modern man to fight. "We dwarves are few in number. The purpose of Ruth and of the Angel Deborah was for us, as humankind representatives, to give you this message of impending evil. We have been taught by Ruth enough about your time to be able to achieve this end. I hope we have done this."

There were nods all around the room.

"We have been given our own task in the battle for the world. We will go to Australia where we believe the last surviving princess from our time, named Shimishi is living. We will kill her if we can for, as we have explained, if she dies then so do her hordes of Spawn and Slavers. That won't be the end of the matter, but it is the best we can hope for."

CHAPTER TWENTY-FOUR
THE CAPTURE

Lowe and Lowin were sat with Queen Elizabeth and Mrs Shaw, having afternoon tea. Mrs Shaw smiled at the dwarves and said "It has been a great honour to have been allowed to meet you dwarves and learn that Man has a future, if we can hold true to the light. The world already owes you a great debt of gratitude, for you have given up so much to bring this message. The world in our time is complex as you can see. The world will meet these threats as one people eventually. Her Majesty [and here Carol bowed towards The Queen] has many allies worldwide. She and others will orchestrate the battle for the souls of mankind. Our task in Australia will be greatly eased by your knowledge and presence in fighting the evil horde that will shortly fall upon us from within our own borders. With your permission we will fly to Australia before the collapse of civilisation and begin the defence of our homes."

They left The Queen who called for her staff to update the Prime Minister on the weekly meetings in the palace.

Lowe, Lowin and the dwarves were mightily impressed with all they had learned about weapons. They particularly liked aeroplanes but were astounded at their ability to fly. Although they had been educated by Ruth, with the Angel Deborah supplying much of the content, it was another matter to see the world in such a new light.

Mrs Shaw entered the 747 in her bright red shoes and the dwarves, who were by now celebrities among the tight security of special service men and guards, followed her up the steps. There was a slight delay before take-off as a discussion took place about the dwarves' need to carry their weapons with them while onboard.

Lowgrim and Joygrim sat together on this their first ever flight. Of all the dwarves, it was these two that were most excited. As the airplane taxied, all the dwarves were talking at the same time. Apart from Joygrim and her brother, everyone else had a soldier next to them for reassurance. The soldiers explained what was happening. Everyone was quite calm and with nervous smiles until the pilot used the radio Tannoy to warn of the impending acceleration. The jet spurted forward. The dwarves as one let out a frightened howl and then everyone was out of breath. It went quiet and then Lowgrim called out, "Can we do it again?"

Pillows, chocolate and plastic cups rained down on his seat and he and Joygrim were fairly pelted with everything to hand. Then it was cheers all around the seating area as all the soldiers joined in the mayhem.

Jono, the officer commanding, had been up front with the cabin crew. "Drinks will now be served. This is not dwarf ale and not so heavy, but you might get a liking for it. This dark ale is called Theakston's Old Peculiar, a dark beer from the home country. If you prefer something lighter, we have Newcastle Brown Ale or for the ladies there is good, old-fashioned lager."

Service was swift and the dwarves were very pleased to be sampling the hospitality of The Queen, as were the soldiers. Before long Lowe proposed a toast to The Queen. Then a toast to his wife. Then all the dwarves toasted each other. The soldiers were next and at each toast glasses were filled and emptied. It was a very happy party on board and the soldiers were very impressed by their guests' ability to hold their ale. A rousing cheer went up whenever a soldier absented himself to be sick in the facilities provided. When the flight had been in the air for 18 hours, the beer finally ran out. No one was awake to see the jet being refuelled by a tanker sent for the purpose.

Lowe winked at Lowin and said, "What a very interesting place our world has become."

Lowin kissed his beery beard and they settled off to sleep. Lowgrim had a broad smile on his face. Joygrim was out cold and using her brother's legs as a footstool.

An hour before landing there was a meal to be eaten and the dwarves all tucked in. Jono marvelled at the dwarves' capacity for alcohol and food. When they had landed, all the dwarves helped their soldier comrades disembark the aircraft. One or two soldiers, believing they were being attacked, threw a few punches at the odd dwarf head and these were met with smiles and understanding. Once everyone was off the aircraft Jono ordered them to sit on the ground. Jono was very relieved their arrival was being met by soldiers from his regiment who alone would witness the cream of Australian special forces regiment unable to hold their beer, as well as dwarves, who as far as he knew had never tasted alcohol. A sing song, started by the soldiers, was cheered by the dwarves and a very happy crowd was loaded into lorries and taken to their destination.

A secret base close to where the first outbreak of Spawn activity was their destination. A training camp for special forces offered the opportunity for jungle war practice in the outback and all sorts of terrain including mountain and desert training. It was also very secure and secret, known only to those who had trained there or were needed there. Carol Shaw was now one of those with need to know. The plans were discussed and activated to meet this old and quite terrifying threat were agreed by the parliament. The shock had been extreme, the evidence gathered overwhelming. Mrs Shaw ordered strikes against known targets and in the past six months the face of humanity had changed rapidly.

Mrs Shaw reviewed the paper documents before her. All computers, together with records and essential operations, were buried deep underground and deactivated together with as much weaponry as was possible in the time given to countries. This was done as a response to the belief that the sun might stop issuing electromagnetic pulse (EMP) waves across the planet at some time in the future. More concerning to governments was the fear that they would no longer be in control of humanity.

Australia, along with countries in the Commonwealth of Nations, took the view that local government was going to be the best defence for cities across the world. Plans were urgently adapted from apocalypse planning as the calm before the inevitable storm arrived. The populous was informed of the danger. The great religions, backed by political allies, worked to support the faithful and direct them to the salvation of mankind. The chaos before the sunbursts spread like fire across the planet. Every nation was in turmoil and social order broke down in most countries. Cities became dangerous places to be. Suicides, murder and mayhem were widespread. Armed forces were despatched as planned to lead the populous. When the first EMP waves struck, many aeroplanes were still in the air, as some countries were taking advantage of the chaos and attacking others.

China launched a sea offensive against Taiwan.

Russia invaded its satellite countries.

America was split once more between north and south.

Australia and New Zealand were on alert against a Chinese invasion expected at any time.

The EMP waves struck and with that all electrical equipment across the world became obsolete. Armies halted, populations prayed, while overhead the world's satellites crashed and burned as their power sources were fried. The world was silenced in an instant and people panicked in huge numbers. It was impossible to stop the destruction of property and with it the lives of millions.

Private armies across the world sprang up. Many were organised locally and were radical groups. Government forces became the only safety net for whole populations and those that could headed for agreed safe areas, identified before the fall of civilisation. Carol, Bill and a few close friends were based with the dwarves.

Carol knew the suffering that was happening around the world but also knew that her own people were among the casualties. With all communication lines cut it was now down to each country to meet the threat of the Spawn and Slavers and heaven knew what else.

It started on the first night. Reports of Spawn outbreaks all over Western Australian were taking place. It happened in every part of the planet. Every large land mass was facing human extinction. Carol thanked her lucky stars that she was not able to hear of the terror across the world. It would have driven her insane.

The microcosms of order that had been arranged in advance began to take effect. Within three months the lines of battle were drawn all over the world. Western Australia was almost overrun by Spawn and much of the defensive capability soaked up hundreds of thousands of Spawn dead until the ammunition ran out and then the hand-to-hand defence began. Carol put down the report and went out into a large common room where the leadership of Western Australia was housed.

Lowe and the dwarves had been very busy since they had arrived with their special forces cousins. It quickly became clear to Lowe, Lowin and the others that while modern man was intelligent, he was also physically weaker in most cases and not prepared either physically or mentally for the sort of battle they were going to have to fight.

When the fighting began, the modern warfare tactics were a wonderful foil for a dull, evil enemy. Lowe and Lowin began their true purpose given to them by Ruth and the Angel Deborah. They began to train their special forces cousins in dwarf warfare, fitness to fight and tactics. General Lee had kindly supplied modern steel axes for all the dwarves and great hammers were issued to every soldier in the command. Lowe and Lowgrim had watched the giant forges spit out the steel and they saw how it was shaped and cut to size before all power failed.

Lowe and Lowgrim rallied the dwarves and set them the task of training and toughening their students. Lowe smiled as the training had begun. The skills of each soldier seemed impressive and Lowe watched them fight each other for an hour before their physical weaknesses were beginning to show.

Lowgrim was teaching six soldiers at a time. He carried light, hard, plastic weapons and fought six soldiers at a time. The soldiers' orders were to take the dwarf down and Lowgrim was relishing the conflict as much as the soldiers. He moved with the speed and certainty of a young dwarf and, within ten minutes, his combatants were forced to retire through hard knocks and exhaustion. Lowgrim was careful not to cause concussions in his students. As a soldier was retired another took his place. Sometimes it was a male and sometimes a female. All were treated with the same respect by Lowgrim.

After an hour and a half there were thirty highly trained soldiers sitting and marvelling at Lowgrim's skills and stamina. As they recovered their dignity, they began to cheer on the soldiers' attempts to take down the dwarf. Big men fell as quickly as small men and women. The last opponent standing was a female. She was number thirty-six. The thirty fifth had been a heavily muscled man of six feet six inches and he had tried to use his reach and weight against the dwarf. Lowgrim retreated one step and, as the man lunged at him with a hammer to strike his helmeted head, he parried the blow and took his legs away with the sweep of his hammer, carefully using the side of the hammer head and not the head of the weapon. Number thirty-five was rewarded for his effort with a stamp to his solar plexus which ended his interest in the sport for that time.

Number thirty-six was sneaky and had attacked Lowgrim at the same time as thirty-five. She had come close to scoring a wounding blow but Lowgrim twisted his body under the blow as it glanced off him. Number thirty-six retreated with good balance and Lowgrim stalked her around the fighting area and, when she was sufficiently tired, he struck and put her on her bottom. The soldiers from one to thirty-six applauded their teacher and trainer. Lowgrim called them to order with a smile and then dismissed them for lunch. Every day since they had arrived, the dwarves took their squaddies, officers and security teams through battle practice.

Lowe was pleased with the results and the soldiers quickly adapted their skills and muscles to imitate the dwarf battle tactics. The soldiers were fit to start with, but now they were lithe and strong and quicker in defence and attack.

Lowgrim spoke to his father and the rest of the leadership team. "Our cousins have done well, father. We now have a thousand soldiers capable of taking battle to the enemy without fear of heavy losses. The modern armour is excellent at deflecting claws and teeth and we have moved on to the heavy hammers and axes. Our cousins can use both hammer, axe and most can fight now for perhaps two hours, hand-to-hand, with the dwarves. They are good with spears and with the bow. I think they are ready."

"Good," said Lowe, "it's time we began to move on the enemy."

Lowe stood at a lectern at the front of the auditorium which had been set up at one end of the command centre. Every modern tool for computing and communication lay at the other end. All were dormant. His audience were the generals and soldiers and leadership team, which included Mrs Shaw and Bill Carruthers. Nearly all were veterans from the second encounter with the Spawn, the first having been disastrous from which there were no survivors.

Lowe looked around the room. His own people were behind the audience and when Lowe spoke he looked to the rear, searching the faces of his people who were in a very strange environment. Lowe knew they were coping well with modern life. He was very grateful for Ruth's understanding of modern man and the effort put in to prepare his people.

"Dear friends we are ready to fulfil our destiny and at the very least make a dent in Queen Yonlik's plans for the world. Our purpose is to find and kill the Princess Shimishi, who lies under the mines of Australia. This we learned from Ruth. This is a battle and a war for the very souls of men past and present. So many have fallen already and many more will do so. We dwarves are gratified that our education has allowed us to communicate freely. The gift of tongues granted to us by the Angel Deborah has enabled us to have true purpose in this timespan of the world. We retain our ability to see evil in people. We have thinned down your ranks to only include those we feel we can trust to join us in this battle. We are gratified that many of you are re-examining your own spiritual beliefs at this time. It is enough for the dwarves that you are good people, and that your decisions are made as free people. It has been a sadness to learn that evil has caused so many people to be slaves of others. We dwarves would not be a party to slavery in any form. The battle above ground is for modern man to unravel. We will do our best work underground.

"It is our understanding that the evil ones have used the years between your time and ours to dig tunnels, join up caverns to network the planet. Every land mass has its own network of caves and these house millions of Slaver eggs which are now hatching. This tells me that Shimishi is also awake and responsible for the organisation of Slavers and Spawn. The attacks upon the western edge of Australia are causing mayhem and casualties are high among the population. Your army is fighting well and will be able to hold on for many months with luck. As in our time, sheer numbers will eventually overcome them. Our best hopes lie in seeking out and destroying Shimishi. This we will attempt together. I ask Bill to step up and explain our plan."

Bill stepped up confidently to the lectern. He had grown in personality, wisdom and old knowledge under the tutelage of the army and the dwarves. His mining experience was as good as it could be, and he had built a great affinity with all the dwarves who spent hours listening and advising and planning with him. He had found truth in the hearts of the dwarves and he now felt the certainty of his role in fighting evil. His former life now seemed so insignificant that he found it hard to believe his own selfish interest in his dealings with the world and he knew nearly all present had experienced something similar.

"Certainty is a wonderful thing and I wish to tell our brothers from the deep past that their coming has galvanised humanity to meet the needs of the age to defeat evil if we can. Our focus is the hunt for the Princess Shimishi, who sounds terrifying. We are told she lives and so we must kill her. Nothing else will save Australia for its people. We have cleared the mine entrance which was blocked on our last retreat. The mine is open. It seems that the entrance where we met the Spawn had been a side entrance and the Slavers were ready for us. Since the assault began by the enemy across Australia, there has been no movement in the mine. We think attention has moved elsewhere. The horde of Spawn and Slavers are attacking on many fronts all at once. Now Mrs Shaw would like to address you."

"Thanks Bill. No need for the Mrs anymore. The government decision to organise defence by regional government has been agreed with cross party support. This is a great weight off my mind and means each region can fight its own battles, as its leaders see fit. Our strongholds against the hordes are well defended and most still have the advantage of superior fire power from our modern weaponry, while stocks last. There is no let up on the EMP hits from the sun so we must do our best. I am no longer Prime Minister except in name. This is as it should be. It means I can concentrate on this very special mission we are about to undertake. I have considered long and hard who should lead this battle plan. General Lee will be responsible for communications above ground and respond to the threats against this base. Our soldiers and populous will be his responsibility. The special forces chosen for our raid on the enemy, when we find them, will be under the command of its officers as usual. Bill and I are not combatant in nature and we are not really fit enough to take the fight to the enemy, but we are going on the mission anyway."

A few murmurs were heard in the room before Carol Shaw continued. "This decision is not up for discussion so please accept it whether you agree or not. Bill and I have been in this disaster from the beginning. We know much and have learned more from our brethren who came to warn us. We will go with the dwarves as advisors from our time and be guided by them in terms of delivering the killing blow to Princess Shimishi, whom we have learned so much about. If we all die in the attempt it will be up to those that follow to attempt the assassination of this evil creature by any means possible. Her demise is our best hope of holding out and overcoming evil in our time."

CHAPTER TWENTY-FIVE
THE REVOLUTION

"Weapons checks please," said Jono, who had the honour of taking his squad, Jane, Ann and Smithy, in the lead group with the dwarves, Bill and Carol. The dwarves followed Jono's squad into the mine. Everyone was quiet and Lowgrim and Joygrim went ahead to scout out the mine proper. The mine was eerily silent and each footfall sounded like a shout to the wary dwarves, who's hearing was so acute. The dwarves moved in the dark and no lights were on in the tunnel. It was a long walk to the entrance hidden in the rockface they had discovered so very long ago. Carol and Bill were both drinking regularly and taking on salt, as were the rest of the force. Joygrim and Lowgrim waited for the party to reach them. Lowgrim had a broad grin on his face and Joygrim punched him in the arm.

"Stop being so happy Lowgrim."

"Can't help it," said Lowgrim. "It's being safe underground that all we dwarves feel so comfortable about." He winked at Jane, Ann and Smithy and ushered them to follow Joygrim and himself through the hidden entrance. The others followed quietly behind. They travelled through the tunnels without incident and came to the cave where the stone door stood.

"Dwarf door," said Joygrim, and she and Lowgrim began to search the walls on either side for signs of a hidden lock. Lowgrim looked above the door and signalled he had found what he was looking for.

"Axes at the ready," put in Lowin.

There was a loud click in the deafening silence and the door swung outwards with barely a sound. Nothing could be seen or heard within. Lowe called for light and torches were turned on. These had been saved from damage by the EMP waves from the sun and were lead-lined with rubber grips. They sent forth pencil light, which was sufficient to see perhaps twenty feet ahead. The group moved through the door and on, down the pathway.

Before long they came to a wide cavern and Lowe ordered all lights switched off. Bill and Carol gasped as the cavern slowly filled with a faint glow. The rocks glowed with a luminescence that showed thousands upon thousands of stalactites forming the high ceiling of the cave. The sight was truly beautiful and as the soldiers moved into the cavern there were involuntary sighs when they saw the marvels and beauty all around them. The dwarves were all smiling. They could not have been happier. Their confidence underground was complete. They confidently moved around the cavern, checking for exits on every surface.

Lowin spoke for the dwarves. "Right then. This is our first drop off point. Officers to me."

When they were assembled before her, she spoke again. "This will be our fallback position. It seems that there is only one way into the cavern and one way out. I will leave the details for defence to all of you. You know your business well. When we return, we will very likely be under attack ourselves, so you need to be sure of your targets. Anything not dwarf, or other man and woman, is your legitimate target. If we can signal you, we will before we enter this place. If the enemy send men against you, you will be doing them a favour by despatching them to the judgement of the Creator. If you hesitate you die. It's really, as simple as that. "Right then, Let's get to it."

Once more Lowgrim and his sister took the lead, this time with Jane, Ann and Smithy in tow. These five had formed close ties of understanding and made close friendships with each other. Bill and Carol followed on with dwarves all around them. Bill was comforted by the care being given to himself and Carol.

The luminescence dimmed somewhat but they could see one another. Their route was downwards, always downwards. The way was wide enough for comfort for three broad shouldered dwarves to move in comfort on each side of Bill and Carol. Down they went, only taking breaks for water and salt as needed. They marched until Carol was very tired. When she slipped on a rock in the floor an attentive hand steadied her. She smiled at the dwarf gratefully and continued. Lowin was mindful of the limits to Carol's strength and called a halt ten minutes after she tripped.

The company came together and sat in a circle and dwarves guarded the path both up and down for their protection. Bill asked the question most burning in his mind. "Did dwarves build this tunnel Lowin?"

"In a manner of speaking they did," she replied. "The cavern where we left our defences was clearly an early home to dwarves. The stalactites have grown long and many have fallen, but it is clear that the spot was chosen for its luminescent prospects. Dwarves in our time sought out such places and, where there was no light, the family would breed fireflies that fluttered on the ceiling to provide light. Sometimes we used lava in the rock to the same purpose. The temperature tells me this was not used here. The path we sit upon has been widened by dwarf craft and was probably dug as an escape route in the dark times of attack by the hordes of evil. This path goes a long way down into the earth and I suspect we will find the signs of dwarf delving will soon cease. At one time there must have been another way up and out and it could be behind us or in front of us. Escape routes are carefully disguised."

Bill was delighted with this answer and settled down to his cold meal and was lost in his own thoughts. He would have loved to have seen the families of early man that had made the cavern their home. He sat pondering such a simple existence and he smiled at Carol, who was looking at him, as if guessing his thoughts.

"Amazing isn't it," she said, smiling herself. Carol and Bill were now very close. Lowin nudged her daughter as she ate her meal and Joygrim nudged back, hiding the pleasure etched in her eyes at the happy couple's comfort with each other and love. When all was made tidy the group settled to rest and sleep if they could. The dwarves were asleep in minutes, as was Bill. Carol listened to the heavy sound of breathing coming from the group. Slowly her eyes closed. She could fight off sleep no longer.

After four hours the company moved on down the tunnel. The dwarves and the rest of the company now moved with caution. Their pace slowed to a gentle stroll, always moving down the slope. Joygrim, Lowgrim and the soldiers returned from their role as scouts and reported that they were only a few hundred yards from another cavern. They reported the latest cavern to be smaller than the one behind them. Joygrim reported that it appeared to have two entrances running off it. The company moved on cautiously, being as quiet as they were able.

The cavern was once more lit by a breed of firefly, not seen above the earth for aeons. The dwarves were now all wary. They risked a little light. The light shone out and all were met with a beautiful array of stalagmites and stalactites, forming from the floor and ceiling and in many cases they met to form natural columns as if placed there by an ancient civilisation. The ceiling glittered in the light of diamonds and quartz of many colours refracted from the torch light as it hit them, creating the most beautiful mosaic of all the colours in the spectrum. The whole company looked up in sheer amazement and joy for the honour of seeing something so rare and beautiful. For a few moments even the dwarves allowed their emotions to overtake their protective roles for the company and all forgot the anxiety that their adventure carried within them. The cavern was perhaps thirty metres deep and as many wide, in a roughly oval shape. Two small and dark patches on the far wall were the only exits that could be seen. They were only the size of a normal doorway. The dwarves went to them and checked them for movement or sound. There was none.

"Okay," said Lowe, "we will take a break and decide what to do."

Everyone settled down and the soldiers and dwarves took out rations. These were all modern but cold. The dwarves had warned against aromatic hot food due to the enemy having an acute sense of smell. They drank and ate and sat around Lowe and Lowin, who sought responses from all present. Jono spoke for the soldiers. Bill and Carol kept their council. Both were very happy to let those with experience in matters of security make the decisions. Lowin was concerned about breaking up the group and Lowe was adamant that they had to use both passages. He argued that using one might cause them to have no warning of a trap from that direction. The debate was calm and reasonable, and Lowe won the day. Lowin had misgivings about Lowe's plan. She wished to send Lowgrim and Joygrim ahead in each tunnel to check them out. Lowe argued that the tunnels might split many times, so it made sense to him to gamble with two parties from that point, with the aim of giving the other party a fighting chance to escape if one party was discovered. Lowin and Lowe split the party into two groups.

Lowgrim and Joygrim were to take Bill and Carol into the right exit. With them were Jane and Ann with two other soldiers and six dwarves. Lowin was insistent that her children lead the group because she knew they would make brave and bold decisions if they needed to. Her confidence in their abilities had been much enhanced since the start of their adventure together. Her last words to them were, "Stay safe."

This left Lowe and Lowin with the remainder of the dwarves and Jono with the rest of the party. Lowe said several times, "Remember why we are here. We must find and kill Shimishi, if we can., at all costs, but don't throw your lives away. If we can kill her the world has a better chance, for the Spawn will likely be paralysed and die, along with the Slavers commanding them."

Lowgrim led his party into the tunnel with Joygrim at the rear. Carol and Bill were behind two dwarves. Ann and Jane were behind Lowgrim. They had great confidence in the dwarves and they were, in turn, granted the honour of being Lowgrim's support should he need it. The tunnel straightened after four hundred metres and went on for another eight hundred quite straight. Lowgrim stopped dead and Jane and Ann pulled up sharply. Ann put out a warning hand to Carol and Bill to alert them. The party went quiet. Joygrim joined her brother at the front. Lowgrim spoke quietly to his sister, "I smell Spawn." Before him was a split in the tunnel. Joygrim moved past him into the right-hand tunnel and then returned and went into the left tunnel.

She returned after a minute or so.

"We have a choice to make brother. The smell is in both tunnels but less intense in the right one. I think we should use that one as it feels likely to hold less risk of exposure before we need to meet Spawn. My instinct tells me the left holds an army of Slavers and Spawn and I always trust my instincts," said Joygrim, with a grin.

Lowgrim moved into the right tunnel and now Joygrim was behind her brother. The company now knew the danger was nearly upon them. Bill and Carol exchanged looks and Bill grinned with excitement, with the adrenalin he was feeling, beginning to prepare his body for action. Carol was surprised at her own courage and in the ease with which she smiled back at Bill. Lowgrim moved without much sound, carefully placing each foot on the rocky and dusty floor. Joygrim was grateful for the dust, as it dulled the small sounds from their boots as they moved.

A loud roar went up that funnelled down the tunnel towards them. The scream of Spawn fighting and dying came to their ears. Even the dwarves were startled by the noise and Carol and Bill jumped so abruptly as to almost fall over. In all their minds was the thought that the other group were fighting for their lives against terrible and hopeless odds. For the first time Carol wondered why on earth she was here. It must have shown fear on her face for Bill gripped her hand and put his forehead on hers. He whispered to her. "It's okay, nothing has happened to us yet." His voice was steady and his touch reassuring. She smiled back weakly and squeezed his hand in thanks.

Lowgrim took the opportunity to move forward faster now that the noise ahead of them was covering any risk of them being heard. The noise of battle continued for ten minutes and then slowly faded away. Now only a rumble of voices from Slavers and Spawn could be heard. Lowgrim moved forward another hundred metres until a sharp tug from behind stopped him. Joygrim moved back to see Carol collapsed on the floor. She was shaking with fear. Bill was pale but in control, as were Jane and Ann. Joygrim gripped her into a firm embrace and moved back the way they had come.

After twenty metres Carol spoke. "I'm feeling better," she said.

Joygrim put her down and, as the others joined her, she ventured to speak just loud enough for all to hear her. "Carol has given us the advanced knowledge that we are close to the Princess Shimishi, she is clearly very sensitive to the pheromones released by the evil one."

Lowgrim agreed and ordered the dwarves to the front. He turned to the soldiers. All four were readying their weapons.

"We dwarves will go forward with Jane and Ann. You soldiers are to guard Carol and Bill with your lives."

The soldiers nodded. They took Lowgrim to be an officer in charge and they knelt either side of Carol and Bill for their protection.

Carol whispered to Smithy. "Why are they taking Ann and Jane with them?"

"Two reasons," said Smithy. "They are like you, Carol. They will feel the fear before the dwarves do and it will aid their approach to whatever is at the end of this tunnel."

"What else?" asked Carol.

Smithy smiled and said, "They trust them to tell them when they feel terror creeping over them." Smithy smiled and put a hand on her shoulder as he spoke, then turned to concentrate on his duty.

Lowgrim, his sister and the others, moved forward at a steady walk. The sounds of battle had all gone. A single voice rang out and was not loud enough for the dwarves to hear what was said. They moved further along the tunnel and then an evil voice replied to the first voice. This too was muffled. Even so Jane and Ann together took an involuntary knee. Joygrim smiled at both and used hand signals to tell the other dwarves to take Jane back to a safe distance, while she and Lowgrim scouted ahead. All the dwarves knew that Shimishi was very close now. Lowgrim and his sister reached the end of the tunnel and lay on the floor so that they could hear what was said without being seen. The smell of Spawn and Slaver was strong, rather like burnt pork. Both peered over the edge to witness the scene. They were twenty metres above the floor of another glittering cavern. This one was filled with thousands of Spawn, Slavers and a few hundred winged females in the image of the figure that sat on a throne of bones. Behind Shimishi, for it was she, was a gigantic form of an ancient cretinous evil, that smelt like death. It was the once mighty Queen Yonlik.

Joygrim shuddered at the sight and smell. "Yonlik," was all that she could utter.

Lowgrim did not move or respond. He was looking at movement coming into the cavern far below.

Six feet in height, the Slavers brought bundles into the middle of the cavern next to the throne. Each was tied hand and foot and made to kneel before the princess. Shimishi stood up in surprise.

"What is this? What are dwarves doing in this time frame?"

This was unexpected and was a shock to Shimishi. The soldiers that had accompanied were kneeling beside the dwarves. The only one not there was Jono.

"Is this all of them?" asked the princess.

"One got away my princess. It was a soldier of these times," said a nervous Slaver.

"No matter," said Shimishi. Her voice was cold and cruel. "We will have these for our next meal. Dispatch them now.

Without a second thought the Slavers present ripped the soldiers to pieces.

Lowgrim gripped his axe far above but was stayed by Joygrim, who whispered, "Not yet brother."

Princess Shimishi ordered the muffles removed from the dwarves.

"Stand and face your doom dwarves. Now tell me, how have you come here? Your kind are all long dead or should be. Who are you?"

Lowe stood forward with Lowin. They leaned against one another as if to help each other with the terror that they were experiencing. Lowe spoke for the first time. "Remove my bonds Shimishi, I would speak freely to you as one of your oldest enemies."

The princess was perturbed but she was unafraid of these creatures from a bygone age. She gestured to the Slavers to release his hands. Once free, Lowe put a loving arm around his wife.

"My name is Lowe and this is my wife Lowin. We are free people. We have come to kill you Princess Shimishi and that is our only aim. It was we that wounded you so badly in your lair. We are all sad to see you survived the ordeal. We had hoped to end you."

"Very bravely put," sneered Shimishi. "I don't remember you or your wife. Enlighten me."

Lowe felt energy return to his arms and legs, although his legs were still bound. "It was my plan to meet your sister in the gorge. It was my kin that attacked your hiding place and it was my family that embedded the axes into your flesh all those years ago."

Lowe laughed in the face of Shimishi. "It was we dwarves who butchered your sisters. They weren't so lucky as you. Those wounds we gave you might have killed you too. I am sad to see that you live still, although you have lost your good looks and replaced them with a foul stench!"

Lowe 's voice prompted the other dwarves to stand in unison. His children were shaken free from their fear by his brave words. They knew he was baiting Shimishi.

Princess Shimishi stood and looked into her enemy's face and saw no fear in his eyes. "Where does this courage come from? You dwarves are human and none have been able to resist me before. I would learn more from you Lowe."

Lowe spoke again. "I am at least pleased to see that the arch nemesis of the world behind you appears near to death. You do not appear to have been caring for your family as you might Shimishi. If I didn't know better, I might guess you are quite pleased to see Yonlik in such a state. May I watch her die before you kill me? It would make an old dwarf exceedingly delighted."

Shimishi gave an evil smile filled with pure vitriol. "Aah, my mother has done Satan our master a great service in his absence and she will shortly join him in Hell."

Yonlik did not stir from her deep slumber.

In a cold and cruel voice Shimishi sneered at the dwarf. "Yonlik has finally succumbed to her own folly. She demanded a million daughters from me. She took every one of my offspring. All females. These beauties are those you see before you. Each one has the spiritual essence of Yonlik within them. They are all called Juliana. They are beautiful and they are mine. They are a hive mind like no other. My foolish mother did not spare herself in her insanity and what you see left here is but the last essence of her spirit. My horde and my daughters are spread all over the planet. We are ready to finally enslave the whole world."

Shimishi turned to her mother, Yonlik, and said cruelly. "Time for you to go Yonlik. I will take things from here."

As one, the Juliana sprang onto the unmoving body of Yonlik and fed upon her until there was nothing left but bones.

Lowe looked on with distaste. The smell in the hall was vile. He glanced around and up. Behind his right shoulder, he looked directly at the point where his children lay listening and watching. He opened his hands in a gesture. It was as clear as him asking for an axe as if he had shouted it.

Lowgrim gripped his heavy axe and threw it down to his father. The axe went swirling down to Lowe, end over end. Lowe timed his grasp onto the hand of the axe and in the same movement hurled it into the back of Shimishi who screamed as the blade buried itself between her shoulder blades.

Shimishi was not mortally wounded. She launched herself at Lowe and Lowin and caught them each by the throat. She leapt into the air and crushed them into the ground, breaking both of their necks. The Juliana closest to the dwarves dispatched the rest of the company. Lowgrim and Joygrim silently praised the bravery of their parents as they made ready, lying on their backs and pulling axes and hammers to hand, ready to leap from on high upon the form of Shimishi.

In the meantime, Shimishi returned to her throne and sat now on the high throne of Yonlik. One of the Juliana came forward and pulled the axe from her back. As she walked away from Shimishi, she licked the blade that was dripping with blood. "How did the dwarf get the axe?"

The nearest Slaver reported that it appeared in his hand from nowhere. His head was ripped from his shoulders by the Juliana nearest to him. The Juliana moved as one towards the princess. Shimishi was in terrible pain but knew she would survive the wound. She looked at the Juliana with surprise as they joined her all around the throne.

"What is this? I have not asked for your help."

The Juliana continued toward her, faces all serene in a form of beauty. They reached hold of Shimishi as one. Shimishi suddenly realised their intent. She struck out at them, even as they gripped her and held her arms, legs and wings. More and more Juliana joined their sisters. Shimishi screamed in rage and fear for them to release her.

The Juliana spoke in reply as one. "We are the Juliana of our grandmother. Yonlik wishes you to know that your treachery has long been suspected. She wished us to say that we do not need a queen. We are the Juliana."

With that the Juliana ripped Shimishi to shreds. They passed pieces to all the Juliana present before standing before the now silent and fearful Slavers and Spawn. The Spawn and Slavers were silent but showed no sign of dying themselves now that Shimishi was dead.

"They aren't dying," said Lowgrim.

"Come on," said Joygrim with tears flooding down her face,

"let us get out of this hell. We must warn the others and then get to the surface."

To be continued...

The end of Book One.

PRINTED AND BOUND BY:
Copytech (UK) Limited trading as Printondemand-worldwide,
9 Culley Court, Bakewell Road, Orton Southgate.
Peterborough, PE2 6XD, United Kingdom.